NO LIMIT

SUSAN HAYES

ABOUT THE BOOK

Three hearts. Two worlds. No limits.

Tyran Varosa and Braxon Torr are on a mission. Find an inhabitable planet. Start a new colony. Escape the archaic rules and traditions of the Vardarian homeworld. They never expected to find their mate along the way, and they never imagined she'd be a diminutive human female with pink hair and a warrior's spirit.

Phaedra Kari has been called a lot of things in her life: trouble, cyber-jockey, lunatic, hacker, but never someone's mate - not until an alien prince and his best friend arrive at the Drift. She's got plans of her own, and they don't include mating anyone, not even a pair of gorgeous aliens whose every touch tempts her to say yes.

When corporate backstabbing progresses to real-life murder, these three will need to come together to ensure the survival of their plans, their friends, and each other.

No Limit (The Drift Series - Book 5)

First E-book Publication: May 2018

Cover Design: Melody Simmons ~ ebookindiecovers.com

Editor: Dayna Hart

Published by: Black Scroll Publications

ISBN: 978-1-988446-14-1

DEDICATION

For my Mum and Dad, for supporting me no matter where my dreams lead. And for my dear friend Karen, who set me on this path so many years ago.

PROLOGUE

Out on the edge of civilized space is a rag-tag collection of space stations and platforms known as the Drift. It's a haven for the hunted, the lost, and those seeking second chances. The people who live there hail from every species, class, and corner of the galaxy, but they all have one thing in common: they don't belong anywhere else.

There's nothing beyond the Drift but wild space and an asteroid belt full of ore-rich rocks. The asteroids are mined by hundreds of vessels and their hard-working crews. When the ships deliver their haul to be processed, those crews hit the infamous bars, casinos, and pleasure houses that are the Drift's primary source of income... and only source of entertainment.

It's a world of its own. One where corporations rule, the laws are flexible, and everything is for sale, for the right price.

Welcome to the Drift.

<hr>

CHAPTER ONE

<hr>

BRAXON TORR WAS FLOATING in zero gravity several feet above his favorite chair as he reviewed the latest data from the long-range scans on a wall monitor. The observation lounge was one of the few rooms on the ship big enough to allow him to stretch his wings, which made it his current favorite place to work.

His attention was drawn away by the sound of the only other being onboard stomping up to the door to the lounge, each boot fall landing in time to a litany of decidedly unprincelike curses. Being away from court had been good for Tyran, even if the boredom was slowly driving them both a little insane.

"Braxon! How many times do I need to tell you to quit switching the *qarfing* gravity orientation in the corridors? I just slammed my head on the ceiling again."

"Sorry. I forgot to switch it back after I was done."

"Done what? Why did you need to be walking on the ceiling? And why are you floating? Something wrong with the furniture?" Tyr stood in the doorway and gestured to the unused chair below Braxon. He was sufficiently annoyed that his skin was a brilliant shade of silver. For anyone else, that would have been a warning to step carefully, but Braxon had been the prince's *anrik*—his blood-bound companion and protector—since Tyr was ten years old. He knew he had nothing to fear.

"There's nothing wrong with the furniture. I was just looking for a change in perspective." The only thing wrong with the furniture was that he'd seen it every day for more than three months. In that time, Braxon had explored every inch of the ship. There wasn't a chair, bed, or room he hadn't spent time in. When he had agreed to Tyr's suggestion that they escape the Vardarian Imperial Court and go on this scouting mission, it had sounded exciting. Finding a new world to colonize would be an adventure. Only, they had yet to find a single inhabitable world, and instead of adventure, they faced a daily grind of dull routine.

"As for what I was doing that required me to flip the gravity, I was repairing a power conduit. It was easier to swap gravity than find a ladder."

"Next time, change it back. There's nothing fun about stepping into a corridor only to discover up and down have been reversed." Tyr rubbed the top of his head, making his short black hair stand up in unruly spikes.

"It depends on your point of view. To me? That's funny. I'm sorry I missed it."

"In that case...." Tyr gestured with one hand, and Braxon dropped out of the air like a stone.

He landed in a sprawled heap of wings and limbs across the chair he'd been floating over. "*Bakaffa*. That was uncalled for."

Tyran snorted with laughter. "I thought it was funny. Must have been my point of view."

Braxon flicked two of his fingers up in an obscene gesture before retracting his wings and arranging himself more comfortably in his chair. "Point taken. Next time I'll put it back."

"Thank you." Tyr entered the lounge. "Did you find anything of interest on the scans?" Tyr claimed a seat near one of the floor-to-ceiling windows that gave a breathtaking view of the galaxy outside.

They were currently light-years from any star system, surrounded by the velvet blackness of deep space. The stars gleamed like distant gems, and in orbit around one of them had to be the planet they were searching for. If they found it, they could escape the demands of the imperial court and the Vardarian empress, Tyran's twin sister, Neha.

"Maybe." Braxon visualized the data he wanted and the nanites within his body linked to the ship's computer. A hologram of the area where scans had shown something out of the ordinary appeared in the air in front of him a second later.

"What am I looking at?"

"A map," Braxon retorted.

"I can see that. What's so special about this area of this map?"

Braxon reached up and manipulated the image, expanding it and then zeroing in on a sector. "The scans are picking up some kind of signal from this area. It could be more cosmic noise or a natural phenomenon, but the computer projects a sixty percent likelihood it's not naturally occurring."

Tyr leaned forward, his hands on his knees as he stared at the display. "Sixty percent?"

"It could be another pulsar or a star nursery, but it's the strongest lead we've had in weeks. If there's intelligent life over there, I vote we go find them. I'm dying for a conversation with someone I haven't known for most of my life. You already know all my best stories."

"Agreed. I caught myself having a long, in-depth conversation with one of the servo-droids this morning. Let's go see what's making all that noise. Where there's life, there have to be life-supporting planets."

"That's the theory." Braxon took another look at his friend and frowned. Tyr's sleeveless vest had a ring of gemstones affixed to the collar, and the flowing fabric was dyed green and black, the traditional colors of the Varosa royal family. There was something more bothering Tyr than just a bump on the head. "I know that look. And that outfit. You've spoken with your sister, haven't you?"

He nodded. "Neha wants me to stop this 'frivolous pursuit' and return home."

"You've been at her side her entire life. She doesn't understand why you're not there now, giving her your counsel and support."

Tyran shook his head, and the light in his blue eyes dimmed for a moment. "Neha relies on the counsel of others too much. She rules by committee, which is no way to run an empire. So long as I am at court, she'll never come into her own."

"And the longer she listens to those *vipa* she calls her counselors, the harder it will be to wrest control away from them," Braxon added. Tyran's twin sister might be the eldest by a matter of minutes, but she had always relied on her brother's support and advice. Now she had ascended to the Imperial throne, she still continued to look to Tyr, and it was causing unrest and confusion at court. Treasonous whispers had circulated more than once suggesting Tyran would make a better ruler.

"It's time for me to step away. Neither of us would be happy spending the rest of our lives at court, and if I am not there, no one can try to put me on a throne I do not want."

"She still doesn't suspect what we're trying to do?"

"No, but we're running out of time."

"Did she order you to return?"

"Not yet. But she will soon."

If they returned without finding what they were looking for, they would never get another chance. Declaring a diaspora and leading a group of colonists to a new home would allow them both to live free. For Tyran, it meant escaping a life of court intrigue and the expectations that came with his rank. For Braxon, it meant being away from those who would judge him for his ancestry.

He wasn't a pure-blooded Vardarian. Anywhere else in the empire, that was the norm. Their species had scattered across the stars centuries ago, finding new worlds to inhabit, new alliances to forge, and occasionally finding races genetically compatible with them. But Braxon lived on the Vardarian homeworld, where everyone was judged by their lineage.

Tyr got to his feet and walked over to the hologram. He touched the location with one finger, and a set of coordinates appeared. A moment later, the ship's main engines powered up.

"We're going right now?" Braxon asked.

"Why not? This might be our last chance. We'll make the journey in three or four jumps. That should give us time to stop and assess as we get closer."

"And if the computer's right and there's someone out there?"

"If they're friendly, we start first contact protocols. If they're not..."

Braxon grinned. "If they're not, then you steer, and I'll shoot."

The Vardarian empire was relatively peaceful, but that didn't mean they were pacifists. Their ship, the *Santar*, was a royal cruiser equipped with enough fire-power to protect itself and its occupants. By approaching in a series of jumps they'd have time to gather information and begin the process of translating any new languages into Vardarian. If this weren't another false reading, they'd be ready by the time they arrived at their destination.

Please, don't be another false lead.

PHAEDRA STARED into her cocktail glass and tried to banish her bad mood. This wasn't the day for reflection and regret. Today was the best day of her best friend's life, and she should be celebrating with Alyson and the others. They had so many reasons to celebrate. The corporations were finally being held accountable for their past choices. Arrests had been made, and more would be coming. The remaining cyborgs had been freed, and the station where they were being experimented on had been shut down. The good guys were winning.

Still, she couldn't shake the feeling their winning streak wouldn't last. There were still too many unknowns. Too many nameless players with stakes in a secret game Phaedra and the others were only just started to figure out. Vic and Ward, the two cyborg assassins once known as the Reaper, were still working to retrieve their memories of who had taken them, and where they'd been held. They were still here on Astek station, but they didn't socialize with anyone other than their batch brothers, Jaeger and Toro. The corporations were still destroying lives, and it haunted her that she couldn't do more.

As happy as she was for Alyson and her three new husbands, her head was still full of dark memories she simply couldn't shake.

She had left the Drift full of hope and determination to save the cyborgs still held prisoner. *Save.* The word made her laugh, now. Freeing the cyborgs they had found had been relatively easy. The Reamus research station was already abandoned by the time the IAF ships had arrived. Someone had tipped them off, and the bastards running that hellish place had vanished, taking all their data and most of the evidence with them. The only thing they had left behind were their test subjects – the cyborgs Phaedra had come to save. Only, it wasn't as simple as showing up and declaring them free. Saving them...she didn't know how to do that, and no one else seemed to have any ideas, either. So here she was, brooding instead of dancing and celebrating her friend's wedding day, her only companions a steady supply of drinks provided by the Nova Club staff. Since she currently lived in the residential area above the club, they knew her preferences well.

The bar had been transformed for the reception, full of flowers and the flickering light of a hundred or more holographic candles. Even the fight cage had been decked out in garlands of flowers. That had to be Zura's idea. If anyone else had tried to put so much as a ribbon on those bars, the owners, Kit, Luke, and Cynder would have torn it right back down. Zura's pregnancy was advanced enough she was showing, now, her small frame expanding to accommodate the twins she carried. Her husbands, Kit and Luke, didn't let her out of their sight. Not that Phaedra could blame them.

Zura's babies were unique in all the galaxy because she was the first non-cyborg to ever carry medi-bots. Her children would be the first to be born with nanites running through their bloodstream, repairing any damage and keeping the children healthy for the rest of what might be very long lives. They represented change coming to the human race. A change the corporations had tried to prevent through any means necessary.

Her musings were interrupted by an upbeat male voice. "I'm going to ask you a really stupid question right now, but I swear it's not a pick-up line. Don't I know you from somewhere?"

Phaedra turned and was about to offer up an acidic comment, but one look at the man standing there with a drink in his hand and smile on his face made her stop. He was cute, with dark skin, a mischievous grin, and hazel eyes that did seem familiar. Okay, she *did* know him, but from where?

"Uh. Maybe?" She eyed his dress uniform, noting the silver, five-pointed star that marked him as a member of Nova Force. The only IAF soldiers she knew on sight had been part of the mission she'd returned from three days ago, and there hadn't been any Nova Force officers onboard.

He caught the direction of her gaze and chuckled. "I think we crossed paths before I joined up. My name's Eric Erben."

The name sounded familiar, but she still couldn't place him, and she didn't feel like sorting through her onboard data stores to figure out who he was.

"Sometimes I went by Magi. In those circles, you were known as Phreak, right?"

"Magi? Holy *fraxx*, I didn't recognize you! What the hell are you doing in the IAF? The last time we crossed paths we were..." She trailed off before saying anything incriminating. She and Eric were cyber-jockeys, their bodies and brains wired with tech that allowed them to interface with computers on a level no other being could match.

"We were doing what we do best." He winked and claimed the seat next to her.

"Looks like you changed sides, though." She pointed to his uniform.

"Not long after I saw you last, I screwed up and got caught. I was given two choices: sign up or go to prison with a total ban on access to all technology." He shuddered. "Can you imagine?"

"That's a fate worse than death," she agreed.

"What about you? This isn't your usual crowd, or your usual look, either." His gaze dropped to the sapphire blue bridesmaid gown the brides, Alyson and Lieksa had cajoled her into wearing for the occasion. It was backless, strapless, and she'd only agreed to wear it once the brides gave in to her request to wear her favorite pair of boots with it. She'd buffed them to a high shine, and they were a whole lot more comfortable than high heels.

"One of the brides is my best friend. I wouldn't miss her big day."

Eric's eyes widened. "Which one?"

"Alyson. The one who just married the galaxy's sexiest triplets, lucky girl."

Eric burst out laughing. "How the hell did you end up best friends with Triple C's little sister?"

"Who?"

Eric pointed across the bar to a handsome blond man drinking at the bar. "Lieutenant Crispen Caldwell. He's the reason I'm here. Cris is a teammate and he scored us all invites to the reception."

"Small galaxy. I went to college with Alyson. She called in a favor a while ago and had me look into some corporate shenanigans."

"Holy *fraxx*, that was *you!*" He glanced around and lowered his voice. "I know what she's been involved in. The cyborgs, the corporations, the stolen DNA. If you're part of that, then I'm betting you're the one who hacked the IAF and found out about the Vault of the Fallen."

"How do you know about that?" she hissed.

"My team was sent to investigate the thefts. That's where I got these." He pushed up his left sleeve to show her a freshly healed set of burn scars that surrounded one of his data ports.

"Whoa. That had to hurt. How did it happen?"

"My last mission, the DNA theft investigation, went a little sideways. Buy me a drink, and I'll tell you all about it."

She waved a server over. "Hey, Echo. When you've got a moment can you bring me another Sunsprite's Delight and grab my friend here a-- what are you drinking?"

"Something with the word sin in it. Red. Tasty. Packs a punch."

"You're drinking Cynfuls? Remind me to introduce you to the lady that's named after later tonight. She's one of the owners."

"She single?"

Echo laughed and gave Eric an appreciative glance. "Don't even think about it. Her husbands would kill you... if she didn't end you first."

"I don't want to be ended. I'm too young to die."

"Too cute, too." Echo flipped her blonde hair over her shoulder, winked at him and left to fetch their order, leaving them alone again.

"Alright, then. Our drinks are on the way. You tell me how you got those scars, and I'll tell you what I can about how I went from hacking the IAF to going on a mission with them."

Eric nodded. "You have yourself a deal, Phreak."

"Since we're in the land of the normals, why don't you call me Phaedra?"

MEETING ERIC TURNED out to be the best part of her night. The time they spent catching up and talking about their various adventures helped to remind her she had made a difference before, and she would do so again.

She wasn't a norm. She operated outside the rules, living by her own personal code of honor and fighting the battles no one else could. *Veth*, she fought battles no one else even knew about. Without her help, no one would have known where the cyborg DNA had come from, or that the IAF had inadvertently been involved in a war effort they swore they had no part of. It had been too long since she'd talked with someone who understood what her life was like, and by the time they parted ways, she felt energized.

The party was winding down by the time she hugged Eric good night. He caught her hand in his and kissed it, bringing the data ports in their wrists together long enough to send her a brief databurst message.

Don't be a stranger. I need at least one non-norm in my life.

Along with the note was a few lines of code that included a way to contact him whenever she was jacked into cyberspace.

She scanned the information before they'd even finished their hug and sent him a brief message back.

Same here. You'll be hearing from me.

"I could walk you home," he offered.

There'd been a time where she would have accepted his offer and everything that might come of it, but not tonight. Eric was handsome and brilliant, but she wasn't feeling more than gratitude and friendship for him. She decided to point him in a different direction. "I am home. I'm staying here at the Nova Club for now." She leaned in and whispered. "And if you leave with me, Echo will never give me another free drink. She's waiting for me to go so she can tell you that while Cynder unavailable, she is very single."

He grinned. "Yeah?"

"She's very selective who she flirts with, so I'd say you've got a shot. Go on, tell her she's pretty and then offer to show her your new battle scars."

He stiffened. "You think she'll still think I'm cute when she sees the data ports and the scars? Norms don't really go for our kind, you know?"

Phaedra nodded. "She's not a norm, though. Echo is a cyborg."

Eric's eyes widened. "She is? But she's so…"

"If you say the word normal, I'm going to call you a hypocrite and kick your ass."

"I was going to say gentle. Most of the cyborgs I've met have been big, glowering mountains of muscle, like your friend's new husbands."

"Fair enough. Compared to them, Echo is a delicate flower." She nudged him in the direction she'd last seen Echo. "Go. Have fun. And keep in mind that if you piss her off, she can break you in half with one arm."

Eric's grin broadened. "Sounds like a good time."

"Anyone told you that you have dangerous taste in women?"

"More than once."

They parted ways, and Phaedra spent a few minutes saying her goodbyes to the staff and remaining guests. By the time she was done, she was only a few feet from the private door that led to the back rooms of the club, and to the elevator that would deliver her to her simple but incredibly secure room. She had slept better in the last few months than she had in years. The club was one of the most secure places she'd ever seen, and once she'd added a few of her own modifications, it was damned near impenetrable.

She had transferred her access code from the key card she'd been given to her internal systems, and a quick wave of her hand over the keypad opened the door. It was so much easier than trying to remember to bring her key card with her everywhere she went. Of course, she had added a few extra levels of access to her implant in the time she'd been staying here. Thanks to her visits to her friends at Corp-Sec, the Drift's version of law enforcement, she had managed to give herself access to every door, communication system, and even some of the surveillance cams on the station. How could she keep herself and her friends safe if she didn't know what was going on?

She stepped through the door, and a half-second later, a siren started to wail and whoop. For a moment, she thought she'd set off some kind of alarm, but a quick look around made it clear it wasn't for her. Judging by the hurried departures of several IAF officers, something serious was happening elsewhere on the station.

She ducked down a side corridor and headed for the back door - the one club employees used to bring in fresh supplies of booze, food, and licensed pharma. If something interesting was about to happen, she wanted to be there. Even if she hadn't been invited.

CHAPTER TWO

Tyran sat in the cockpit and tried not to watch the chronometer tick away the seconds. How much longer until they got a response? They had sent a message of greeting to the massive space station they chose to approach first, but so far there had been no reaction.

"Do you think we screwed up the translation? What if we didn't say we come in peace? What if we said we're here for your vegetables or something?" Braxon was perched at the edge of his seat, absently twirling a dagger between the fingers of his left hand.

"I don't think they'd believe we came all this way to steal their produce. Besides, we recorded nearly a hundred hours of transmission, more than enough for the computer to start working on a translation matrix. It verified that the message we sent was a non-threatening invitation to talk."

Braxon pointed the dagger's tip at the screen. "So, why aren't they talking?"

"Perhaps we selected the wrong station? This entire area is full of ships, stations, and platforms."

"But this one had the most military ships docked, which means it's most likely a command center of some kind." Braxon started spinning the blade again. "Of course, that also means we have a good chance of getting blown to atoms if we did screw up that message."

"We're not getting blown to atoms. My guess is they're observing us right now. Or maybe they're in the middle of a sleep cycle, and everyone of rank is being roused from their beds."

"Not the way I'd like to be woken up. Let's hope they don't hold it against us."

The central monitor flashed several times, alerting them to an incoming message.

"Looks like they're awake and ready to talk." Tyran ran the message through their rudimentary translation program and started smiling as he read their response.

Braxon leaned in to read it too, and when he reached the end he sheathed his blade. "There are four species living together on these stations? Well, at least we know they're not xenophobic."

"We've got docking instructions, too."

Braxon chuckled and pointed to the viewscreen. "I think I can guess where, too. Three ships have left one of the docking rings, and it looks like a few more are activating their engines. They're clearing an area for us."

Tyran began navigating the *Santar* into position, then glanced over at Braxon. "Now might be a good time to get dressed and try to make yourself look a little less...disreputable."

"I'm your personal guard. I'm supposed to look threatening."

"You're also representing our entire race." He looked pointedly at Braxon's bare torso. "At least put on fresh garments."

"That, I can do." He got to his feet and held out his left arm, his hand closed into a fist. "May we make our ancestors proud today."

Tyran reached out to touch the scars on his wrist to the matching one on Braxon's. "And may they guide us to our heart's desire."

Braxon left to prepare for their meeting, which Tyran knew would also include arming himself in case things didn't go as planned. Braxon always prepared for the worst possible outcome. It was in his nature to be suspicious, and that caution had served them both well over the years.

It took time and some careful piloting to get the *Santar* positioned at the docking ring, and a little longer to establish and ensure a secure seal between the ship and the station. It appeared that while their technology was not an exact match, it was close enough to be able to make it work. It was a promising start.

A few more communications back and forth had included information about atmosphere and other environmental data. The language barrier forced both sides to keep their inquiries and explanations simple, but it appeared that they would be able to breathe and move without a problem while on the station.

Now, they were standing at the door, waiting for the signal to exit.

"We ready?" he asked Braxon, who had reappeared

moments before docking. He'd donned his best clothes, braided his hair back and tied it up in a clubbed queue, and looked every inch the part of an intergalactic emissary.

The illusion shattered the moment Braxon spoke. "Bet's still on, right? Fifty *koldar* that we meet at least one female at this ceremony who finds out you're a prince and immediately starts to flirt and simper."

"It will be a pleasure to take your money while proving to you that not every female in the galaxy is interested in money and power."

Braxon snorted. "Your optimism in the face of years of evidence to the contrary is impressive. You are going to lose, my friend."

"I have a good feeling about this meeting. For the first time in generations, we have made first contact with not one, but several new species. Even if I do lose the bet, it will take more than a little simpering to ruin this moment."

A sharp rap on the hull announced their moment had arrived.

Tyran raised his head, squared his shoulders, and activated the door. It glided open, revealing a stretch of open hallway that opened into a wider space that seemed quite crowded with curious onlookers packed in behind a more sedate-looking greeting party comprised mostly of humans. Matching uniforms of blue and silver marked several of them as military, and there were others not in uniform that were clearly there as representatives of their species. A slender female with striking blue coloring and silver eyes, a massive male with blue-black hair and eyes as dark as the void outside, and a tall, lanky being with yellow skin bedecked with thorny growths. Included in the messages had been generic pictures of each species but seeing them all in the flesh was different.

Behind him, Braxon exhaled sharply. "That's a lot of beings."

"And they're all here to meet us. Amazing, isn't it?"

"Let's just hope they're not disappointed when they discover we're not that different from them."

"Ah, but we *are* different. Follow my lead." Tyran stepped through the door and partially unfurled his wings as he raised his hand in greeting. There was a collective murmur that rippled through the crowd, echoed a few seconds later as Braxon appeared and unfurled his wings as well.

A well-built human male with silver in his hair stepped forward as they approached the greeting party. He wore a uniform, and there were enough ribbons and metallic decorations to indicate he was of high rank. When he spoke, he used the language they had heard most often in transmissions, though it was clearly spoken and used a slower cadence.

"On behalf of everyone present, I bid you greetings, and welcome to Astek Station. My name is Colonel Scott Archer, and I represent the Interstellar Armed Forces."

Tyran nodded and spoke the simple phrases he had been practicing. "I am Prince Tyran Varosa, and this is Braxon Torr. We are of the Vardarian Empire, and we thank you for your greeting."

The one called Archer's expression softened and he offered a slight smile. "Well spoken," he said in a low tone before continuing at a more normal volume. "What is the reason for your visit?"

This had already been mentioned in their communications, but Tyran knew this was for the benefit of the crowd watching them. It appeared these beings understood the art of ceremony and showmanship. "We are here as emissaries. Our mission as scouts is to seek out new planets to colonize and to ally ourselves with new races we may find. We seek trade and friendship. Nothing more."

The mood in the room relaxed, and soft murmurs started to ebb and flow through the crowd. Archer took the lead, introducing Tyran and Braxon to each of the other members of the greeting party. The names, races, and affiliations were more than Tyran could keep in his head at the moment, but his nanotech enhancements were recording everything so he could play it back later.

He took a steadying breath and caught a teasing whisper of something that tore his attention from the diplomatic niceties unfolding in front of him. He glanced around, not even certain what he was looking for. The scent seemed somehow familiar, and yet how could there be anything familiar here? Was there another Vardarian present?

This place was strange in every aspect. The ceilings were too low, the material in the carpet that appeared to have been hastily laid out was nothing Tyran had seen before. The languages being spoken around him were strange, and the air carried a dozen odors he didn't recognize. Faint traces of cooked food, the unfamiliar tang of alien beings, and...that. He caught the scent again.

"What is it?" Braxon asked in their own language.

"I don't know. A scent. Something I should recognize but don't."

Colonel Archer caught the interaction. "Is there a problem? A concern?"

"No. Nothing of concern. I am sorry. There is so much to take in." Tyran raised his hands to encompass the room and the crowd.

"Of course. Perhaps we should continue this conversation somewhere quieter?"

"That would be pleasing. I am still trying to learn your language. It is easier when there is less – everything."

Archer smiled. "I imagine it would be. Come with me. We have a space set aside already. There we can discuss how best to proceed. Perhaps you would like a guide? A liaison. Someone to assist you? I could arrange someone to be assigned to you."

"That would be pleasing as well," Tyran said.

Braxon waited for the exchange to finish, then whispered to Tyran. "I smell it too. I don't understand. It can't be."

"Can't be what? What is it?"

Braxon inhaled deeply, and his golden skin began to shimmer with agitation. "Our *mahaya* is present. How can this be?"

Tyran breathed in again, and this time the scent was stronger. Strong enough to confirm what Braxon was telling him. Somehow, against the odds, they had found their mate in a place where no Vardarian female should be.

"Find her." A jolt of raw need put an edge to his words.

Braxon nodded sharply. "I will."

Seeing that both his guests were agitated, Colonel

Archer deemed it time to move them to a smaller venue. He couldn't have any idea what was truly bothering them, and Tyran wasn't sure he even had the words to explain. He let the human male lead them away through a corridor lined with guards.

Archer was still speaking, but Tyran was too distracted to hear anything he said. All his focus was on that elusive scent. Where was she, and how was she here at all?

A QUICK INTERFACE with a data node allowed Phaedra to acquire the information she needed. She skimmed the pertinent details from the datasphere, a simple act that didn't even require her to make a hard connection. The station was about to have unexpected visitors. It was a first contact situation, which explained the alarm, but since no shots had been fired and a number of high-ranking corporate and IAF members were being sent to greet them, it looked like they were friendly.

A quick review of the station's schematics and security cams was all it took for her to figure out exactly how to get to the site without running afoul of security.

If Mac and Dash had any idea how much information about the station and its occupants she'd acquired while she was helping them track down the assassin known as the Reaper, they'd probably toss her ass in a cell...or out the nearest airlock.

She made her way to the site down a flight of stairs and through a maintenance corridor that ran beneath the main passage. The area was crowded with conduits and pipes that looked like they were at least twenty years older than she was. Some of them were leaking fluid that dripped onto the floor to form incandescent puddles that she took great care to avoid.

She reached the spot that should have been her exit, but instead of a nice easy staircase like the one she'd descended, there was nothing but a series of steel bars secured to the wall. "A *fraxxing* ladder? In this dress? Are you kidding me, universe? This is how I'm going to die, isn't it?"

She continued muttering as she tucked up her skirt as best she could manage, baring her legs almost to the hip in the process. She made the climb slowly, hands locking around each rung with a death grip that she had to force herself to release each time it came to reach up again. *Veth*, she hated heights.

Thankfully, there was a nice, stable platform at the top where she could stand as she unlocked the door and opened it a crack to see what was on the other side. She could hear the murmur of a crowd, but a quick check showed her that they were all facing away from her. *Perfect.*

She slipped in behind them, closing the door with care so there was no noise to attract attention her way. She straightened her dress as best she could, checked her hair, and did her best to act as if she had every right to be there. The crowd of onlookers appeared to thin down to her right, so she started making her way in that direction, trying to get close enough to be able to see what was going on.

"I don't want to know how you got here, do I?" a deep

voice rumbled as a massive hand came down on her shoulder.

"Hey, Zale." She tried to sound nonchalant as she smiled up at the big half-Torski.

"Hello, pipsqueak. You're not supposed to be here."

"And you are?"

"We were with Archer when the first message arrived. He invited us to observe with the rest of the aides and entourage types."

She huffed. "You were having a meeting about what to do with our new friends, weren't you? Why wasn't I invited? I'm being shut out, and it's really starting to super my nova."

"It was just a casual conversation over drinks at the reception. You weren't invited because Archer's still annoyed with you for hacking into his communications." Zale gave her a look that reminded her of her mother – if her mother had fangs and all-black eyes, that is. "If you stopped irking him, you might be surprised how supportive Archer is to the cyborg cause."

"I don't like secrets, and he's keeping too many," she declared.

"Which is exactly why you're here, isn't it?" Zale's cousin Denz turned around to wink at her.

"You know me so well." She gave Zale her sweetest smile. "Can I use you two as cover? You're big enough no one will see me if I stay behind you."

"That way at least we'll know where she is," Denz pointed out quietly.

"Fine. But behave yourself. This is important."

"First contact, I know. I'll behave." She wedged herself into a small gap between the two of them, then sighed.

"Problem?" Denz asked.

"I can't see a thing from here. I don't suppose you'd consider moving closer?"

"Don't push your luck, pipsqueak." Despite his grumbling, Zale started moving closer, and the crowd melted away without a word of protest.

There were serious advantages to being over seven feet tall and looking like Denz and Zale. It didn't matter that both were men of science, not action. People took one look at them and moved out of their way. If she had tried on her own, no one would have given her an inch. No one was afraid of a tiny human woman with pink hair.

She'd gotten to know the cousins on the mission to Reamus research station. As the only civilians, they'd spent a lot of time together, and their bonds had deepened once they'd discovered the situation at Reamus.

The crowd suddenly hushed and she stopped talking to focus on the scene unfolding in front of her. The door to the newly arrived ship had opened, and a hot-as-hell male walked through it. At first glance, he appeared almost human, with short, black hair and a neatly trimmed beard. His skin was a shimmering silver, though, and he was taller than most of the humans and Pheran present. Another male followed after the first, and she had to bite her lip not to sigh in appreciation. The second male was a little taller and broader than the first, and his skin had a golden sheen to it. His hair was long enough to be tied back, but his beard was as closely cropped as his silver companion's.

"They don't look much like aliens."

Zale grunted. "Maybe not to you."

That was the moment both males unfurled their

wings. Holy *fraxx*. They had wings! "I take it back. Wings are definitely alien."

"Wing's, scales, and I do believe I just spotted fangs," Denz said.

"Scales?" she narrowed her eyes, but human eyesight wasn't as good as Torski. She'd have to wait until they got closer to get a better look. Fortunately, she'd have a good vantage point to watch the impromptu welcome ceremony. With Zale and Denz shielding her from view, she could appreciate the appearance of the two males as they began speaking with Colonel Archer and the other delegates.

Alien or not, they were breathtaking. They both wore sleeveless vests that highlighted their well-muscled arms. The garments were clasped at the top but parted in a gentle V to show off two sets of sculpted abs. The vests had slits in the back to accommodate their wings, which were vaguely bat-like in design: a thin membrane supported by a network of lightweight bones. It was hard to tell, but she guessed that if they were fully extended, they'd have a wingspan of well over twelve feet.

The silver one looked around as if he were searching for someone, and for a moment she felt as if he were staring right at her. It was a strange sensation, like something inside her was reaching for him, but then his gaze moved on, and the feeling vanished. *Weird.*

A short time later the ceremony came to an abrupt end as Archer signaled for an escort. IAF soldiers in dress uniforms appeared, and the various representatives were ushered past the crowd and toward the nearest exit. It was yet another subtle reminder that the military was calling the shots these days. Until the investigations into the corporations were over and everyone with blood on their hands had been taken into custody, the Drift was under an informal kind of martial law.

As the two alien visitors passed by, the one called Braxon broke rank and came straight toward her. His pale green eyes narrowed. She idly noticed that his irises had black rims, and his pupils were slightly oval instead of round, but after that, she was too concerned by his approach to take note of what he looked like. The entire group came to a stop as he reached the edge of the crowd and uttered something in a language she'd never heard before.

"*Mahaya*?" His voice was tinged with confusion as he stared at her.

Zale and Denz stood their ground, but Braxon ignored them. He reached between them and caught hold of Phaedra's arm, pulling her forward.

"Hey! Hands off!" she yelped.

"Don't touch her," Zale rumbled.

"Is there a problem?" Archer asked. She couldn't see him, but she'd know that ring of command anywhere.

"No."

"Hell, yes!" she retorted, trying to tug herself free of his grasp.

"Phaedra Kari. Of course. Who else would be in the middle of this mess?"

"You're blaming me?" Instead of trying to free herself, she pushed between her two stalwart guards to face Archer. "I was just standing here, and suddenly tall, gold and winged here marched over and grabbed me."

Instead of responding to her, Archer turned to

Braxon. "Is there a problem? Why did you wish to speak to this woman?"

Another voice joined in, speaking what sounded like the same unknown language as Braxon. She glanced over to find Tyran had joined them. There was a brief exchange, and then Braxon's gripped eased, though he didn't let go completely. The two aliens looked at each other, and then at her. She could have sworn they both inhaled, too.

"Would someone please tell me what's going on?" She demanded, tugging her arm free.

"I will explain soon. Please be patient. First I must ask question." Tyran turned to Archer. "Colonel Scott Archer, would it be acceptable for us to select the guide to assist us during our time here?"

Archer looked pained, but he nodded. "It would be acceptable, of course, but might I suggest someone with more diplomatic skills and training?"

"That is not necessary." He gestured to Phaedra. "We chose this one."

CHAPTER THREE

BRAXON COULDN'T TEAR his gaze from the diminutive, pink-haired female. She was their mate?

"*This one* has a name, and she'd like to be asked if this is acceptable to her, thank you very much."

"You do not wish to be our guide? Tyran is a prince. His sister rules an empire."

He found himself transfixed by a pair of emerald green eyes as she turned her attention to him. "So? Royalty or not, it's still nice to be asked."

Archer uttered a strangled croak before composing himself. "Prince Tyran Varosa and Braxon Torr, may I introduce Phaedra Kari."

Tyr dropped into a formal bow, but not before Braxon caught the bemused smile on the prince's face. He knew that look, and it didn't bode well. The prince of Vardaria was smitten.

"It is good to meet you, Phaedra." Braxon performed a cursory bow but kept his eyes on Phaedra the whole time.

Was she truly their mate, or was this some sort of biological malfunction?

"Hi, and uh, welcome to the Drift." Her hand rose, then lowered again as if she were unsure what to do next.

"I apologize for making assumptions. Would you agree to be our guide?" Tyr asked.

"Apology accepted." She cocked a bright pink brow. "So, what, exactly, would I be required to do?"

Tyran was beaming now. "You would work with us. Show us this place, teach us your language, help us to negotiate with the beings that live in this part of the galaxy."

Her eyes widened. "You'd want me to be part of any negotiations?"

"We'd need your help. There are..." Tyran paused as he struggled for the word he wanted. "There are subtle twists in your language."

"Twists is a good word for it," Phaedra agreed.

"Will you help us, Phaedra Kari? Will you be our guide?"

Her stance softened. "Yes. I will."

"I am pleasured by your decision." Tyran beamed and offered her his hand.

She laughed, and the sound was sweeter than any music Braxon had ever heard.

"You mean pleased. Pleasured is..." Her cheeks turned red as she took Tyr's hand. "I'll explain that another time."

The moment she touched Tyr, a fresh wave of her pheromones flooded the air. She was reacting to them as if she were their mate, yet it appeared she was unaware of it. *Strange.*

He expected her to walk away then. Instead, Phaedra turned to look at him. "You haven't said much, Braxon. Are you okay with this? If not, I'm sure Colonel Archer would be *very* happy to find someone else for this gig. I should probably warn you both that I'm not really the obedient, order-taking type."

Surprised at both her concern for him and her confession, Braxon found himself nodding. "I agree with Tyran's choice of guides."

Of course, it was really the only thing he could have said. Tyr had already made his choice. At least this way, they would be able to speak to Phaedra alone. Then maybe they could find out why they were reacting to her as if she were their *mahaya*. It had to be some sort of mistake. They were Vardarian warriors. This delicate human female was not built to withstand the passion of one of their kind, never mind two.

THE SMALL GROUP started moving again, and Tyran was pleased when Phaedra came with him willingly, her hand still captured in his. As far as he was concerned, it would take the explosive force of a supernova to make him relinquish that small connection with her. He still couldn't believe it. They had found their *mahaya*.

They had come across light-years in search of a new home for their race. A place they could be free of the traditions and rules that bound their homeworld. Neither of them had spoken of it, but Tyran knew he and Braxon both hoped that a new colony would give them a chance to find their mate - and they had. Not a Vardarian, but something far more precious and rare. A female of another genetically compatible species.

The ratio of males to females on Vardaria was skewed heavily to the males. That imbalance had triggered the first diaspora, when thousands of unmated Vardarian male lefts their homeworld to claim mates from the newly discovered Ferrym race. Another exodus had occurred when they had come into contact with the Vinu. Now, it appeared there may be another fully compatible race in the galaxy – humans like Phaedra.

He glanced down at their joined hands and tried not to think of where else he'd like to be touching her right now. She was wearing a dark blue garment that hid her legs but left her upper body delightfully exposed. The pale gold skin of her shoulders was utterly smooth, and he wanted to caress her and learn if it was as soft as it looked. She was small but curvy, with eyes that gleamed like green gems. Her hair was several shades of pink, and he wanted to run his hands through it and play with the vibrant curls, too. Could it be her natural color? No other being present had hair that shade.

"What is it that brought you to this part of the galaxy, Prince Tyran?" Colonel Archer was clearly trying to continue his diplomatic efforts, but all Tyr wanted was to steal Phaedra away and learn everything he could about her. *Soon*, he promised himself as he forced his attention back to the colonel.

"The Vardarian Empire has allies and trade agreements with several other races." He gestured around them. "Something like you have here, I think. We were on a scouting mission, looking for new planets to colonize, and of course, to attempt to connect with any new races we find." He'd rehearsed that statement for days and was rewarded by an appreciative nod from Colonel Archer.

"You have learned a great deal of our language for someone who only recently learned of its existence."

"The computer learned it first, then learned – no, teach?"

He looked at Phaedra, who nodded. "Taught. The computer taught you our language. Well, one of them."

"It is the most used language, yes?" he asked.

"It's the one all species use to speak to each other."

"The most useful one. We thought so." Braxon finally joined the conversation. He hadn't said a word since agreeing to Phaedra as their guide.

"Right through this door." Colonel Archer directed. The corridor they were in was clearly not a public area. The walls were marked and dented, the floors showed signs of wear, and there were empty crates of various sizes stacked against the walls.

Once through the door, though, things were very different. Plush red carpeting muffled his footfalls, and the air was cool and freshly filtered, carrying no discernable scent. The walls were painted a neutral cream, and images of landscapes from what appeared to be dozens of worlds were displayed at regular intervals.

As if sensing his interest, Phaedra squeezed Tyran's hand. "We've arrived at Astek's headquarters. They're the corporation that owns this space station. Everyone else here pays them for the right to be here. Even the air we breathe comes at a cost."

Colonel Archer frowned at Phaedra, but she merely lifted her shoulders in a brief shrug.

"What? It's the truth. If they wanted someone diplomatic, they would have taken your advice and picked someone else to be their liaison."

Tyr didn't care if she was the most undiplomatic female in the galaxy. She was *their* female. She simply didn't know it, yet.

"We need to be alone with the human female," Braxon pitched his voice low and spoke in Vardarian.

"Soon. We'll be able to tell her the good news once we are back on the *Santar*."

"There is nothing to tell her. Not until we have more data. There are still tests that need to be done," Braxon pointed out.

"Do you doubt what your senses tell you? She is our *mahaya*."

Braxon pursed his lips. "Perhaps."

"Your language is lovely. I don't suppose your translation program could teach me to speak Vardarian? It might help us communicate better."

"It would take some time, but I believe it is possible." As their mate, she would need to speak Vardarian eventually. The sooner she started, the better.

"If our technologies are compatible, I don't think it would take me that long at all."

"How?" he asked, uncertain what compatibility would be necessary.

"I'll explain later." She glanced around at the group of dignitaries surrounding them. "Not here."

"We need to speak alone about many things. Soon." Unable to resist any longer, he drew her hand to his mouth and brushed a kiss across her fingers. Her flavor exploded on his tongue, sweet and decadent, like his favorite desserts all combined.

Her teeth dented her lower lip and he heard her utter a whisper soft sigh before withdrawing her hand. "Soon," she whispered, and it sounded less like agreement and more like a promise.

They filed into a meeting room as elegant and lush as the corridor outside. A long table of polished wood, matching chairs, and a side table with elegantly designed carafes containing different beverages. He and Braxon were ushered toward two chairs at the end of the table, but he chose to ignore the suggestion and claimed a spot in the middle that ensured Phaedra was seated between himself and Braxon.

She flashed him a grateful smile as she claimed her place at the table, and he knew he'd do everything in his power to give her reasons to smile like that every day of her life.

PHAEDRA'S MOTHER had taught her to seize every opportunity and hold on tight, and that was what she was going to do. Granted, Myra Kari probably hadn't meant literally hanging onto a prince's hand, but it was working for her. She had finally found a way inside the corporation's inner circle. From here, she might be able to find a way to fight for a future for the cyborgs she'd helped to rescue. Not to mention, she was now assigned to two sexy, intriguing alien males who could turn her on with just a look or a touch.

She wanted to find out why Braxon had grabbed her, and why he kept looking at her with unease while Tyran looked at her like she was a present he wanted to unwrap.

Why had they noticed her at all, never mind selected her to help them? There were so many questions she wanted to ask about their world, their lives, and their wings. She leaned back in her chair to get a better look at those wings, but Tyran's were gone. A quick glance at Braxon showed the same thing.

Curiosity got the better of her, and she reached out to place a hand on Braxon's back. *There.* She could feel his wing beneath her hand, at least, she thought that's what she was feeling.

Braxon exhaled sharply and snapped his head around to look at her. For a second, his green eyes glowed with obvious desire as he leaned into her touch, but then he moved away again.

"Sorry. I shouldn't have touched you without permission."

Braxon's brow furrowed, but instead of barking at her, he nodded. "I also touched you without permission. Now, we are equal. Next time, I ask."

"Did I hurt you?" she asked as she withdrew her hand.

He gave her a panty-meltingly hot smile. "You did not hurt me. That was - I think the word is - pleasurable."

Holy *fraxx*. He was flirting with her. At least, she thought he was. If he was flirting, did that mean he and Tyran shared? The idea of being the filling in a sexy alien sandwich flipped switches she didn't know she had. It also made her wonder what, exactly, her new duties entailed. Was sexplomacy a thing? Was it even a word?

A corporate lackey came by and set down a glass of ice water in front of her and the other guests. She picked up the glass and nearly dropped it in surprise. So *cold*.

She got a firmer grip and took a drink. That's when she realized what the problem was. It wasn't the temperature of the water. It was her. She was running hot and hadn't even noticed. Did she have a fever? *Veth*, she hoped not.

Archer stood, and the buzz of conversation died away as he began to speak. "Now that we're all comfortable, I was hoping that you could answer a few questions for us. I intend to keep this meeting brief, as it's the middle of the sleep cycle for many of us, but I'm sure there are questions on both sides."

He inclined his head toward Tyran and Braxon, though she noticed his gaze never left the prince. "On the walk here, I asked what brought you to this part of the galaxy. I'd like to ask a follow-up question if I may. How did you know where to find us?"

Braxon answered, forcing Archer to look at him. "We followed your communication traffic. So many ships and stations create noise. The closer we got, the louder the noise. Eventually, we heard your transmissions clearly and knew we had found others like us."

"And you came here alone? No military back up?"

Phaedra listened to Archer's questions and wondered if the man ever thought beyond his role as a military officer. He had been like this on the mission to Reamus station, too. Everything he saw was processed through the same filter.

"We are a scout ship. Scout ships always travel alone," Braxon replied.

"What if we had been hostile? What if you had been attacked instead of welcomed?"

Braxon grinned, baring a set of fangs she hadn't seen until now. "That's why we listened and learned your language before making contact. We believed you to be not hostile. If you had attacked, our plan was simple. Tyr fly. I shoot."

His answer was met with chuckles from around the table. Archer leaned back in his chair, apparently satisfied. "Thank you. Do you have any questions for us?"

Tyran answered this time. "We have not had time yet to review the information you sent. Now we have Phaedra to help us translate, I believe we will have more questions soon. For now, I would like to know, is there a way for us to claim a planet in this part of the galaxy? To make a new home. A place for trade."

The question was greeted with silence and Phaedra wanted to stand up and scream. This was why the cyborgs they'd rescued were still locked away in cryo-sleep. Neither the IAF nor the corporations wanted to give up one of their precious planets. Tactically important locations. Mineral rights. Future considerations. She'd heard all the excuses.

Well, not heard. Read. No one wanted her opinion or allowed her to attend their meetings. Once she had hacked into Reamus station's main systems, deactivated the automated defenses and ensured what little data remaining on the servers was secured, she'd been shut out. Everything she knew about the cyborgs and their plight she learned from Zale and Denz or from her hacks into Archer's communications. She learned long ago that the galaxy's greatest currency was information, and she gathered it like a dragon hoarded gold.

Tyran leaned forward and placed his hands on the table. "We would not expect it to be a gift, but part of a larger agreement. Perhaps a trade? Our technology and knowledge, as well as the opportunity to trade with the Vardarian empire and its allies?"

The atmosphere changed instantly. Reluctance turned to interest. Everyone leaned forward, their attention suddenly fixed on Tyran.

"How many planets would you need?"

"What technology could you offer?"

"What about weaponry? Star maps?""

The questions came all at once, and she decided it was time to remind everyone present what her role was. She raised her hands, and when that didn't work, she put two fingers to her lips whistled.

Silence fell.

She smiled sweetly as some of the most influential beings on the Drift gaped at her. "Perhaps everyone here has forgotten that our esteemed visitors have only been speaking Galactic Standard for a few weeks. If you wish to ask a question, you will need to proceed one at a time and make your meaning clear."

To her surprise, Archer nodded in agreement. "Now is not the time for detailed questions. Let's keep the queries general and easily understood for tonight and save the rest for later. Negotiations like this will have far-reaching consequences and will take time."

"I assume that future meetings will be by invitation only? Restricted to those of us who have a part to play in these negotiations?" The question came from a heavy-set man with ring encrusted fingers who looked pointedly at Phaedra.

Tyran took Phaedra's hand in his. "We are here to negotiate with *all* beings who wish to speak with us. We chose Phaedra Kari, a human, to assist and guide us. She will accompany us at all times."

Phaedra felt a rush of warmth and gratitude toward Tyran. She couldn't remember the last time a stranger had stood up for her.

"I see." Mister rings-galore looked like he'd swallowed something moldy and possibly toxic. "And what, exactly, are her qualifications for that position – apart from the obvious?"

Her temper hit the stratosphere. "Let's see, I speak five languages, have an augmented memory that allows me perfect recall, and experience working with hardware and software from a variety of worlds. As for my obvious qualifications, I have to assume you were referring to my implants."

She held out her free hand palm up so that the data port embedded in her wrist was clearly visible. "I'm a fully jacked cyber-jockey, which means I should be able to interface with our esteemed visitors' computer systems. That means I can learn their language and figure out how to make their tech play nicely with ours. *Those* are my qualifications."

Archer cleared his throat. "If there are no other questions, I believe we'll wrap this up for now. An agenda and invitations to attend negotiations will be prepared and sent out as quickly as possible."

He got to his feet and gave Phaedra a steely-eyed look. "If our guests and their liaison could stay until everyone else has left, I have a few security issues to discuss before you return to your ship."

She should probably be worried about what Archer was going to say once the others left, but she was distracted by the way Tyran kept stroking his thumb over the back of her hand.

Braxon reached for her hand but stopped before making contact. "I wish to see your arm. May I touch you?"

She was tempted to tell him that if kept being this nice, he could touch her anywhere he liked. What the hell was wrong with her? First, she was overheating, and now she was feeling weirdly giddy.

The weirdness jumped another notch when Braxon touched her arm. All he was doing was running his fingers around the data port, but it felt like a sensual caress.

"You are enhanced?" Braxon asked.

"I am." She hadn't meant to tell them this way, but at least they seemed to be taking the news well. Better than many humans, actually.

"Why? What purpose?"

"To interface with machines. I can go inside them, to what we call cyberspace. The place where information is stored and artificial intelligence exists."

"You can connect directly?"

"I can."

He pointed to Tyran, then himself. "So can we."

"You can? How? Show me!"

"Not like you. Similar, but smaller." Tyran joined in. "Much smaller."

"Inside your body?" She felt like she'd fallen into a wormhole and come out in a world where everything that made her different was suddenly the norm.

"Yes. Microscopic," Tyran stretched out the word as he struggled to pronounce it.

"Medi-bots. Nanotech. That's what we call it." She lowered her voice. "I have that, too."

"Which is a secret you were told not to reveal, Kari." Archer reminded her.

Braxon scowled. "Why is it a secret? All of our people have such enhancements. It is how we adapt ourselves to new worlds and environments."

"Nanotech and augmentation are not common among beings in this part of the galaxy. Most of those who do are cyborgs, and they're a relatively new species."

"They are not a different *species*. They're humans," she retorted. Those were her friends he was talking about.

"Cyborgs?" Tyran asked, looking uncertain. "I do not recall hearing anything about them."

"I'll explain about them later. Then I can introduce you to some."

Archer surprised her by agreeing with her again. "Good thinking. Make sure Zale meets them, too. In fact, I'll send you a list of names. You'll need to find a way to ensure everyone meets with our guests for at least a few minutes."

"Me?"

"You're their guide, liaison, and translator. I'll arrange for security, but everything else will require your input. At least I don't have to worry about you being unduly influenced by the corporations. You wouldn't have been my first choice for this position, but now I've had time to think about it, you might be exactly the right person for the job."

Archer being complimentary? The theory she'd landed in an alternate universe was starting to look more and more likely.

"Forgive me, but I struggle to see what the issue is. Phaedra is more than qualified." Tyran said.

"I imagine that your empire has different factions? Groups of people with similar interests, who work against those who do not share their goals?" Archer asked.

Tyran and Braxon both nodded. "The imperial court is full of such factions." Tyran said.

There was no missing the disdain in his tone. He didn't like political games. Was that why someone of his rank was out scouting the galaxy instead of staying home? "We have the same dynamics at play here." Archer splayed his hands wide. "Everyone has their own interests and biases. Phaedra is..." Archer shrugged looked her way. "Kari, you should be the one to explain matters, and give them a crash course in politics and factions while you're at it. And for the love of whatever you hold dear, try to stick to the facts without adding your own colorful commentary."

"Of course I will. I'm a good little galactic citizen."

He merely arched a brow in response, his silence speaking volumes.

"I'll keep the spinning to a minimum," she offered.

"Acceptable." He turned to Tyran. "I will have a security team assigned to guard your ship and accompany you on any excursions. They'll be there mostly for crowd control. I believe you will be the focus of a great deal of attention."

"I am Prince Tyran's *anrik*. It is my duty to protect him."

Phaedra stepped in. "Protecting Tyran may be your duty but protecting you both is Colonel Archer's. It would make it easier for you to explore the station and move around if there was someone to ensure we had space to move."

Tyran squeezed her hand. "It is also our duty to protect you. As our mah—our guide — your safety and comfort fall to us." He looked over at Braxon and uttered a few words in their language.

"Very well." Braxon rose from his chair, and once again Phaedra was struck by how big the two males were. If they were duty-bound to protect her, she was going to be one of the safest women on the Drift.

"You will accompany us back to our ship and we will talk about matters, yes?" Tyran asked her.

"Talk tonight, then send me a report tomorrow morning with as much information as you can." Archer ordered.

Phaedra got to her feet. "What's the magic word, Colonel?"

He ran a hand through his salt-and-pepper hair and grunted in irritation. "Send me a report tomorrow morning, *please*."

She grinned. "I'll make sure it's the first thing on my to-do list."

"I'm starting to rethink your suitability for this assignment already," he grumbled as he rounded the table and shook hands with Tyran and Braxon. "Phaedra will see you back to your ship, along with two guards. I'll speak with you both again tomorrow. And once again, I'd like to welcome you to this part of the galaxy."

The moment they were alone, Tyran and Braxon started speaking to each other in their own language. She didn't need to speak it to know that they were having some sort of debate. She let it go on for a few minutes and then tugged at Tyran's hand until he stopped talking to look down at her.

"We should continue any conversations you might want to have on your ship." She gestured around them. "This is not a secure area."

Braxon nodded, and she thought she detected a hint of respect in his expression. "You are right. The ship is the best place for us right now."

Taking that as permission to leave, Phaedra started for the door and Tyran followed after her, still holding her hand.

There were two IAF soldier's waiting in the corridor. "We're going back to the ship, now. Please lead the way," she asked, and they nodded without uttering a single word.

The three of them fell in behind the soldiers with Braxon walking a few feet ahead. The slits in his vest gave her glimpses of his back, and every once in a while, she saw part of a wing. It appeared to be folded tightly against his body, and once again she found herself tempted to reach out and touch him. Maybe once they knew each other better she'd ask to see their wings. Hell, given the way they were acting, maybe she'd get to see a whole lot more than that. The idea made her heart race and a surge of desire coursed through her, leaving fire and need it its wake.

Braxon glanced back at her like he knew what she was feeling. His gaze locked with hers, and for the second time that night she felt like something inside her was reaching out, trying to connect.

"*Mahaya*." Tyran uttered the word with near reverence.

"*Cahan tesk a jeza*," Braxon replied without looking back.

She glanced up at Tyran. "This would be more fun if I spoke Vardarian. What are you saying to each other?"

"I will tell you when we are alone. We have much to talk about."

"We do. And fortunately for us, I don't need a lot of sleep. I'll explain more about that when we're alone, too."

"I look forward to knowing all about you, Phaedra Kari. Tonight will be the first of many conversations," Tyran said.

They were almost back to the docking ring now. She hadn't realized how big Astek's headquarters were until now. The main entrance was closer to the station's center and several levels up.

"I want to know more about you, too. Both of you. I want to make sure you get the best possible deal for your people, and maybe you can find a way to help me get a deal for some of my friends, too."

"Whatever you need of us, *mahaya*, all you have to do is ask."

She wanted to ask what *mahaya* meant, but their escort came to a stop outside the door that led to the alien's ship. They'd made good time, due in part to the late hour and the route they'd taken. Anyone still awake would be on the main promenade, enjoying the entertainments on offer.

"Our orders are to remain outside and to escort you if you leave the ship," the taller one declared.

He didn't look familiar to her, but there was more IAF

personnel around these days. Things had been quiet since they had captured the Reaper and rid the Drift of the illegal pharma called Crimson, but everyone knew it wouldn't last. There was too much tension between the corporations, the planetary governments, and the Interstellar Armed Forces. Something was going to break soon, and when it did, it was going to get ugly.

Usually, ugly was her cue to pull up stakes and move on. She didn't stay in one place too long. She couldn't. She had made too many enemies over the years and uncovered too many secrets. This time, she was staying. Her friends, and the cyborgs they'd rescued, needed every ally they could find.

The guards stood aside, allowing Braxon to access the door panel and pass his hand over a sensor. The door opened, and the three of them stepped inside the most elegantly appointed ship Phaedra had ever seen.

CHAPTER FOUR

Braxon was waging an internal battle to stay in control - and he was losing. Tyr had already succumbed to the allure of the tiny human female.

When a Vardarian mated to another Vardarian, they formed an unbreakable bond that lasted the rest of their lives. When the mate was of another race, the outcome varied. With the Ferrym and the Vinu, the bond was for life, but with the Reekar, the bond rarely lasted and never produced children. Reekar matings were sexually intense at first, but unless the couple or trio could build a lasting relationship outside the bond, it ultimately ended in heartache. Until they knew what kind of bond they could have with Phaedra, he wasn't ready to accept her as their mate.

"This ship is huge!" Phaedra exclaimed, looking around her in wonder.

"This is the *Santar*, a royal cruiser class vessel. Fast, well-armed, and only for use by members of the royal family." Tyr patted the gleaming white wall of the outer hull. "This has been our home for many of your months."

"It's beautiful. I've never seen anything like it." She stretched her arms out and spun in place. "There's more room in this corridor than I've seen in some personnel quarters."

"Though it can be flown by a single being, the *Santar* was built to carry many. Crew, passengers, court followers, and those who assist them."

She dropped her hands back to her sides. "Those who assist them... do you mean you have servants?"

Braxon didn't know the word, but her reaction made it clear it wasn't something she approved of.

"What is a servant?" Tyr asked.

"Someone who serves. Who works for those with money and power and does the jobs the rich one doesn't wish to do. Cook. Clean. Help them dress."

Braxon took a long look at the human female, and this time he saw more than her attractive features and small stature. During the meeting, she had been dismissed by the others and had to fight to be acknowledged. Now, she expressed distaste for something any court-raised Vardian female would consider her due – servants. Phaedra Kari was becoming more intriguing by the minute.

"There are what you call servants at the Imperial Palace. There are none on this ship, though. It would not be fair to ask them to leave their friends and family when we are capable of taking care of ourselves," Tyran explained.

"But, you do have servants?"

Tyran answered before Braxon could stop him. "Of

course. I'm a prince. I was raised with any number of servants and staff."

"And what about Braxon? What is he to you? For that matter, what am I? Did you have him pull me out of the crowd because you thought you needed someone to look after you while you're here?"

He'd never seen the expression on Tyr's face before. It was a tangled mess of emotions, including dismay and confusion. No one had ever pushed back at the prince like this. Well, no one but Braxon.

"I am his *anrik*." Braxon pointed to the scar on his wrist. "I am not his servant. We are blood-bound companions."

"My friend," Tyran added. "The only one I can trust."

Phaedra's expression softened. "So, not his servant?"

"Never," Tyran replied. "And you are not servant, either. You are our *mahaya*."

"I think it's time you told me what that means."

"It means we are powerfully attracted to you. Your scent drew me to you, helped me find you in the crowd. I thought I was looking for a Vardarian female, but I found you," Braxon explained.

Tyran shot him an irritated look before turning his gaze to Phaedra. He took her hands in his and drew her close to him. "We are more than attracted to you, Phaedra. You are our *mahaya*, our mate. You will bind yourself to us and we will be a family."

She jerked her hands out of Tyr's and backed away from him in the direction of the door. "Whoa! I'm not binding myself to anyone. We just met!"

Braxon sidestepped to put himself between Phaedra and the door. This close to her, the acrid scent of her fear was strong. "Calm. There is nothing to fear here, Phaedra Kari. The choice to bind with us is yours to make. You will not be forced."

"I'm not afraid," she protested. "But I'm not calm, either. What he said. Is that true?"

"I don't know. It is possible. There are tests we can run to be sure."

Tyr started to speak, but Braxon silenced him with a warning look. Tyran might be convinced, but he wasn't the one they needed to worry about right now. If she *was* their mate, then scaring her away was not in their best interests. Not if they wished to hang on to their sanity.

"What kind of tests?"

"Medical tests. A scan, then—" he tapped his wrist. "Blood?"

She straightened her shoulders and nodded. "Do it."

She certainly sounds like the mate of an imperial prince, he thought to himself as he set off toward the medical bay. "Come. We can explain more as we run the tests. It won't take long."

"Why will neither of you accept what you know to be true?" Tyr asked.

Phaedra had started to follow Braxon, but she stopped to speak to Tyran. "I don't *know* anything yet. I feel mild euphoria when I'm around you, and there are some other weird physical reactions, but that doesn't mean I'm destined to spend the rest of my life with you. With either of you. Both? I'm going to need more information."

"We would both claim you as our *mahaya*." Tyr held out his arm and showed her the scar on his wrist. "We are bound by blood. When – " he paused. "I mean if you chose to join with us, we would bind you to us the same way."

They started walking again. The med-bay was on the main floor near the stern of the ship. It wouldn't talk long to get there. Phaedra continued to ask questions along the way.

"You said you're bound by blood. Does that mean you share your nanotech, too? The small machines in your bodies."

"We do. We have mixed ourselves together," Braxon tried to explain, hoping she understood.

"So, you carry each other's blood and nanotech. What if you did that to me and our tech didn't react well?"

Braxon paused. He hadn't considered that. Of course, they hadn't considered much of anything. There hadn't been time to. "If the tests prove you're our mate, we'll ensure the binding would be safe for you."

"I have a friend, Zale. He's the one that designed the nanotech I carry. He'd be able to help with that. I mean, he could, if this is real, and if I say yes."

"I don't understand why you both keep saying 'if' this is real. It is. I am sure of it," Tyr said.

"Because Braxon and I aren't sure I'm this *mahaya* thing, even if you are." She sighed. "All I was supposed to do today was witness my best friend get married to the men of her dreams and celebrate for the rest of the night. How did I end up here?"

"Our ancestors brought us together for a reason. You are destined for us, Phaedra. And then, together, we will lead the new colony," Tyr said.

"Whoa again. Who said anything about leading?"

"You do not wish to lead?" Tyr sounded perplexed by

the idea, while Braxon grew even more intrigued. He had never met someone who cared so little for power and all its trappings.

"I NEVER SAID I didn't wish to lead. I said no one mentioned it until now. When you said we had things to talk about, it was something of an understatement." Phaedra was having trouble staying focused on the conversation. She'd been hit with so much new information already, and her physical response to them was distracting as hell. Not to mention the fact she was standing on an alien vessel with two aliens, one of whom seemed keen to marry her and the other who wanted to run tests.

Braxon paused in front of a large doorway and it slid open a second later. He walked through the door and gestured for her to follow.

Alyson was always trying to warn her that her habit of jumping in with both feet was going to catch up to her someday. It looked like that day had come. "Don't make me regret gatecrashing your welcome ceremony."

"What is gatecrashing?" Tyran asked as he followed her inside.

"It means that I wasn't supposed to be there. I snuck in." She got her first look at the medical bay and uttered a low whistle. "I'd say your medical technology is aeons ahead of ours. Make sure you remember that when the bargaining starts. The corporations will be at each other throats to get a piece of all this."

There were four beds, each set into its own alcove and

surrounded by monitors and machines she couldn't guess the purposes of. In the center of the space was a circular console with seats and more monitors. As they entered the room, a hologram flickered into existence. The image was of a kindly looking female with golden scales, wings, and dark hair. She spoke in a calm, friendly voice, though Phaedra didn't understand a word of it.

"Let me amend my earlier statement. The corporations won't just be at each other's throats, they'll be willing to commit murder to get their greedy paws on your tech." She pointed to the hologram. "If that's an interactive diagnostic program, it's probably worth a planet all by itself."

"Too many unfamiliar words," Braxon said, shaking his head. In the brightly lit room, his scales gleamed like newly minted gold.

"That is a hologram, right? A projected image connected to a computer program. One that can determine how to treat someone who is sick or injured?"

Braxon nodded. "If we are injured, the program will heal – treat us on its own."

"Our medical technology is not nearly that advanced. At least, not that I'm aware of. My friend, Alyson, is a doctor. She'd be able to give us a better idea of its value. These tests. How will it work?"

Tyran pointed to the nearest bed. "If you lay there, this can be done quickly."

"And then we'll know if I'm your mate?"

"I already know this, but Braxon wishes to prove it to himself, and to you."

"I'm glad he does, because I need some proof. We're not the same species. We don't even know if we're uh, physically compatible." She walked over to the bed, which was far too high for her. Before she could ask for a stool, Tyran stepped in and lifted her onto the bed. It was the closest contact they'd had, yet, and she had to bite back a moan as his arms closed around her, holding her close to his body for one exquisite moment.

When he set her down again, her pulse was racing, and her skin felt like it was on fire. Tyran was breathing heavily, too.

"Is this feeling part of being mated?"

"What are you feeling?" Tyran asked without moving away from her.

She censored her response because the last thing she wanted to admit was that she was turned on and feeling like she'd taken some premium bliss-inducing pharma.

"Hot. Giddy, like I'm a little intoxicated, and my skin is sensitive."

Tyran chuckled, a deep, satisfied sound that made her breath hitch. "You are experiencing the *sharhal*. The mating fever. You are reacting to what you call pheromones. It means your body recognizes what you do not yet accept.

"My body is not to be trusted. It's got a lousy track record," she muttered, then lay back on the bed. It was the most comfortable thing she'd ever reclined on, and she made a note to include the design as yet another thing they could offer in trade. The way things were going, they could probably afford to buy a whole *fraxxing* system full of planets.

Above her lights activated, and she closed her eyes to shut out the glare. "Be still, please. The scan will not take long, and you will not feel anything more than a mild warmth." Braxon's tone was almost gentle, and she knew he was trying to reassure her.

"If I feel anything else, you'll be the first to know."

As promised, she didn't feel anything more than a bit of heat during the scan. A few more tests, all just as gentle as the scan, and she was done. Sitting up, she let her feet dangle off the edge of the bed as she looked around. "How long until we know?"

"Not long. Maybe one-quarter of your hours." Tyran moved in and offered her his hands to help her down. She took his hand and hopped off the bed, once again thankful she wasn't wearing heels.

Instead of letting her go, Tyran pulled her in close and looked down at her, one hand lifting to stroke a loose curl away from her face. "Never did I dream our *mahaya* would be so beautiful."

"We still don't know that's what I am."

"I know."

"You might be right, but that doesn't change the fact we're strangers. All I know about you is your names. This might be how it works for your species, but that's not going to be enough for me."

"But you feel the pull between us." He stroked her cheek again. "Tell me that my touch doesn't bring you pleasure."

She turned away from his touch. "Pleasure is one thing. Together forever is something very different."

"She is right, Tyr. We should not rush this."

Braxon moved beside Tyran and bowed low. "I am Braxon Torr of Vardaria. Son of Kalis and Anjira."

Tyran stepped back and then performed his own graceful bow. "I am Prince Tyran Varosa of Vardaria, member of the Imperial house, brother to Empress Neha Varosa, son of Talus and Kess." He straightened and gave her a smile that made her brain melt a little around the edges. "But you can call me Tyr. If you introduce yourself to us, then we will no longer be strangers."

She managed a passable bow of her own. "I am Phaedra Kari, daughter of Myra and Timothy."

"What world do you call home?" Braxon asked.

"None of them. I was born on a space station called Plaisa IV."

Tyran frowned. "Then who holds your loyalty?"

She laughed and shook her head. "My loyalty is to my mother and my friends. No one else."

She was met with perplexed stares.

"Remember when Colonel Archer said I should explain why I'm not going to be welcome at the table during investigations? This is why. I have no loyalty to any faction, government, or world. I chose to live outside what most consider normal society. I don't follow rules or even laws if I don't believe they're right. I want to make things better for everyone. Hacking is how I do that."

She pointed to the data port on her wrist, then pushed back the hair behind her ear to reveal her second one. "I told you, I have implants that let me interface with computers. Not long ago, I used that ability to help expose secrets the corporations were trying to hide. Some of them suspect I was involved. They don't like or trust me, and I don't like or trust them."

"You want to make things better, so you defy authority?" Tyran was grinning now, and she got a good look at the delicately curved fangs sat in the same spot humans had canine teeth.

"Yes."

"That is why we are here. Things on our homeworld do not change. The empire is strong because we are many different species, but on Vardaria, there is no many. Only purebloods and a few who are considered lesser. It is wrong." Tyran looked at Braxon, whose expression hardened for a moment before dropping his head in a slight nod.

"Braxon isn't treated the same as you because he's not a pureblood? Then how is he your -what did you call it – *anrik*?"

"My father chose Braxon because he believed he was the best choice. Later, he told me it was also because he wanted to be sure that at least one of his children understood that there were more important virtues than someone's bloodline."

She read between the lines. "Your sister doesn't share that belief, does she?"

"She struggles with the idea. My father's lessons have been weakened by the influence of her counsellors." Tyran's shoulders slumped, and his blue eyes darkened.

"And this colony you want to start, it will be different?"

"That is our wish," Braxon confirmed.

"See, that's the kind of thing I want to know. You might be willing to trust pheromones or fate, but I can't do that."

"We want to know about you, too." Braxon pointed to the data port behind her ear. "Did you get that the same time as the nanites?"

"No. I got my first data port when I was a teenager –a young woman, not even an adult yet. The medi-bots, I mean the nanites, were given to me by a friend to protect me from harm if the corporations retaliated for what I've done. I've only had them a few months."

"Will you tell us more about what you did, and what secrets you revealed while we give you a tour of the ship? Are you thirsty? Hungry?"

"I'm fine. I was at a party tonight, with more than enough food and drink to keep me going. I'd like to see your ship, but what I'd really like is to look at your computer system. You said you had a translation program. I'd like to see if there's a way I can access it."

The two males looked at each other and had a quick conversation she couldn't follow. "It might be best if you did that from here," Braxon said.

"This could be dangerous to you. I don't want you to be injured." Tyran seemed less than thrilled with the idea, but she had her medi-bots and years of experience hacking into alien systems.

"If I'm going to be truly useful, we need to be able to communicate quickly and without risk of misunderstanding. It will be fine, Tyran. Accessing systems is what I'm best at. Before I do this, can one of you write down the name of the program in your language so I know what I'm looking for?"

Braxon moved to one of the stations and entered a few keystrokes, which appeared on the monitor above it. The figures were lovely, ornate, and completely incomprehensible to her, but if she could reference the pattern, she could find the program.

"Phaedra, I don't want you to do this." Tyran stepped in and put his arm out, blocking her from getting closer to the computer stations.

"Then you should have picked someone else for this job."

"I forbid it."

She looked up at Tyran and frowned. "You might be a prince, Tyran Varosa, but you're not *my* prince. You can't forbid me anything."

He frowned, blinked, opened his mouth, then closed it again, while Braxon tried, and failed, to stifle a bout of laughter.

"What's so funny?" she demanded ready to pick a fight with him, too.

"I believe I owe Tyr fifty *koldar*. I have never seen a female defy him before. Usually they are too taken with his charm and title to refuse him anything."

"Titles don't impress me." She shrugged. "And I'm not good at following anyone's orders. I believe I warned you about that already."

Tyran stepped back and let his arm fall back to his side. "I was only trying to keep you safe, *mahaya*."

"I have bad news for you, Tyran. Even if I am your mate, you still don't get to boss me around." She turned to Braxon. "Can you inform your system that I'm about to make contact? Maybe tell it not to treat me as an attacker at least?"

He nodded, and then both he and Tyran went to a workstation and began making entries. After a few minutes, they stopped and looked at her. "We have done what we can."

She took a seat and lay her hand over what she guessed was the data node. It would take a while, but she was determined to get this done. They might have chosen her because of pheromones, but that didn't mean she wouldn't take her new role seriously. She had been looking for a way to fight for the cyborgs and be heard. This was her chance to make a difference. When the tests came back and proved that she wasn't their mate, then she would still be of use to them.

It was the only plan she had.

TYRAN WATCHED as the female closed her eyes and went still. It was as if the essence of her was suddenly gone, leaving only an empty shell behind. Without a word, he moved to her side and placed a hand on her bare shoulder. A moment later, Braxon did the same, and the two of them sat in silence as she traveled through their ship's systems.

Their nanotech allowed them to interface with the ship in a different way, and while he understood what she was doing, he couldn't imagine what it would be like, or what problems she might come across. Their technology was different. He wasn't even sure she'd be able to manage what she sought to do.

After a few minutes, Phaedra inhaled sharply and woke from her fugue. "Your system is beautiful. *Veth*, I could spend hours in there."

"Did you find what you needed?" Braxon asked.

"Are you uninjured?" Tyran added.

"I'm fine, and no, I didn't. I wasn't even jacked in. That was just a test run to see if it was possible."

"And is it?" Tyran asked.

Her delicate features folded into a frustrated frown. "I think so, but I've never seen technology quite like yours before. It's a crystalline lattice design like the Pherans use, but it's different enough I can't access it. Not yet."

She drummed her fingers on the keyboard. "Until I can, we'll have to make do."

"The program will continue to improve our abilities. The more we listen, the more it learns. We already speak better than we did, yes?"

"I noticed that. So, you were linked to this system even while you were away from the ship? That's amazing!"

It bothered him that she was more interested in the technology than in her mates. Maybe Braxon was right and this wasn't a true mating. How could it be, when she continued to resist them? It didn't make any sense.

Tyran lifted his hand from her shoulder and stepped back. Even that small bit of distance felt wrong, but he no longer trusted his instincts.

Braxon watched him, then shook his head. *"Having doubts of your own, now?"* He asked, using their subvocal communicators.

"She denies the mating bond and will not listen to me."

Braxon barked with laughter, then answered aloud in Vardarian. "Welcome to my world. This is what it's like for those of us who weren't born an emperor's son with the world at his feet."

"I don't like your world. Mine's easier." He glanced down at Phaedra. "If the test results prove she is ours, what then?"

"Then we give her a reason to choose us. As for how to make that happen, I don't have any suggestions. The females at court deemed me unworthy, remember?"

"Phaedra is not like them."

"No, she is not. But that won't make this any easier."

"Hello? You two realize that my name sounds the same in your language, right? So I know you're talking about me. Which is rude. Did we discuss that yet?" Phaedra shrugged off Braxon's hand and turned to face them. "I'm here. You can ask me anything."

"We were discussing the test you took," Tyr said.

"Cold feet already?" She crossed her arms over her chest and lifted a brow in question.

"What does the temperature of my limbs have to do with anything?" Tyr asked.

"It's an expression. It means to have second thoughts. Doubts. You're starting to think it would be better if I wasn't your mate. It's okay. Most people have that reaction. I'm an acquired taste."

He didn't know how to answer her. Lying was dishonorable, but if he admitted his doubts, she'd be hurt. Braxon was silent, too.

She rose from her seat, her smile bright but her eyes shadowed. "Yeah. Cold feet. I thought so. I think it's time for me to go. I have a report to write and work to do. Do you guys sleep? When should I come back?"

"You're leaving?" Tyran hadn't expected that. He hadn't expected any of this.

As she nodded, the console chimed. Her test results.

"You should stay for this," Braxon said.

"Please," Tyran added, earning himself a look of surprise from his *anrik*.

"If it comes back negative, will I still be allowed to be your liaison?"

"Of course." Both he and Braxon spoke at once.

She grinned. "If I didn't know better, I'd say you practiced that. Okay, I'll stay and hear the results. And uh, thank you for not firing me. I mean, letting me stay on as your guide even though I'm sure we're not mates."

Braxon glanced at the screen, frowned, and tapped the monitor several times. The data displayed changed, but his expression didn't. "Tyr. Look."

"What is it, what's wrong?" Phaedra asked.

Braxon flicked his fingers and the information on the screen appeared in the air in front of them. "You're are a perfect match for us, Phaedra Kari. You are our *mahaya*."

"I can't be. Do the test again." Her rejection stung, but not as much as the fear he heard in her voice.

"The tests have already been run twice. Three will not change the answer. You are our *lia jeza*. A miracle."

"So that's it, I belong to you now?"

"Would that be so bad? To be ours? We Vardarians dream of the day we will find the one who will complete us. This is a joyous moment," Tyr said.

She backed away from them. "For you maybe it's joyous, but five minutes ago you both had doubts. This doesn't change anything."

"It changes everything, *mahaya*." He reached for her, but she continued to move away.

"You can't make me stay here with you. You can't *make* me do anything. Right now, my choice is to go. I'll be back tomorrow."

Braxon moved toward the door. "I will show you the way out."

After they left, Tyran walked over to the nearest wall and punched it with enough force to leave a dent. Being parted from Phaedra was already difficult, and that would only get worse as time passed. In a matter of days, they would all be completely in the thrall of the *sharhal*. If she refused their claim, they'd descend into a madness that they might never recover from.

He ran a hand through his hair and muttered to himself. "Only a fool goes into battle with a single plan and expects to win." It was one of his sire's favorite expressions. They needed a new plan – or plans. She wasn't the soft-spoken, gentle female of his dreams. She was beautiful, fierce, and strong-willed enough to walk away from them forever if they didn't convince her to stay.

CHAPTER FIVE

PHAEDRA HAD SPENT the last hour or so hiding in her room at the Nova Club. At least, that's where her body was. Her mind was adrift in cyberspace. It was a distraction-free place for her to work as she slowly unraveled the mysteries of Vardarian technology. It was like trying to undo a tangled knot while standing in the middle of the threads. Eventually she'd find the right thread and the knot would loosen, but right now she was stuck.

She came out of cyberspace with a growl of frustration. "I have one damned job, and I can't even do that very well. They're learning our language so fast that soon I'll be totally useless to them."

"And hello to you, too. I was starting to wonder if you'd died in there."

Phaedra nearly levitated out of her chair with surprise, then spun around to glare at her visitor. "Damn it, Cynder, I swear to god I'm going to sew bells into every scrap of clothing you own."

"I'd be more afraid of that threat if you could actually

sew." Cynder drawled, her long legs stretched out in front of her as she slouched in the only other chair in Phaedra's quarters.

"Who says I can't?"

"The missing buttons on your favorite jacket. You do realize we have tailors on the station, right? We even have droids that could fix that for you."

"I'm a wee bit busy keeping the unwashed masses away from the winged wonders right now to worry about buttons. Speaking of which, are they downstairs?"

Cyn nodded. "They're with the guys. Well, the ones not currently on their honeymoons. So, why are they getting a night off and you're up here, working?"

"Because they need some downtime before we do any more meetings. It's the same thing every time. Whoever we're meeting tries to get them to agree to an exclusive deal before negotiations even start. It's crazy, and it's making Tyr and Braxon cranky."

"Mmhmm. That only answers half my question. Those are two seriously hot males, and they clearly want you to be the cherry on their sundae, so I'll ask again. Why are you up here, alone?"

"Because I have to figure out how this translation program works so I can do my job. We're just waiting for some high-ranking executive from Axion Corporation to get here before starting negotiations, and I still can't speak Vardarian."

"Before you continue down this path, might I remind you that as a cyborg, I know if you're lying before you've finished speaking, and that includes half-truths."

Phae huffed. "Fine. I'm avoiding them. Happy now?"

"No." Cyn frowned and sat up. "Did they do something to you? Do I need to hurt them?"

"Cool your boosters, no need for violence." Phaedra hadn't told anyone about the *mahaya* thing yet, but she probably should, and she wasn't going to interrupt Alyson's honeymoon to talk about the weird twist in her love life.

"Then why avoid them? Can't choose between them? Or is it something else?"

"Choosing between them isn't an issue. Choice is the issue."

"A little less cryptic for those of us who spent our formative years shooting anything that moved instead of studying philosophy."

"Tyr and Braxon are linked for life and share everything...including a mate. Vardarians find their mate through pheromones, and once they find her, that's it. She's with them for the rest of their lives."

"So, once they find her, they'll have no choice but to leave you."

"They've already found her. It's me, Cyn. I'm their *fraxxing* mate."

The cyborg blinked and then grinned. "Is that why they hauled you out from behind Zale that night? I feel like I should be congratulating you, but since you're hiding from your mates, there's clearly a problem I'm not seeing."

"Choice."

Cyn looked blank for a moment, then sighed. "Aha, I see the problem. In this scenario, you don't get a choice. Are they sure this is real? I mean, you're not even the same species."

"They're sure. They ran some tests the first night. I'm their *mahaya*. Their mate. I'm supposed to abandon my life and my friends to go with them, and they don't understand why that's not okay with me."

"I get wanting some choice, and a little courtship might be nice, but how do you feel about them? Toro and Jaeger had to work hard before I agreed to date them, but I already knew I liked them, I just didn't want to admit it." Cyn gave a wry grin. "I didn't really admit it to myself until Jaeger got himself stabbed trying to protect me. I guess what I'm asking is, do you like them that way?"

"Tyr's bossy, and Braxon's got brooding down to an art form."

Cyn snickered. "Tyran's a prince. I'm pretty sure expecting everyone to do as he says is part of the lifestyle. On the plus side, if you end up mated to him, that means you get to boss people around. And you didn't answer my question."

"I don't know. I think so? We haven't had much time alone. There have been so many meetings and briefings and introductions, and when we're not doing that, I'm supposed to be scheduling more meetings. It doesn't give us a lot of time to get to know each other."

"And yet, they're downstairs, relaxing, and you're up here. Hiding." Cyn pointed to the door. "We're continuing this conversation downstairs. With drinks and friends."

"Zura?" Phaedra loved Cynder's sister-in-law. The feisty blue-haired woman was quick to laugh, even though her pregnancy had advanced to the point that she couldn't hide it any longer. Word of her condition was spreading, and they were expecting the corporations to react any day now. They were not going to be happy to learn that the first humans to be born with medi-bots would not come from the cyborg women they had tried – and failed - to make infertile, but from a human woman, the wife of the cyborgs they had always claimed were mindless machines, incapable of emotion.

"And River, if I can get her to answer me. It's too bad Nya took that mining job. With her gone, there's a lack of fun females around."

"I'm going to miss Nya, and you're right, River needs a girls' night more than I do. I'm not sure she'll want to spend time with me, though." River was the representative of the cyborgs they had found at the station. The others had chosen to go into cryo-sleep until a place could be found for them, and they had entrusted River with the task of finding them a home.

"Naw, she likes you. She just doesn't know how to show it. She spent years submitting to every order and repressing every emotion she had because every time she reacted emotionally they reset her programming and wiped her memories."

"I wasn't sure how she felt about me. I went there looking to be a hero and free a grateful group of prisoners. I wasn't prepared for what we found."

She would never forget seeing the cold, cramped metal boxes where River and the others were housed, or the stories of degradation and abuse they suffered at the hands of the scientists and staff. The experiments and tests. The brutality and indifference.

The females were forced to tend to the newly matured cyborgs, cyborgs created long after the corporations were supposed to have stopped production. They taught them the rules, tested their abilities, and endured their violent outbursts. As the new soldiers were made increasingly violent, the females grew to fear them. So much so, that when Phaedra and the others arrived, River and the others came to them and warned them not to wake any of the males from cryo-sleep until there was a safe place for them to recover.

"Hey, without you, we still wouldn't know where they were. You're the reason they're free."

Phae slammed her hand down on the desk. "That's the thing. They're not free. They're sleeping, waiting for a group of people who don't care about them to commit time, money, and resources to giving them a home. That's why I agreed to be Tyr and Braxon's guide. I thought it would get me in a better position to help."

Cyn just grunted and pointed to the door. "We need drinks to continue this conversation. Come on. First round is on me."

Phaedra rose and laughed. "Since you own the damned bar, I vote the first two rounds are on you."

"Deal. River says she'll meet us downstairs, and Zura is on her way."

THE NOVA CLUB was relatively quiet, but no matter how busy it got, there was always a table in the VIP section set aside for the owners and their friends. Cyn led the way, greeting regulars and touching base with the staff as they made their way through the crowd. The gaming tables all had crowds of onlookers and gamblers, and everywhere she looked, Phaedra could see couples and groups crowded together, eating, drinking, and laughing.

Tonight, it was a social crowd, but on fight nights the place was packed with visitors from every race and social class on the station. Phaedra had been around for one of those events, and the electric atmosphere had sucked her in despite her reservations. She had thought it would be hard to watch her friends fight and risk injury, but the energy and exhibition of skills and power had been intoxicating. Cynder had fought that night, while her husbands cheered her on from the outside of the cage with so much pride and enthusiasm it made Phaedra envious.

She looked over at the fight cage. The flowers and ribbons from the wedding celebration were gone, and it was back to its stark, foreboding appearance. It seemed like an age ago they'd been sitting here, celebrating the wedding. So much had happened since then.

River was already seated and talking to Zura by the time they arrived, and Phaedra was pleased to see the newest member of the group was looking more at ease. The bustle and noise of the club were hard on her enhanced senses, and she ate her meals with hurried, frantic speed, as if expecting it to be taken away at any moment. She was tall and lean, like Cynder, with black hair and deep brown eyes. Since coming to Astek, she had cut her hair so short it was barely visible, and all her outfits were overlarge and unflattering. She did her best to keep everyone at arms-length, but she was slowly adjusting.

"Hey, River." Cyn dropped into a seat and grinned at the cyborg. "Glad you could join us. How you doing, little blue momma? Those babies of yours letting you get any sleep?"

Zura waved in greeting. "They're just like their fathers. They never stay still very long. I've already told the guys that next time, they're in charge of the manufacturing stage."

"Did they run screaming from the room?" Phaedra asked as she claimed a seat across from River. "Hi, River. Nice to see you. It's been a while."

River shrugged. "I've been around. You haven't been. Your new assignment keeps you busy, and there haven't been any updates or briefings on the plan for my brethren in days. Not since your aliens arrived."

"They're not my aliens. I agreed to be their liaison because I thought it would give me a chance to talk to the people who are supposed to be making decisions about you and your group, but so far, it's not working that well. They barely acknowledge me, and all they want to do is talk with Tyran and Braxon about trade deals and tech. I hope that changes when the real talks start. If Werner Tice, the Vice-President of Axion ever gets here. The man owns his own star cruiser. How can you be late when you have a ship that can travel all of known space in a matter of days?"

"People like him have so much wealth and power they know they can be late, because nothing can be done without them." Cyn waved over a server who took their drink and meal orders.

"People like him are my favorite targets. They always have secrets."

"You like to live dangerously." Zura had firsthand experience in how dangerous secrets could be. She and her brother had nearly been killed over one, and when Kit and Luke had given her a transfusion of their medi-bots in a desperate attempt to save her life, it led to the uncovering of secrets the corporations had been keeping for years. They'd lied about everything from the source of the DNA used to create the cyborgs to their attempts to block the female cyborgs' fertility. Another of those secrets led to discovering the existence of cyborgs like River – prisoners who had never been freed despite all the promises the corporations had made.

Phaedra shrugged. "Taking risks is part of the deal. Uncovering the truth means making enemies. I came to terms with that a long time ago. It's why I don't usually stay in one place too long."

"And yet, you're still here," Cyn said.

"Why do you stay?" River asked. "You did your part of the job already."

"No, I haven't. The IAF asked me to help them secure the station's AI and help retrieve any data I could. That was what they wanted me to do. Having been there, I know that isn't enough. You and your kin need somewhere to call home. Somewhere safe from anymore corporate insanity. I want to help you find it."

"Why?" River asked. "Why do you care what happens to us? No one cared before."

Zura gasped and Cyn rocked back in her seat. "It's not that we didn't care! We didn't *know*. They kept lying to us, covering up what they'd done. It took years, and luck, and a lot of risks to find out you were still out there. Once we knew, we came after you. You have to believe that."

River shook her head. "We were abandoned. Forgotten. I had batch brothers who never looked for me. They just accepted the story they were told about my accidental death and went on their way. I've met your brothers. They wouldn't have accepted anything without seeing your body. That's why I'm angry. You didn't know, but some of the cyborgs had to have suspected. And the humans..." she turned her focus on Phaedra.

"What about the humans?" Phaedra asked. She could guess where this was going, but River had been holding on to her anger too long already. If this was the moment she finally opened up about it, then she wouldn't stop her.

"It was the humans who let this happen to us. They didn't care about us, because we weren't their family and friends. We were just fighting machines, dying so that they didn't have to."

"All true." Phaedra spotted their server coming with a tray full of drinks and thanked the universe for good timing. They were going to need booze.

No one said anything until the drinks were served. Then Phaedra looked at River and raised her glass. "My mother had a lot of expressions, but this was one of her favorites. "Regretting the past is like poking a pig. It feels like you're doing something, but you're not accomplishing anything worthwhile."

River stared at her. "I –I don't think I understand."

"Me either. Why would anyone poke a pig?" Cyn asked.

"Forget the pig. It means that being angry about the past won't change anything, but it can distract you from doing something to make the present better."

River frowned. "Then why didn't she say that?"

"There's a long, complicated answer to that, but the short one is easier. My mom was quirky."

"Well, that explains a few things about you, doesn't it?" Cyn hid her smile behind her drink.

"So, you're saying I need to stop being mad and do something? What? What can I do?" River asked.

"Find a way to make them listen to you. That's what I'm trying to do right now, and I'll keep trying until I make it happen."

Cyn set down her drink. "And while you're doing that, you don't have to think about Braxon and Tyran, right? To borrow from your mom's saying, isn't that just poking one pig while ignoring two others?"

River groaned. "There are too many pigs in this conversation."

All of them burst out laughing, and for the first time in two days, Phaedra finally felt better. Cyn was right. She needed this break.

BRAXON TOOK another sip from the large glass of liquor his host, Kit Armas, had just handed to him. "What did you say this was called?"

"Torskian Ale. Go easy, that stuff has a kick." Kit paused. "Never mind. I forgot, you have nanotech, too. No hangovers for you." He raised his own glass. "I'm glad Phae encouraged you to hang out with us tonight, though I admit, I'm surprised. I thought you'd be too deep in negotiations to get away."

"They haven't started yet." Braxon said, trying to keep the frustration out of his voice.

"What?" The cyborg called Jaeger exclaimed. "You've been here two days. What the *fraxx* have they been doing if not negotiations? Phae's been working non-stop, and you two have hardly been seen since arriving."

"We're in something called preliminary meetings. Countless ones with the corporations, the military, even representatives of the other races. Phaedra attends all meetings with us, and when she is not, she is working on the program that translates for us." Tyran drummed his fingers against his glass. "She keeps finding ways to be busy."

Jaeger arched a brow. "I take it you wish she wasn't always busy?"

Tyran tensed. "She is our *mahaya*, and she will barely speak to us."

"What's a *mahaya*?" Toro asked. He was another cyborg. He and Jaeger were mated to Cynder, the sister of Luke and Kit. Phaedra had introduced them all this morning, and Braxon had felt an instant camaraderie with the enhanced warriors.

"Our mate," Braxon explained. "We caught her scent the moment we left the ship."

"No way. Phae's your mate? So that's why you pulled her out of the crowd? Does Zale know? He's been grumpy ever since that happened, it would cheer him up if he knew why," Toro said.

"I don't know who Phaedra has told, if anyone. She is not happy about it. Not at all."

Jaeger chuckled. "Welcome to the club. When we first met Cyn, she had zero desire to go out with us. It took a lot of work to get her to change her mind."

"And then you *fraxxed* up again and had to go chasing after her," Luke pointed out.

"Like you did any better? How long did it take for you two to make a move on Zura?"

"Too long," Kit admitted.

"But you have your mates now." Tyran sat up, his drink cradled in his hands. "How did you do it? How did you make them care for you?"

"Charm."

"Flowers."

"Chocolate."

"A little begging." Each of them offered a different answer.

Tyr swore and set down his glass harder than he had intended. Those little losses of control were happening more often – to both of them. As the need to claim Phaedra grew more intense, their emotions would become more volatile, and their control would continue to fray.

"Easy, my friend." He reached instinctively for Tyr, setting his hand over the prince's forearm to calm him. It wasn't something he'd done before, but it seemed to work.

Tyr nodded to him, then uttered a frustrated growl. "Nothing about this is easy."

All four men were looking at them in confusion, and Braxon decided explanations were in order. "With our species, mating is not a matter of courtship. It's based on pheromones. When we meet our mates, we claim them and learn about each other afterward."

"That sounds a lot simpler than our way," Toro muttered.

"Yes. When only our species is involved. Phaedra is human. We think she's feeling the effects of the mating fever, but she's fighting it." Tyr said, his tone edged with frustration.

"You're going to need flowers *and* chocolate. Maybe booze. Definitely jewelry. Cyn likes jewelry. We'll help. Won't we, guys?" Toro looked around at the others, who nodded. "Phaedra's done a lot for us. She deserves a little happiness in her life."

"What's this about a mating fever?" Jaeger asked.

"The *sharhal*. It affects all Vardarians as we mature. It's a need that drives us to find our mates, and once we do, it intensifies until the claiming is complete." Braxon explained.

"And you're both feeling the effects of that right now?" Kit asked.

"Yes. And it's damned distracting."

The four cyborgs looked at each other and grinned. "You thinking what I'm thinking?" Luke asked.

"Cage match," Toro said, and the rest started to chuckle.

"First, we give them a crash course in human dating rituals, and *then* cage match."

"I don't understand." Tyr interjected.

"Cyborgs were built for war. To do that, they dialed up the hormones keyed to aggression. Those also happen to be linked to our sex drive. Before we were married, we spent a lot of time sparring and fighting in the ring to take the edge off. Do you think that would work for you?" Jaeger asked.

"Sparring is fighting for practice, yes? What is a cage match?" Tyr asked.

"This club hosts fights. Sanctioned events between fighters like Toro here, and our sister, Cynder. If you two wanted to try and dull the effects of this *sharhal* thing, we could open the ring up for an exhibition match. The customers would love it, and you'd be safe inside the cage we use to protect the fighters from the crowds."

"Who would we fight?" Braxon asked. He hadn't done much combat practice since they'd left on this mad mission. There was nowhere onboard big enough to allow it, nor anywhere that they could take to the air and stretch their wings. It was an oversight they both had agreed would be rectified once they were back home. The idea of sparring to blow off steam, as the humans called, it, was very appealing.

"It would give Archer fewer ulcers if you fought each other. At least the first time." Kit said.

"Think of the crowd we could get in here if they agreed to a match we could promote first," Toro added with enthusiasm.

Braxon looked at Tyran and switched to their native tongue. "I like the idea. This will help us focus. And I haven't had a chance to prove I am the better warrior for weeks now. It's time you were reminded."

Tyr scoffed. "It's been too long if you remember yourself as being the better warrior."

Braxon switched back to Galactic Standard. "We will fight each other. Does this cage have enough room to allow us to extend our wings or fly a little?"

"We can make that happen. Expand the perimeter a bit, lower the floor so that it's a pit-style fight. Will that work?" Luke replied.

"It will." Tyran grinned and drained his glass.

"Then that's the plan. We'll have another round or two, give you a few tips on dating, and then you two can hit the cage for a demonstration match. No weapons. No betting."

"And the winner?" Tyran asked.

Toro chuckled. "I like these guys. They know the importance of bragging rights."

"How are things decided on your world" Jaeger asked.

"First one to bleed loses," Braxon replied.

"You're allowed to make your prince bleed? Why can't we have rules like that here? There are a few leaders I'd love to go a few rounds with." Toro drove his fist into his other hand. "Make 'em bleed, but you know, just a little."

"What kind of leader would I be if I feared having my blood spilled?" Tyran asked, his silver skin gleaming brightly.

Braxon put his hand on Tyr's shoulder and the prince leaned into his touch. "Calm. It was an honest question." He looked over at Toro. "When we are agitated, our scales tighten against each other. It's a form of armor, but it also changes our coloration."

"So, shiny bad. Got it." Toro rose from his chair and crossed the room to offer Tyran his hand. "I meant no disrespect."

"I know. And now you see why we need to claim Phaedra. This will only get worse as time goes on." Tyr took Toro's hand and shook it in the way of humans.

"I'm going to get started arranging things ringside. When you guys are done with the crash course in dating, get these two ready and we'll hit the lights and make an announcement. If we do this right, we can surprise every-one, including Zura and Cyn. They're going to love this." Toro poured himself another drink and left shortly thereafter.

Luke rose and started refilling everyone's drinks. "You know, I'm starting to think we should just write a dating manual and hand it to anyone who wants to be with the women in our lives."

"Bad idea. If we did that, the women in our lives would find it, laugh, and then beat us with it."

CHAPTER SIX

PHAEDRA WAS ENJOYING HER IMPROMPTU GIRLS' night.

They had just ordered another round of drinks and desserts when the lights dimmed. "What the *fraxx*?" Cyn was on her feet in a split-second, looking for the reason for the change.

"Good Evening, Nova Clubbers! We've got a special treat for you tonight. An unscheduled cage match!" The lights around the cage came on all at once, making it the focus of attention.

"Is that Jaeger talking?" Phaedra asked as the club exploded with cheers and many of the customers headed to the fight area.

"It is, and he's got some explaining to do. We're not supposed to have a match tonight."

"Our two fighters tonight are local celebrities, new to the Drift, and ready to put on a great show. For the first time anywhere, I give you, Prince Tyran Varosa and Braxon Torr of Vardaria!"

"Son of a bitch!" Phaedra jumped to her feet and ran

to the edge of the VIP area, which overlooked the fight cage. She ignored her hatred of heights and leaned over the railing to get a better look. River, Zura, and Cynder appeared at her sides, and the four of them watched as the training area doors opened and the two Vardarians entered the club.

Phaedra's first thought was that she was going to kill them for doing this, because when Archer heard about it, he was going to blame her. Her second thought was that they looked incredible, and it was hard to recall why she was fighting her attraction to them.

Both of them were shirtless, their metallic skin gleaming in the light as they made their way down the short runway to the ring. The cage doors were open, but instead of using them, both males extended their wings and flew to the top of the cage, circling once before descending to the floor of the ring.

"Archer is going to have my ass for this. I'm supposed to be making sure they stay out of trouble."

"You're not their keeper, Phae. They might be your mates, but you're not responsible for their actions. If Archer wants to blame someone, he can blame the guys. They were supposed to be having a boys' night in, not this." Cyn waved her hands toward the cheering crowd.

"Mates?" River stared down at the two Vardarians. "They are your mates? When did this happen?"

Zura's silver eyes widened. "No way. Why didn't I know about this?"

"Because I didn't want to talk about it." Phaedra glanced at River. "It happened right after we met. It's a pheromone thing. I'm not ready to agree to anything, though. It's kind of a work in progress."

"Or it would be, if you stopped hiding from them." Cyn narrowed her eyes and stared at Phaedra. "You feeling okay? Your temperature just jumped, and your heart is racing."

"You and your *fraxxing* cyborg senses. I'm fine. This is what happens whenever I get close to them. Now do you see why I've been staying away?"

Cyn arched one dark brow. "You never mentioned the fact that their pheromones are affecting you, too."

"It's nothing I can't handle."

She gripped the railing and stared down at the two males in the ring. They were standing face-to-face, arms raised, wings partially unfurled. The tension between them was so highly charged she was surprised the air wasn't full of sparks. They were going to fight, and she was too far away to do anything about it. As angry as she was that they were risking injury, part of her couldn't wait to watch them in action.

They extended their arms to one another, crossing wrists, and then both of them turned to look straight at her, their expressions primal and hungry.

"You think you can handle *that*?" River asked, her voice edged with fear.

"I know what it looks like, but they're not like that, River. They're actually kind of sweet." At that moment, the fight started and her sweet males transformed into fearsome warriors hell-bent on killing each other.

"I don't think that word means what you think it does," Cyn drawled as she watched Braxon throw a spinning kick that sent Tyr staggering backward. Tyr recovered by spreading his wings and then launching himself into the air, avoiding Braxon's follow-up attack.

"*Veth*, they're fast," Cyn muttered. "I know Archer's going to launch himself into orbit when he hears about this, but if there's any way you can get them to agree to a sanctioned match... we'd make a *fraxxing* fortune."

"I can't watch this." River retreated from the railing, and Zura went with her, offering her support.

After all the brutality and abuse River had been subjected to, it was no surprise she couldn't understand fighting for sport or profit. She'd survived the war, then been forced to train more cyborgs to become killers. Part of that training included having them fight each other, just like this.

"Any word from your men as to how this came about?" She asked Cynder, who shook her head in response.

"They're ignoring me. I'm going to go down there and discuss their poor life choices in person. You coming?"

"I don't think that's a good idea. Proximity makes this fever thing worse, and neither of them need to get ramped up any more than they already are. I've never seen them like this. I don't understand."

"No? Think about it. You're human and this pheromone thing is affecting you. Imagine what it must be like for them. My bet is, they're fighting because it's the only outlet they've got to take the edge off. Cyborgs have the same problem." Cyn left, but her words lingered in Phaedra's mind.

As Tyr and Braxon exchanged blows, Phaedra felt a sickening pang of guilt. She'd been so busy trying to avoid dealing with everything, she hadn't considered what would happen to them.

The crowd was cheering them on, and every kick or

punch that landed sent the onlookers into a frenzy. The combat continued for what felt like forever. Others joined her at the railing, jostling her from side to side, but she kept hold of the rail and refused to be moved.

Her heart was in her throat by the time Braxon ended the fight. He clipped Tyr across the face with the tip of one wing, splitting his lip. As the crowd cheered, someone slammed into her, crushing her against the rail. A second later she was upended, and she uttered a panicked scream as every nightmare she'd ever had about falling became a reality.

TYRAN SPAT out a mouthful of blood and was about to congratulate Braxon when a terrified scream filled the air. It was loud enough to be heard over the cheers of the audience. He shouldn't have been able to recognize her voice, but he knew it was Phaedra.

He launched himself into the air, making straight for the spot where she'd been standing while he and Braxon fought. She wasn't standing any longer. She was desperately trying to hold onto the railing - the only thing stopping her from plummeting to the floor far below.

He cleared the cage wall and swooped down, sending the crowd scattering in all directions. She was falling by the time he reached her, and he caught her just a few feet off the ground. She latched onto him with a frightened cry that tore at his heart.

"I've got you, *mahaya*. You're safe."

He flew straight to the doors leading to the training room. Braxon was already there, holding open the door.

He touched down and kept going, carrying Phaedra into the relative peace inside.

She was shaking, her eyes still closed and her skin so pale it was as if all the blood had fled her face. "Do you wish me to set you down now?"

She nodded and finally opened her eyes. "*Re'veth*, that was..."

Despite what he'd said, Tyr didn't put her down. He wasn't ready to let go of her, yet. "You nearly died. What happened?"

"Someone pushed me. Hard. I think maybe they did it on purpose."

"Someone meant to harm you?" Braxon demanded, appearing in front of Tyr, his gaze locked on Phaedra.

"I think so. It was so quick. I can't be sure."

"I'll tell the others. You have her?" Braxon asked.

"I will protect what is ours."

"I'd argue with the whole 'ours' thing, but given that you just saved my life, that might be kind of ungrateful of me." Phaedra touched his chin with trembling fingers. "You're still bleeding. I thought your nanites would have healed that by now."

"It will heal soon. I am more concerned about you. Are you injured?"

"My heart is beating about a billion times a minute and I'm pretty sure I'm going to crash so hard I'll leave an impact crater once the adrenaline wears off, but I think I'm okay."

"Thank the ancestors." He gave in to the need coursing through him at last, raising her in his arms to slant a hard kiss across her mouth.

They'd nearly lost her.

He half-expected her to resist, but instead of pushing him away, she kissed him back. The clarity he'd managed to find back in the ring vanished, replaced by a whirlwind of desire and carnal needs.

Her lips parted as she uttered a soft moan, and he took the kiss deeper, ignoring the pain of his split lip as he got his first taste of the female who had consumed his thoughts since the moment they met. Their tongues tangled as they kissed, though the moment she brushed against one of his fangs she stiffened in his arms and pulled away.

"You bit me!"

"My fangs descended." He'd been so distracted by the pleasure of having her in his arms he hadn't noticed his body's response to having his mate so near.

"Yeah, right into my tongue. What's that about?"

There was so much he needed to tell her, but it was hard to think past the adrenalin and need. "I'll explain about the fangs later. I promise." He brushed a gentle kiss to her cheek and forced himself to put her down. "For now, I need you to tell me again that you are unhurt."

"I'm fine. Thanks to you. If you hadn't been there…" Her expression hardened slightly. "Which reminds me. What in the name of sanity were you doing fighting with Braxon? You were supposed to be having a quiet night to relax!"

He stroked her cheek, and she leaned into his touch just enough to give him hope. "I will also explain about that, later. Now, we are talking about you. Why would someone try to hurt you?"

Cynder threw open the door to the club and charged in, nearly taking the door off its hinges in the process.

"Phae! Holy *fraxx* woman. I leave you alone for two minutes and you nearly get yourself killed. Oh, and nice catch, flyboy. Also, nice moves in the ring. You and your *anrik* made some fans tonight, and that was before you swooped in and saved the pink pipsqueak."

"How many times have I asked you not to call me that?" Phaedra stepped out of his reach and turned to glower at Cynder.

Cyn just laughed and hugged Phae hard. "Now I know you're okay. I heard the scream and when I saw you falling..." She hugged Phaedra again. "What happened?"

"Someone pushed her." Tyran wanted to find whoever it was and make them understand the depth of their mistake, slowly and painfully.

"Son of a starbeast. Who? Phae, what happened?" Cyn let go of her, and Phaedra immediately stepped back to lean against the nearest wall.

"I don't know. You left. I watched the fight. A few seconds after Braxon smacked Tyr in the face hard enough to draw blood, I got bumped in the back, and the next thing I know I'm living my worst nightmare." She swayed slightly and her hands flattened against the wall to steady herself.

Tyr had her back in his arms in a second, cradling her against his chest. "You need to sit down."

"That might be good, yeah. That crash I mentioned? I think it's started."

"Then I will take you to the ship."

Cyn held out a hand. "Whoa. Corp-Sec is going to want to talk to her before she goes anywhere."

"She comes with me. She is not safe here."

"And now I see why she's not so keen on this whole

mate thing. Cool your boosters, flyboy. Corp-Sec is what passes for law enforcement on the Drift. If someone tried to kill Phaedra, they need to know about it."

"They can do that on our ship."

"It will be easier for everyone if we do it here." Phaedra looked up at him with amusement. "And remember when we talked about how I like making my own choices? You have to stop making decisions for me, Tyr."

The cyborg males had spent much of their recent discussion telling him the same thing. It went against his every instinct. "I know you do not understand this, yet, but you are mine to protect. This is not easy for me, *mahaya*, but for you, I will try."

"I'm starting to understand how hard this is for you." She tapped a finger against her chest. "In here, I'm feeling the same things you are. At least, I think I am. It's messy and confusing."

He tightened his arms around her. "Then let me take you to the ship and I will try to explain."

"We'll do that later. For now, I want to stay here." She placed a hand on his chest and pushed, putting space between them again. This time, he let her go, though he had to grit his teeth when Cynder stepped in to support her.

"I've let the others know we're taking Phae to the main meeting room. It's secure and comfortable. They'll bring Braxon and meet us there."

He nodded and fell in behind them. The way the cyborgs communicated with each other intrigued him. He and Braxon relied on implanted throat mics and receivers to speak to each other the rare times they were separated, but the cyborgs' method was more direct, and much harder to detect.

Braxon's voice sounded in his ear. *"I'm on my way. We scoured the club, but there was no sign of anyone suspicious. The cyborgs have already downloaded the surveillance footage and are reviewing it. How is Phaedra? Should we take her to the Santar and have her checked for injuries?"*

"She insists she is unhurt and wishes to stay here and discuss what happened with her friends and those who enforce the law here."

"Our mate has the spirit of a warrior."

"She is also as stubborn as a mogat."

Braxon was silent for a moment. *"What happened?"*

"I failed to heed the advice we were given earlier tonight."

"You really need to remember that the only person in this part of the galaxy who has to obey you is me. Do I need to bring chocolate?"

"No, but perhaps you could have some delivered to the ship for when we return."

I'll see what I can do."

Tyran ended the transmission and caught up to Cynder and Phaedra. They would stay with their mate and help with the investigation any way they could. Then, they would take Phaedra back to their ship and have a long talk. He touched his now healed lip. And hopefully she'd allow him a few more kisses. Having had a single taste of her, he wanted more.

"WHAT DO YOU MEAN, there's nothing on the vids? Someone came up behind me and pushed me over the railing." Phaedra was so frustrated she couldn't sit still. Her medi-bots had cleared the last vestiges of adrenaline from her system and helped stabilize her once she started to crash, but there was nothing the nanotech could do about her current mental state. She was a mess. Anger, fear, and horror were all swirling inside her gut like some kind of toxic cocktail, and beneath all that, there was this constant state of arousal that had started when Tyr kissed her. It had been a hell of a kiss, sure, but she couldn't stop thinking about it, or him, or Braxon. It was making her crazy.

"There was a crowd of people around you, and we only have a few cameras pointed in that general area. We'll address that issue tomorrow, but it doesn't help us now. None of the footage showed anything useful." Kit didn't look happy about the lack of evidence, either.

"Maybe Corp-Sec can pull some trace evidence off my clothes." She had already given her statement and handed over her clothing to the officers assigned to the investigation. Echo had offered to get her a fresh change of clothes from her room upstairs and Zura had gone with her to unlock the door.

Braxon and Tyran hadn't left her side since the incident. They would've followed into the side room she used to change clothes if she had let them. Having them close was comforting, but it also meant her libido was in overdrive.

"Do we know anything at all?" Cyn asked, her frustration evident.

"Whoever it was, they were careful, which means it wasn't likely an accident." Luke pointed out.

"That doesn't make any sense. I wasn't planning on

being at the club tonight. It was a last-minute decision, and so was Braxon and Tyr's match. No one could have known any of it was going to happen," Phaedra pointed out.

Everyone muttered in agreement. "Then it was a matter of opportunity. Someone wants to hurt Phaedra and simply took advantage of the situation." Braxon looked at her with a look of such concern it made her shiver.

Luke interjected. "I've seen the footage of her fall. She was sent over head first. Sorry to be blunt, Phae, but if you'd hit the floor, your skull would have cracked like a walnut. Not even your medi-bots could repair that kind of damage."

"Great. So, someone's not trying to hurt me. They're trying to *kill* me."

Braxon uttered a sharp hiss of displeasure. "That is not going to happen."

"Damn right it's not," Zura exclaimed before turning to point a finger at Phaedra. "You need to figure out who might have it in for you, and yeah, we all know it's a long list. I'm starting to understand why you stay on the move if this is what happens when you settle down somewhere for too long."

"If you wish to leave the station, we'll take you," Tyr offered.

"I'm not going anywhere." She looked at the two males who had stood at her side all night, guarding and supporting her and comprehension struck like a comet.

It wasn't them she'd been running from, it was what it would mean if she said yes. She'd been moving around her entire adult life, free to do whatever she wanted, however she could manage it. Agreeing to mate with Braxon and Tyr meant trading that freedom for something new, and very different.

There was a sharp knock at the door, and all conversation stopped.

"Someone let Archer in," Phae said.

"How do you know it's him?" Cynder asked, already heading toward the door.

"Because he's the only one I know who pounds on the door instead of using the door chime." Phae said.

"Good point." Cynder opened the door and stepped back to let the colonel enter. He was out of uniform, but somehow, he still managed to project an air of authority.

Phaedra got to her feet as he walked into the room. "Sir, if you're here about the fight—"

He shook his head. "I wish I were. That would be a minor matter. I was just briefed on what happened here tonight. The attack on you would be cause for concern in any circumstance, but given what else has happened, it suggests a pattern."

"What pattern?"

"What else happened?"

"Has there been another attack?"

The questions came from several directions at once.

"Not on the station. We've located the Vice-President of Axion Corporation. Or, more accurately, we've located what's left of his cruiser. Based on preliminary reports, it appears that the ship suffered a catastrophic explosion while being powered by its FTL drive."

Jaeger frowned. "At those speeds, there can't be much left of the ship or anyone onboard. It's going to be a bitch to come to any conclusions on what happened."

"And his ship had every safeguard imaginable. The odds of it being a malfunction are less than one percent. Someone killed him." Archer said, looking straight at Phaedra. "And now someone's made an attempt on you, too. I don't like it." He rubbed the back of his neck for a moment, and for the first time, she almost felt sorry for him.

"We've been targeted before. We know what to do," Cyn said

Zura groaned. "I'm going to be cooped up in the club again, aren't I?"

"You know it. No one goes anywhere without an escort, and that goes double for you, little one," Kit said.

"I'll let Royan know what's going on. Speaking of which, where's Owen? He'll want to be part of any security changes," Zura said.

"Good thinking. I'll let him know," Toro said.

Archer looked around and then shook his head. "You people are surprisingly calm about this."

Cyn shrugged. "This is not our first assassination attempt. Hell, it's not even our second."

"Then I hope I can rely on all of you to be smart, watch your asses, and if it's not too much trouble, try to keep my two VIP guests from tearing each other apart in the ring again until this mess is cleared up?"

"We won't cause any further disruption," Tyr said.

"Good. We're going to start negotiations the day after tomorrow. Axion will have to assign someone already here to represent them. With all that's going on, we can't have any more delays. The longer we've got VIPs on the station, the more likely there's going to be another attack."

Braxon set his hand on her shoulder and she leaned into his touch without thinking about it. *Apparently, my hormones are calling the shots now. Wonderful.*

"I think Phaedra should stay on the *Santar* with us. We can protect her there, and the ship is already well guarded," Braxon said.

"Agreed," Archer answered before she could say anything.

Kit coughed sharply, and she was almost certain the words 'ask her' were embedded in the sound.

A second later, Braxon squeezed her shoulder. "If you will agree, Phae?"

"The Nova Club is perfectly safe. I don't need to stay with you." If she stayed with them, then the temptation to give in without thinking things through would win. She wasn't strong enough to resist, and before she said yes, she needed to be sure this was the right choice for all of them.

"You were attacked here, in the club," Archer pointed out.

Tyr crouched in front of her so they were eye-to-eye. "Stay with us, *mahaya*. Please?"

"No pressure, right?" she asked as all her good intentions crumbled to dust.

"None," he answered, his eyes never leaving hers.

She gave in to the inevitable. "I'll need to get some things from my room before we go."

"Whatever you wish, *mahaya*." Tyran leaned in and kissed her cheek before rising to his feet again.

"Did I miss something?" Archer asked.

"Phaedra is our mate, Colonel Archer."

The big man groaned. "She's your what? How? No,

wait. Don't answer that. I don't want to know. I've got enough to deal with as it is." He looked around the room. "Everyone stay safe, watch your backs, and try to stay out of trouble."

"Yes, sir!" most of them answered in unison, and he left quickly, muttering under his breath as he went.

"We'll take you to the *Santar* now?" Braxon asked, his hand still on her shoulder.

"As soon as I pack. Come on, You can even escort me to my room and make sure no one leaps out of the shadows at me." She got to her feet and they took up position on either side of her, each of them taking one of her hands in theirs.

"That's so sweet. I remember when Kit and Luke were that attentive," Zura said with a grin.

"You should remember it quite well. It was only this morning." Luke bent to kiss his wife's brow before walking them to the door. "You take the night off, Phae. We'll keep working on things here. If we find anything, we'll send word right away."

"We'll see to it that she rests." Tyran glanced down at her with a tender smile. "And I will rest better knowing you are nearby and safe from threat."

The three of them left the others and headed toward her room upstairs. She didn't know what the rest of the night would bring, but if she was going to be in close proximity to Tyran and Braxon, then sleep didn't seem very likely. Not with the way they made her feel.

CHAPTER SEVEN

BRAXON STAYED on high alert until the door of their ship sealed behind him. Once they were safely locked inside, he finally allowed himself to breathe a little easier. Now the three of them could finally talk. Not that talk was at the top of the list of things he wanted to do with Phaedra. She had kissed Tyran, and he was more than eager to taste her for himself.

"Which room is mine? And, uh, how far away is it from where you two sleep?" Phaedra asked.

"Your quarters are down the corridor from ours. This way." Tyran pointed down the hallway toward the front of the ship.

"How far down the corridor from you?"

"Not far," Tyran said. "We can be at your door in seconds."

Her lips thinned. "Is there somewhere else I can sleep? Maybe the crew quarters?"

Braxon set down the bag full of her things he was

carrying and turned to face her. "Why do you wish to be away from us?"

"Because I do." She pulled away from him, tugging free from both their hands. Even as she moved, though, the air thickened with her pheromones. Why was she denying this? Denying them?

His control slipped a notch and he moved with her, recapturing her hand in his. "That's not an answer. You push us away, but I know that's not what you want. I can smell your desire for us."

"Braxon, we're not supposed to push," Tyr reminded him as he set a gentle hand on his shoulder.

"I am not pushing. I am asking a question."

"You're pushing," she said, standing her ground and looking him square in the eye. "But since you've already figured out the problem, I'll answer you. I want some distance between us because otherwise, I won't be able to sleep. Being near the two of you is distracting, and tonight it's gotten much more intense. I can barely keep a thought in my head, and my skin feels like it's too tight, and every time one of you touches me, I don't want to ever let go. *That's* why I want some distance."

"It's the same for us. Every hour that passes, it gets harder to resist the *sharhal*." He tugged on her hand and she took a step toward him.

"Cyn said it might be something like that." She tossed her hair back and stepped even closer. "How do we make it stop?"

"We can't." Tyr moved in beside them, not stopping until he was brushing shoulders with Braxon. "Once we find our mate, the only way to ease the need is to be with each other."

"And if we don't?" Phaedra looked between them, her eyes full of doubt.

"We can't know what will happen to you, but for us... It could drive us mad." Braxon hadn't wanted to tell her this way, but they were past the time for delicate explanations.

"So this feeling. It's going to get worse? And you've been feeling like this since we met?"

They both nodded.

"Then why was mine bearable until tonight?"

"*Qarf!*" Tyran cursed.

"What?"

"It must have been when I kissed you." Tyran reached up to touch his lip.

"And that's what set me off?"

"No, *mahaya*. Not the kiss. My blood. My lip was still bleeding."

Braxon frowned. "You should have been more careful."

"I know. I was focused on her and I forgot."

"What the hell are you two talking about?" Phaedra demanded.

"When you kissed him, you came in contact with his blood. It wasn't enough to bind you to him, but it was enough to increase your response. Amplify? I think that's the word."

"And there's no stopping it?" Phaedra asked again.

"I'm sorry, but no." Braxon wrapped his arms around her. "There is no going back from this. Not for any of us."

"If I – I mean, if we – if we do this. How far does it have to go? Can we be together but not do anything, uh, permanent? I'm not ready for that."

Braxon looked down at the female he craved with every cell of his being and tried to imagine what this was like for her. "If you are not ready, then we will not initiate the bond. I give you my word, I will wait."

Tyr went still, then sighed. "It will not be easy, but I also promise not to initiate the bond until you are ready."

She took a deep breath, then nodded. "Then I don't need a room of my own. Take me to one of yours. I'm tired of ignoring this pig."

He had no idea what her last words meant, but his query died unspoken as she gripped his shoulders and pulled him down to her level. She rose on her toes until her lips touched his, and the second they connected, he knew he'd never let her go again. She'd given herself to him. Him, the one no one thought was good enough.

"Mine," he whispered the word in Vardarian, but she seemed to understand, because she laughed softly and shook her head.

"Not yet," she reminded him.

"But soon." He switched to her language then kissed her again before she could answer. She laughed again, and he slipped his tongue into her mouth, too caught up in the need to taste and touch to speak again. Her scent wrapped around him, filling his veins with fire and fogging his mind with lust.

Her tongue tangled with his and he hauled her in closer. When that wasn't enough, he shifted his hands to her ass and lifted her into his arms, walking her backward until she was pressed against the wall.

"They were wrong. We didn't need chocolate." Tyr was laughing as he joined them. He stroked Phaedra's hair back from her face, involving himself without interfering.

"Oh, you might still need that. After all, you two have a serious amount of wooing to do, yet."

Braxon raised his head to ask, "What is wooing?"

"It's an old-fashioned word for getting to know a woman and finding ways to make her feel special."

"You are very special, Phaedra Kari." He kissed her again, then looked at Tyran. "Your quarters?"

"I think that would be best." Tyr stepped back and went to retrieve Phaedra's belongings, leaving Braxon holding their mate.

"You are safe with us. You know this, yes?" he asked as he lifted her higher in his arms, cradling her to his chest.

"I'm not afraid of you or Tyr."

"Then why have you pushed us away since that first night?"

"Because I don't know anything about living like this. A permanent home. A permanent relationship. I haven't had a home since I was seventeen, and I have never done the relationship thing."

"Neither have we. This is new to all of us."

"Never?" Some of the worry faded from her eyes at his confession.

"Never." He carried her carefully down the corridor, heading for Tyr's rooms.

Tyr fell in beside them. "How could we, when we knew we were destined to find our mate someday? Any female we were with would also be fated for another. To seek pleasure is one thing, but with our species, there will only ever be one mating. You are the one we have waited for."

Phaedra blushed until her skin was almost the same color as her hair. "I think you're getting the hang of this wooing thing."

If all it took to have Phaedra agree to be their mate was to tell her the truth about how they felt, then they wouldn't need the chocolate and liquor after all.

PHAEDRA WAS ALMOST VIBRATING with anticipation. Sex was something she understood. Hell, she was pretty damned good at it, too. If they could be together, clear their heads, and get to know each other for a while, then maybe they could figure out how to be a trio. Her upbringing didn't exactly provide an understanding of how normal relationships worked, but then again, she was with two males who weren't even the same species as her. This wasn't exactly a normal situation.

Tyran opened a door and she got her first look at his private quarters. Holy *Fraxx*. Luxurious didn't begin to describe what she was looking at. Everything was designed to give the occupants a sense of peace and tranquility. From the soft pewter tone of the walls to what had to be a hologram of a stone fountain that burbled softly in one corner, it was a little slice of paradise tucked inside a high-tech cruiser. The outer wall held several viewports, and there was a sitting area with comfortable looking chairs arranged by a floor to ceiling window that looked out over the docking area.

"You travel in comfort," she commented as Tyr lead the way to another doorway. This one was covered only by a sheer silvery fabric that hung in gossamer strips.

"There are perks to being a prince, or his *anrik*," Braxon said.

"Or his *mahaya*?"

Both men stopped and stared at her.

"That's the first time you have used that word to describe yourself." Tyran said, grinning broadly.

"I'm trying to wrap my head around all this." She gestured to herself, then the two of them.

"We know, *jeza*." Braxon set her down with care, then leaned down to kiss her again. She loved the way their beards felt against her skin. The erotic friction made her pulse race. She reached up and buried her hands in the thick mane of Braxon's hair, using it to pull him closer.

Tyran came up behind her, sandwiching her between their bodies. He swept her hair back from her neck on one side and nuzzled the soft skin below her ear. "I've been dreaming of this since the moment I first caught your scent."

She moaned her answer into Braxon's hot mouth as a wave of fire engulfed her. Braxon's lips moved over hers in a possessive claiming as Tyr's mouth branded her skin with a series of open-mouthed kisses. Both of them pressed in on her, grinding the hard lengths of their cocks against her body until the heat between them ignited like a match tossed in rocket fuel.

Their hands were everywhere, stroking, touching, sliding under her t-shirt to reach bare skin. One of them cupped her breast, pausing when his hand touched her bra. "More layers?" Braxon grumbled.

"It's called a bra, and I need it to keep the girls where they look best."

"It's in my way," Braxon retorted as he moved his hand over the garment. "How do I remove it?"

"The clasp is in the—" There was a snap, and her bra came apart in the front. "You did not just break my bra, did you?"

"Your garments are restrictive. Perhaps you would enjoy wearing Vardarian clothes. They are less... cumbersome."

Tyr lifted his head from her neck. "We can discuss her attire later."

Phaedra laughed and let go of Braxon so she could free herself of her shirt and the remains of her bra before they tore anything else. Tyran helped, lifting her shirt over her head and then tossing it away.

The moment the shirt was gone both men growled low in their throats. It was a possessive, primal sound that made her breath catch in her throat. Hands landed on her hips, spinning her to face Tyran. His mouth dropped to hers and sparks of desire danced across her skin as he kissed her. His eyes nearly glowed with desire as he stared into hers.

She stroked her hands over his shoulders, feeling the subtle lines of his scales as she explored his body. His skin was a brilliant silver that shimmered in the light. "I don't think I've mentioned this before, but your coloring, the silver and gold, is amazing."

Braxon nuzzled her ear. "I like your coloring. So delicate and soft."

He let his hands trace down her spine, stopping when he reached the waist of her pants. "Will you let us see all of you, now?"

"I want to see the two of you, too. Especially your wings."

"I will tell you a secret," Tyr murmured between heated kisses.

"What's that?" she asked.

"The spot where our wings meet our backs is sensitive to touch. Especially the touch of our mate."

Armed with that bit of information, Phaedra immediately slid her hands over Tyr's flanks to his back. Her fingers touched the edge of one furled wing and was surprised at how soft it felt. "May I?'

Tyr shook his shoulders, and his wings opened partway. While she was focused on him, Braxon helped her out of her pants, his big hands stroking down her bare legs as he stripped her.

All her attention was on Tyran. She leaned into his chest as her hands moved up his back. When she reached the place where his wing emerged, Tyr shivered and groaned as her fingers caressed the soft skin between his wings. His kisses grew hungrier and more demanding with every second that passed. Braxon moved away for a moment, and when his body pressed to hers it was skin-to-skin contact.

"Where?" Braxon asked in a voice gone husky with need.

"Chair," Tyr replied.

"Not the bed?" she asked.

Tyr lifted his head so he could look into her eyes. "Safer for you in the chair. You do not wish to be bound, yet. Keeping our fangs away from you will make it easier not to give in to our instincts."

"Then chair it is." She appreciated the efforts they

were making to accommodate her wish for more time. It was inevitable that she'd end up bound to them, but that didn't make it easy to accept.

She looked around the room for the first time. It was done in the same subtle color scheme as the main room, but this space felt more masculine. The furniture was sleek, with only a single color and no patterns. The bed was massive, and the ceiling above it was higher than anywhere else. A subtly shifting array of colors was projected onto the ceiling, probably to help the occupants to sleep. Later tonight, she'd be asleep there. The idea didn't make her want to run away, which was a first. She wasn't much for sleepovers. She was more of a 'stay for the fun, then cut and run' kind of lover, but this was different.

"Which chair? The one by the window?" she asked.

"If you're thinking about the view right now, we're not doing this right," Tyr said, then shifted to the left and pointed to a settee-style lounge chair. "That one."

She saw the potential immediately. "Okay."

They walked over together, neither male taking their hands off her body. They craved contact with her. And, she noticed as Braxon's hand brushed over Tyr's, they didn't mind connection with each other, either. Every touch amplified her desires, and by the time they made it to chair she was almost quaking with need.

She knelt on the lounge and let herself sink into the decadently soft cushion that molded itself to her shape. As she started to settle herself on the upward curve of the chair, Braxon stepped in front of her and coaxed her forward until her breasts hung over the curve. She expected to be uncomfortable, but the cushions supported her perfectly. Then she looked up and forgot about everything but the man standing in front of her.

He was beautiful. Hard muscle and broad planes, all gleaming gold. He was staring down at her with rapt fascination, and the wonder in his eyes made her feel like a goddess. She let her gaze drift downward until she could finally see his cock. The golden shade of his skin was darker there, and the thick crown was shaped a little differently than human males, but she breathed a small sigh of relief that there was nothing unexpected about their anatomy.

"You were worried?" Braxon asked, stroking a hand through her hair.

"Maybe a little."

"Don't be. We would never hurt you." He spoke the words like a vow, then looked up and spoke a few words in his own language.

She took advantage of his distraction to wrap her finger around his cock, giving it a gentle stroke.

Braxon froze, every muscle in his body standing out in sharp relief, and she quickly let go. "Did I hurt you?"

He exhaled in a rush, then chuckled. "We have had this conversation before, and my answer is the same."

She reached for him again. "Glad to hear it."

He was so distracted by her touch that he almost missed catching the object Tyran tossed him.

"What's that?"

"Something I think you'll enjoy," Braxon answered, tipping the bottle over and catching the liquid contents in his hands. A new scent perfumed the air. It reminded her of oranges, but there was a trace of spiciness to it, too.

Tyran settled in behind her, his weight making the

cushions shift a bit. "This is *uli* oil. It's a liquid that enhances feelings."

"Feelings, like emotions?"

"No, physical. Skin." Braxon held out his now gleaming hand. "May I show you?"

"Yes."

He ran the tip of one finger around one taut nipple, then caught the hard nub between his thumb and forefinger and rolled it. The oily liquid tingled where it touched her, adding to her arousal.

"Pleasurable, yes?" Tyran asked.

"Wow. Yes. More of that, please."

"As you wish." A warm trickle of oil showered her lower back, and then Tyran started to caress her, using his hands to spread it over her back and then down to her ass.

Braxon added more to her breasts, and soon she was writhing between them as they stroked and teased her. She released her hold of Braxon's cock to rub her breasts, then returned her hands to their place, now coated with the same oil they were using on her. Braxon thrust himself through her fingers, groaning loudly as the oil started to work its magic on him, too.

She turned her head to look at Tyran, who was kneeling behind her. Heat surged through her as she got her first look at him naked, his long, thick cock so hard that it pressed against his abs.

This was going to happen. The three of them. Holy *fraxx*. She was about to find out for herself if Alyson and the others had been telling her the truth about the benefits of having more than one lover at once.

"You've gone quiet. Is something wrong?" Braxon asked.

"This is probably a bad time to mention this, but I've never actually been with more than one man at once."

Tyran made a low growling noise in his throat. "Then we will be your first."

"We will be your *only*," Braxon added, his fingers tightening in her hair as he drew her head back around to look at him. She could see the raw need in his eyes.

"Then show me what that will be like," she challenged them both. The time for talking was over, for now. She needed this. Needed them. Then, maybe she'd be able to think clearly again.

CHAPTER EIGHT

Tyr felt the shiver of excitement that passed through their beautiful mate and knew the time had come. She was right, this wasn't the time for words. They could talk later and start the process of learning about each other. He looked forward to that.

Braxon was already enjoying the pleasure of her hands, bucking his hips against her fingers. It was intoxicating to watch the two of them together, but Tyran wanted to do so much more than watch. He wanted to make their beautiful *mahaya* scream with pleasure and then bear witness to Braxon's pleasure in turn.

He added more of the *uli* oil to his fingers, then slid his hand between her thighs. She gasped as he slowly explored her slick folds, her hips rocking against his touch as he quickly learned what she liked the most.

He found her clitoris and rubbed it hard, his cock hardening to stone as she cried out in pleasure. The air was thick with the scent of her desire, and his fangs had already dropped into position. Every instinct he had was demanding that he claim her. To drive his fangs into her soft skin and let their blood mingle. His dick twitched and throbbed with the need to be inside her.

As her cries grew louder, Braxon stepped in close and started to rub his cock between Phae's oil-slicked breast. His eyes met Tyr's, and they shared a silent moment of triumph as their female shivered and rocked between them. Tyr inserted his thumb into her channel, pushing her closer to release. The room was filled with the sounds of sex, and every breath he took imprinted her scent on his senses.

Watching her teeter on the edge of orgasm was a sight he'd never forget. She had her breasts pushed together, forming a channel for Braxon's cock, and her breaths came in wild, jagged gasps. When the moment came, she pushed back hard against his hand, her body constricting around his thumb and coating his fingers with her essence.

She glanced back and gave him a sensual smile. "You're the only one not getting any benefit here. I think it's time you did."

"As do I." He moved in tight behind her, coaxing her legs into a wider stance. He fisted his cock and pumped it several times, coating himself in the *uli* oil mixed with her essence. The oil amplified sensation, and when he entered her, it was as if every fantasy he'd ever had came together in one perfect moment of bliss.

Phaedra was having difficulty focusing on anything for

more than few seconds. Having the full attention of both her lovers was enough to make her head spin. Braxon's cock rose and fell from between her breasts, but she wanted more. She wanted to taste him. She released her breasts and reached for him, her hands gripping the backs of his thighs as she bowed her head and took his cock into her mouth.

Braxon responded with a few explosive words in Vardarian. She might not speak the language yet, but she got the gist, especially when she felt his hands tremble as they stroked her hair. A light swat to her ass brought her attention back to Tyr.

She growled, and Braxon laughed. "She didn't appreciate that."

"Pity, because her skin turned the prettiest shade of pink."

Before she could free her mouth to comment, Tyr leaned over to press a kiss to her shoulder blade, then started rocking his hips in slow, easy thrusts. The oil they were using made it all too much, and before she knew it she was caught up in a powerful orgasm that tore through her with the force of a comet strike.

After that, there was no more pretense of control or even rational thought. She rode waves of pleasure from one moment to the next, caught between her two lovers in a game of push-me-pull-me that had no losers.

Each one of Tyr's thrusts pushed her forward, letting her take Braxon's cock deep into her mouth. The double penetration was intoxicating, and she uttered moan after moan as she took them both into her body. Tyr's cock was so wide her body had to stretch to accommodate all of him. Each time he buried himself inside her the line between pain and pleasure blurred, then blended together into something new.

"You are perfection," Tyr murmured as he drove into her time and again, her honey coating his dick and running down her thighs as he pounded into her.

"Utterly perfect," Braxon agreed, his words barely more than grunts.

She wrapped one hand around the base of Braxon's shaft and started to pump in time to Tyr's thrusts, working the upper part with her mouth. She traced the thick head of his cock and a few drops of pre-cum hit her tongue. He tasted sweet, like the taffy she'd loved as a little girl. She hummed in pleasure at this discovery, and he groaned in response, bucking his hips against her face and pushing his cock deeper into her mouth.

Tyran withdrew once again, then drove himself in hard enough that their bodies met with an audible slap. She moaned, bracing herself against Braxon's legs as Tyr took her hard and fast, stealing her breath and sending her hurtling toward yet another orgasm.

Spurred by her response, Braxon rocked his hips faster, sliding his cock in and out of her mouth. He uttered a guttural groan and tangled his fingers in her hair as he fucked her mouth.

"I'm nearly there," he warned her.

She hummed again, wrapping her lips around his shaft and hollowing her cheeks as she sucked him in deeper, slipping a hand between his legs to gently roll his balls between her fingers. He came with a roar, filling her mouth with cum. Witnessing Braxon's control shatter was enough to take her over the edge. She came with a muffled cry, her entire body shaking with the force of her release. A few more thrusts and Tyran joined them, his hands gripping her hips hard as he finally emptied himself inside her.

Tyran slumped over her, his breath fanning across her back. She released Braxon's cock and glanced back, and for the first time realized that while they'd been making love, Tyr had unfurled his wings. A quick look at Braxon showed that he'd done the same. It was the sexiest thing she'd ever seen. If she could summon the energy to move, she'd get a closer look, but it was all she could do not to collapse flat and expire from sheer bliss.

Braxon sunk to his knees, murmuring words she didn't understand in reverent tone as he nuzzled her cheek.

"What are you saying?" she asked.

"I'm saying a prayer of thanks to my ancestors for bringing you into our lives, *jeza*.

"Say one for me, too." Tyr pressed a kiss to her shoulder before withdrawing from her body. Even that gentle action was enough to make her gasp.

"What is in that oil?" she asked.

"I don't actually know, but it's potent. If you like, we can bathe together. That will end the oil's effect. If not, no one is going to get any rest tonight."

"Bathe? Your shower is big enough for the three of us?" she asked.

Braxon laughed. "It is. I told you, life as a prince has many advantages, but I don't think a shower was what Tyr had in mind."

"You cannot possibly have a bathtub big enough for three onboard this ship."

"I don't. It's big enough for four or five. My sister likes

to bathe with her attendants sometimes. The bathing area was built with that in mind."

"*Veth*. I'd like to see that." Phaedra could count on one hand the number of times she'd had the opportunity to indulge in a long soak in a real bath. Water and space were both expensive commodities on the stations and platforms where she'd spent most of her life. The few times in her life she'd had enough scrip to buy luxuries, she'd spent it on good food and upgrading her implants.

"You will be able to do more than see it, *mahaya*. You can use it any time you like." Tyr rose from behind her and offered her his hand.

Braxon led the way to yet another wide doorway, and as he passed through it she finally understood the reason. The taller ceilings and wider spaces were to accommodate their wings.

The bathing area was amazing. Gleaming tiles formed abstract mosaics on the walls and the floor, and everything was so clean it was as if it had never been used. There was a raised, circular area that had a number of nozzles covering the ceiling. She assumed it was the shower. Spanning most of one wall was the bath. It was square, with a tiled step built into the side. Another, more elaborate mosaic decorated the tub, and with a single gesture from Tyr, water began to flow from several taps, rapidly filling it with steaming water.

I could definitely get used to this.

As they waited for the tub to fill, she pulled free of their hands and walked behind them. They were standing close enough together that she could put a hand on each of their wings. The skin was soft and free of scales, which explained the duller coloration. They had already explained that their scales were a kind of armor and didn't cover their entire bodies.

"Ever since I first saw you, I've wanted to take a close look at your wings. They're beautiful." She continued her exploration, admiring the simple but powerful design. Tyr had caught her midair without difficulty.

"Any time you wish to look, and touch, you're welcome to," Braxon offered.

"And whenever we can find a space large enough, I would welcome the chance to take you flying."

Tyr's suggestion filled her veins with ice water. After tonight's fall, her fear of heights was worse than ever. No matter how much she tried to distract herself with great sex, the memory of the terror she'd felt was still there.

It might have been her silence, or the fact her hands stiffened, but both males turned toward her with almost identical expressions of concern.

"What is wrong?" Tyr asked.

"I'm not good with heights. There was a gravity malfunction on the station when I was a kid, and ever since then..." She trailed off with a shrug.

Braxon tugged her into his arms. "First, we get you into the water. Then we can talk."

"Yes, please." She let them lead her up the step and into the bath. It was the perfect temperature, and she sank into it with a soft sigh. Tyr and Braxon settled on either side of her, and before she knew it she was sitting sideways in Tyr's lap, with her legs crossing over Braxon's thighs.

"Flying is one of the greatest joys of our lives. It would be our honor to share that experience with you," Tyr said the moment they were settled.

Braxon placed his hands on her ankles, his fingers moving in slow, soothing circles. "We can talk about flying another time. After tonight, I imagine it will be some time before you're ready to consider such a thing."

"You're right about that. I thought I was going to die. It was like every nightmare I'd ever had was coming true." She shivered despite the temperature of the water.

"You have nightmares?" Tyr asked, his tone softer now.

"About falling, yeah." She reached out to take Braxon's hand and then rested her head on Tyr's chest. "I grew up on a space station a lot like this one, only much older. When I was about ten years old, the gravity plates in one sector malfunctioned. Up and down kept randomly switching, and every time it happened I'd fall again. Afterward, they said it had only been fifteen minutes, but to me it felt like forever."

Tyr's arms tightened around her, offering comfort. "How badly were you hurt?"

"I had broken bones, internal injuries, lots of bruising. I spent four days in the medical center. I was lucky. Some people died. I got top of the line treatment because the corporation who owned the station paid for everything. But after that, I hated heights."

"When the day comes that you are ready to fly with us, we will take it carefully." Braxon frowned and corrected himself before she could. "We will go slowly."

"Thank you." She appreciated the intent, though something told her that there wasn't a snowball's chance in a supernova that the word slow was going to play much of a part in any aspect of this relationship. She blew out a breath and let herself sink a little deeper into her lovers' embraces. This was a relationship. For the first time in her life, the word didn't send her into a panic. Despite all the challenges they faced, this felt, different. It felt *right*.

BRAXON WOKE up feeling better than he had in ages. The maddening desires that had affected him since he had first caught Phaedra's scent had faded. They hadn't claimed her, yet, but they'd come close enough to quell the *sharhal*, at least for now. He rolled onto his side, reaching for their diminutive lover, but his hand hit nothing but empty sheets.

He went from quiet contentment to fully alert in a heartbeat. A quick look around confirmed that she wasn't in bed with them. Her scent was faint enough he knew she hadn't been there for a while. Where the *qarf* was she? The station wasn't safe for her right now. She knew that, so where had she gone? Was she having second thoughts? If she rejected him like the others...

He cut off that line of thinking and leaped out of bed. "Tyr! Wake up. Where's Phaedra?"

The prince uttered a groggy groan. "Why are you yelling?"

"Because our mate is not here!"

Tyr was out of bed a second later, his hair on end and his eyes wild. "How? When?"

"I don't know. I was hoping you did."

"When I fell asleep she was nestled between us, and I thought she was already sleeping."

Braxon activated his link to the ship and asked it to

locate Phaedra. Less than a second later, he had an answer. "Thank the ancestors, she's still onboard."

"Where is she?"

"In the medical bay."

"Why? Is she hurt?" Tyr looked at him in utter confusion. "I thought having a mate was supposed to help settle us down."

Braxon shrugged and started for the door, not bothering to dress. "The computer states she's not injured. As for settling down, I don't think that's what the ancestors intend for us. Why else would they choose Phaedra as our mate?"

They jogged to medical, neither of them entirely sure what they'd find when they got there. Why would she go there at all, never mind slipping away without telling them? he didn't know which bothered him more; that she'd left them, or that he had been so deeply asleep he hadn't noticed. It was his duty to protect her, and tonight he'd failed not once, but twice.

The door slid open and Tyr rushed in, cutting off Braxon in his haste to get to Phaedra. "Phaedra!" The volume of Tyran's voice showed the prince's level of concern.

Phae was seated at the same console she'd used that first night. She had her head down on the keyboard, and her mane of pink and fuchsia curls was spread around her head like a halo. At the sound of Tyr's voice, she sat bolt upright, looking around with a dazed expression. That was when Braxon saw the cable that ran from the port behind her ear to the console.

"Phae, no. You should not have done this alone." He felt the sting of rejection like a flow of acid across his heart. She hadn't even trusted him to watch over her while she went into what she called cyberspace and tried to bridge the gap between her technology and theirs.

"I wasn't." She touched the cable with one finger. "I had a friend helping me. He gave me some coding that brought it all together. And well, I'm a fan of the idea that sometimes it's better to ask forgiveness than permission."

"He?" Tyr questioned in a voice gone cold.

She glared at Tyran with all the authority of an empress. "Yes, he. I have male friends. That's not going to change just because you two came into my life."

It took Braxon longer than it should have to realize that she was speaking Vardarian - fluently. "It worked?" he asked before Tyr could say anything more.

Phae beamed at him. "It did!" She started to rise from her chair, then stopped long enough to disconnect herself from the cable before bouncing over to him, looking so pleased with herself he almost forgot why he'd been unhappy with her.

He drew her into his arms. "You shouldn't have done this alone. Your friend couldn't have helped you if something went wrong. It is my duty to safeguard you. How can I do that if you won't tell me what you're doing?"

"You were both sleeping, and I wanted to get this done." She waved toward the console. "Now I can be useful. Really useful."

"So you went and asked this friend of yours to help instead of us," Tyr said.

She twisted around in his arms enough to be able to look at Tyran. "If either of you knew how to help me with this, you would have already offered. And you have no reason to be jealous of Erik. He's not even on the station anymore. He and his team left this morning to oversee the investigation into what happened to Axion's ship on its way here."

"He was here, though?" Tyr asked.

Braxon was tempted to tell him to drop it before Phaedra took offense, but one look at their *mahaya* told him it was already too late.

The joy and pride in her eyes faded away, replaced by something darker. "Is that all you care about? I just found a way to bridge our technologies. I can speak Vardarian now! I can translate and speak in close to real time, but all you want to talk about is the fact I dared to talk to one of my friends. I've known Magi a lot longer than either of you, and I'm not going to stop talking to the people in my life just because they're the opposite gender."

"No one is asking you to do that," Braxon said before Tyran could say anything more. He glared at his prince over the top of Phaedra's head and hoped he got the message to back down.

"No, of course not. I didn't mean..." Tyr scrubbed a hand over his jaw and sighed. "I was worried about you. It made me choose my words badly."

"Was that an apology?" she asked, her tone softer now.

"It was."

She gave Braxon a quick squeeze and moved away. He didn't want to let her go, but he had to. She went to Tyran, but instead of hugging him, she set a hand on her hip and stared up at him with a look of frustration. "You may be a prince, Tyran, but that can't be all you are when you're with me. I want the man, not the prince. No orders. No expectations of obedience. We're all equal partners in this. We have to be, or this isn't going to work."

For a long second, the room was silent. Braxon had never heard anyone speak to Tyran that way, and he wasn't sure how he'd respond.

"I will try to remember that." Tyr reached out to stroke her cheek. "And, I'm sorry I spoke as I did. This is very new for all of us."

The tension between them melted away and Braxon breathed a near-silent sigh of relief. "Tell us what you've done, and how it works. Can we use this as well?"

"The hard part was creating the interface. I wasn't having any luck, but Erik gave me a piece of coding he'd developed for working with Pheran technology. It wasn't a perfect fit, but it was close enough I could make it work with a few tweaks." She touched the port behind her ear. "I also found a way to piggyback onto the signal you use to stay connected to the ship, so I don't need to be jacked in to use the program."

"You were only away from us for a few hours. How did you manage to do so much?" Braxon asked.

"I was motivated. Now that we're together, no one is going to believe I serve any purpose other than as your girlfriend, mate, whatever. I had to find a way to make myself useful, so I wasn't shut out of the meetings or ignored."

"We'd never let that happen. You are our guide as well as our mate. Where we go, you go," Tyr declared.

"How much good would I be if I were there, but no one talked to me? You've already seen that happen more than once."

Braxon knew what she meant. He'd dealt with the

same thing since the day he'd been chosen to be Tyran's *anrik*. "When you find a way to complete the program so that we can speak and understand other languages more fluently, I think we should keep it a secret, at least for now. That way, we can understand more of what is said, even when they think we are unaware."

She grinned, and he caught the gratitude that flashed in her eyes. "That's a good idea. Everyone else will use every advantage they can get in these negotiations, we should, too."

"Yes, *we* should." Tyran caught her hand and pulled her in for a kiss.

"But for now, we should sleep. Medi-bots and nanotech might keep us on our feet for days as needed, but nothing replaces real rest, and I suspect that's going to be in short supply soon," Braxon pointed out.

When the kiss finally ended, Phae glanced over at Braxon and nodded, her eyes bright and her cheeks flushed. "I'm happy to go back to bed, but I'm not ready to sleep yet. I want to celebrate, first."

Her words reignited his desire in an instant. "We'd be happy to help you celebrate." If it came to a choice between sleep and making love to Phaedra, sleep would always lose. She was the star at the center of his orbit, now. He just hoped that eventually, she'd feel the same way about him.

CHAPTER NINE

PHAEDRA SPENT the next day on the *Santar*, making tweaks to the interface and working on a way to add other languages to the matrix. Tyr and Braxon helped her with some of the stranger Vardarian pronunciations, and she was confident that by tomorrow, they'd be ready. The only downside was the discovery that staying in constant connection with alien tech while running a real-time translation program resulted in a low key, but constant, headache.

Pain-blockers helped, and her medi-bots kept the problem from getting any worse, but for now, she'd have to limit the amount of time she used the translation matrix. Eventually she'd find a way to reduce the strain and fix the issue. Until then she was trying to learn as much of their language as she could while teaching them Galactic Standard at the same time.

Even with the headache, it had been one of the nicest days she could remember. She had learned more about their cultures and history. Now that she could understand their language, it was easy to access their databases and find out more about their species, their planet, and their empire.

The best part, though, had simply been the chance to talk to the men that wanted to spend the rest of their lives with her. She finally got a chance to know what they were like when there was no one around. Tyran had a wicked sense of humor, and the normally uptight Braxon had the ability to relax and become the most Zen-like being she'd ever met.

Tyran disappeared more than once over the course of the day. When she asked about it, Tyr explained that his sister was seeking his advice on a problem back home. The third time it happened, she asked Braxon what was so important she needed so much of Tyran's time. He'd made a gesture she was starting to learn was the Vardarian version of a shrug. "Neha tends to be dramatic. I doubt it's anything important at all."

She hadn't pressed for more information. She had enough to adjust to without throwing in family dynamics just yet.

Their brief period of downtime was over now. True to his word, Archer had scheduled the negotiations to begin today, whether the corporations and governments had their reps in place or not.

According to the report that had arrived last night, security had been doubled, travel corridors had been identified and secured, and everyone attending had been assigned a military security detail. No other security would be allowed in the room. Archer was taking no chances. Usually she'd be the first one to call the colonel paranoid, but after her near-death experience, she was grateful for the added security. Both for herself, and for her lovers.

"Are you sure this is on right?" she asked Braxon as she tugged at the Vardarian-style outfit she'd picked out to wear today. They had suggested that since she was representing Vardarian interests, it might help if she looked the part.

Tyran looked over at her and gave her a smile that made her heart race. "You are wearing it perfectly, and it looks incredible on you." He crossed the room and set his hands on her shoulders so that they framed the gold and silver collar of her new shirt. To their amusement, she'd had the computer make almost every item of clothing jet-black. She also had the slits in both the front and the back reduced in length. She didn't have wings, so she didn't need them to go all the way up. This way she could wear a bra. The collar had real gold and silver woven into it, anchoring the flowing fabric. She felt half-naked, but she had to admit, it looked good, especially paired with the flowing pants she'd selected. The only other part of her outfit that was familiar was her combat boots. They were mostly hidden under the pants, but they were the most comfortable shoes she owned, and today was going to be a long day.

He wrapped one of her curls around his finger and pressed a kiss to the crown of her hair. "How's your head? Do you need another dose of pain-blocker before we go?"

"I'm fine. Braxon's bringing something for later, though. I'm sure I'll need it before this day is over."

"I imagine we're all going to have headaches in a few hours. Negotiations and diplomacy are the same no matter what species are involved. It will be worth it though, if we can get an agreement for a new colony.”

“A colony you and Braxon would run, right?”

“And you, too. There will be enough work to keep all of us busy.”

She blew out a breath and leaned back, into the solid wall of his chest. “Would there be room for others in this colony of ours?”

“What others?”

“Cyborgs.” There hadn’t been a good time to tell them about River and the other cyborgs, the ones with no place to go. This was the first step. Tonight, she’d talk to them and see if there was a way they could find room for the cyborgs on whatever planet they ended up claiming. Surely there would be enough room for both species. There had to be, because this was the best idea she could come up with.

“If some of your friends are considering leaving this place, they’d be welcome to join us.”

“Thank you. Maybe we can talk more about that tonight?”

He nuzzled her hair by her ear and murmured. “Whatever you like.”

What she’d like would be to stay here and spend another day with her lovers. Now that they were starting to bond, she regretted keeping her distance those first few days.

“By all the winds that blow. you look beautiful, Phae-dra.” She turned her head to see Braxon standing in the doorway. He was wearing his hair tied back again. It gave him a more hard-edged look, and she couldn’t help noticing that he was wearing a dagger at his hip. It was almost hidden by the dark green and black top he'd chosen to wear, and the black hilt and sheath blended with his usual black pants. Still, she wasn't sure that security was going to allow him to wear it in the meeting.

"You're going armed?" she asked.

"We all are." Braxon held out two daggers and walked toward them. One had an intricate pattern of green and black on the sheath and handle, while the other was smaller and pure black, save for a large green gem embedded in the hilt. Tyran took the larger one and put it on.

"I'm better with a blaster than a blade," she commented as she took the dagger.

"I'm sure you are, little warrior, but no firearms are permitted at these meetings. Nothing was said about *weapons*, however." Tyr said, as Braxon came around in front of her and crouched at her feet before offering her the blade with both hands.

She took it, and both men made a soft noise of approval. "Did we just do something symbolic I wasn't aware of?"

Braxon winked at her as he stood again. "Maybe."

"If we just got married or something, I'm going to use this dagger on you."

"Nothing as serious as that. It's a tradition to gift a new mate with a weapon. It's a symbol of our promise to keep you safe."

"Any other traditions I should be aware of? I guess I should've been reading up on that instead of the history of your empire."

"There's one other thing. Once we are bound to each

other, we exchange armbands. They are much like your human custom of exchanging rings."

"I like that idea." She turned so that she could see both of them. "When the time comes, I want everyone to know you two are spoken for."

"We feel the same way. Between the scars and the bands, everyone will know you are ours."

Whoa. "Scars? What scars?"

Braxon and Tyran looked at each other in confusion, then extended their arms so that she could see the matching set of circular scars on their wrists. "These are from our blood bonding ceremony. When we bond with you, you'll carry both our marks for the rest of your life."

"We really need to work on our communication." She fastened the dagger in place before continuing. "One more question before we go. Is this bonding going to hurt?"

Tyran shook his head. "Not at all. All you'll feel is pleasure."

"A great deal of it," Braxon added.

"Well, that's good to know." There were more questions she wanted to ask, but for now, they were out of time. She shook her hair back over her shoulders and held out a hand to each of them. "Shall we go find you a planet?"

TYRAN FELT like he was the at the center of the universe as they were escorted to the first round of negotiations. His dreams were on the brink of becoming a reality. A new colony, a new life for his people, and all of it with Phaedra at their side.

Even the IAF soldiers accompanying them seemed to have a bit of swagger in their stride as they escorted them. Beings came out of the shops to get a look at the newest arrivals to the Drift. He caught snippets of conversation, some commenting on their wings, and a few times he heard reference to the Nova Club and their sparring match.

Kit and Luke had already asked them to consider fighting again, but they had declined for the moment. As enjoyable as it would be, they'd have to leave Phaedra unguarded, and that wouldn't happen until they were certain the one who attacked her had been caught and punished.

The meetings were being hosted by Astek Corporation at their headquarters. Unlike their previous visit, this time, they would be going in through the main doors, which was two levels up from their assigned docking space. The fast, silent ride on the mag-lifts gave them all a few moments to compose themselves. Once they stepped through the doors, everything he, Braxon, and Phaedra said or did would be remembered and examined for meaning, even if none were present. This was the part he hated the most. A sneeze or an itch at the wrong moment could send these talks spinning out of orbit.

As the doors opened, Phaedra squeezed his hand. "This will go better if you remember to breathe."

Braxon burst out laughing. "And this is why you are perfect for us."

"Indeed she is."

Their security detail walked them to the high,

gleaming doors that marked the main entrance to Astek's headquarters. Once inside, there was an immediate change in the atmosphere. While just as crowded as the station outside, sounds were muffled here, and the air was cleaner. The sights and scents of the station were gone, and Tyr found that he missed the chaotic bustle and hum.

The lobby area was all gleaming surfaces and bright lights. It reminded him of the palace back home. Everything deliberately designed to create a sense of imposing elegance.

"Just like home." Braxon's sub-vocalized voice sounded in his ear.

"This is strange. You're talking but I can't see your lips moving." Phaedra joined their private conversation.

The hologram in the med-bay had performed the minor procedure yesterday, and now she had her own throat mic and receiver implanted and keyed to their channel. Her medi-bots had healed the small incisions almost instantly, leaving no mark or bruise that would hint at what had been done. It was one more advantage they'd have going into these negotiations.

There was an entire bank of reception desks, and they chose one at random. A dour human male made a note on his tablet before directing them to another set of mag-lifts. "Fifth floor. You'll be met." He paused for a brief second before adding. "Your escort is welcome to remain in the lobby or depart, but there isn't room for everyone. The Colonel has been advised of this change."

One of the IAF soldiers pulled out his comm unit, and they waited in silence until the order was confirmed. "We'll be here, waiting for you. If you need us, Use the comm-units you were provided with. Our channel is programmed in already."

The soldiers escorted them to the doors of the mag-lift and stayed until everyone was safely inside. It was clear from their expressions they didn't like the change in plans, but Tyran wasn't surprised by the move. It was a reminder from their hosts that they were in Astek's territory now, and subject to at least some of their rules. The negotiations had already begun.

"We didn't even get to the elevator before the power plays started." Phaedra used her throat mic to make sure they weren't overheard.

"I hate such petty demonstrations. Why can't everyone just say what they want and work out a deal that works for everyone?" Braxon grumbled.

"If we actually get a planet and start our own colony, I vote we make it a law that all deals are made Braxon's way," Phae suggested.

The mag-lift slowed, then stopped. The doors opened, and they stepped out into a smaller scale replica of the lobby they had just left. They approached the desk, and a slender, Pheran male took note of their arrival, rising from his seat to greet them. "You must be Prince Tyran Varosa and Braxon Torr. Welcome." He froze when he spotted Phaedra. "And you are not supposed to be here."

"Of course I'm supposed to be here," she retorted.

"Phaedra Kari is our translator and guide. We require her presence," Tyr added.

"You should have been told downstairs that no members of your escort were allowed at the meeting. That includes this female."

"This female has been assigned as the official liaison and translator for the Vardarians. How much negotiation do you think is going to happen if I'm not there?" Phae demanded, moving between them to confront the male.

The employee gestured to a scanner set on his desk. "If you're supposed to be here but somehow are not on my list, then all you have to do is place your hand on the scanner. All invited members of this meeting have had their palm prints entered already."

"We were never asked to provide palm prints." Tyr informed the male as Braxon growled something unintelligible.

The male's coloring darkened almost to indigo. "You should have been."

"Well, we weren't," Phae said.

"It's a requirement for all attendees to complete the scan each day for security reasons. Clearly, the two of you are who you say you are." His hand fluttered to one shoulder. "The wings, you see."

"Indeed." Tyr was growing impatient.

"Will you vouch for your ah, translator?"

"Of course."

The Pheran nodded sharply. "Excellent. Then I'll need to have each of you record your palm print."

"That will be fine," Tyr said, pleased to have the matter resolved.

"No, it won't be." Phae's refusal surprised him and flustered the Astek employee.

"Uh, but it's protocol."

"I don't care what it is, I'm not doing it."

The Pheran's silver eyes widened. "Then you will

need to return to the lobby. Only registered guests are permitted on this floor."

"She comes with us."

"Then she needs to register her palm print."

He glanced back at Phaedra. "We need you with us. Just do it, *mahaya*."

"But Tyr –"

"There can be no negotiations without us, and we cannot do this without you."

"Please, Phae?" Braxon added.

"Fine." She stalked over to the desk and slapped her hand down on the scanner, while he tried to understand. The word she used indicated agreement, but her body language and tone were far from agreeable.

When she was done, she moved aside so that the two of them could register as well. Then, the Pheran directed them to the left, down a short hallway with several Corp-Sec officers standing guard.

One of them greeted them. "Good morning. Please hand over any firearms and they will be returned to you when they leave."

"If I was armed, I'd have shot someone already," Phae informed the young male, who blinked in shock, then waved her through.

"Our mate is not pleased with you." Braxon murmured as they approached the open doors to the meeting area.

"I'm aware. Any idea why?"

Braxon grunted. "You don't know?"

"No."

"I'll explain later. But the next time she doesn't wish

to do something, perhaps you should consider asking her why before demanding her obedience."

"But we need her."

Braxon sighed. "Later."

BY THE TIME they broke for lunch, Phaedra was ready to scream with frustration. Everyone at the table had an agenda, and if she hadn't figured out how to interface with the translation program, she would have been hard-pressed to help Tyr and Braxon navigate the nuances of language some of the members were using to gain an advantage. While many of the representatives chose to eat together, Phaedra had already requested a private room for the three of them so that they could discuss anything that came up.

Upon entering the room, Braxon checked it for listening devices. Surprisingly, there weren't any.

A generous buffet had been set out for them, and they helped themselves before seating themselves around a table and digging in. While no one had bothered to inform them about the palm print scan requirement, at least they had checked to see what kinds of food were appropriate to serve to their alien guests. There was a mix of delicacies from all over the galaxy. Well, her part of it, anyway. The room was restful, done in dark colors and old-fashioned style furniture. The wood was real, too, and she kept running her hand along the well-polished surface of the table. This far out, natural materials were rare. Why ship a heavy tree when you could have a replica made for far less hassle?

They ate in relative silence, all of them clearly enjoying the chance to relax. She went back for seconds, even though her pounding head made it difficult to enjoy the meal. While she was still making her selections, a knock sounded on the door.

Braxon rose to get it, and by the time she turned around their temporary sanctuary had been invaded by two representatives, Tadeus Grasi from Astek, and Raymond Gunns from Torex. Tadeus was the unpleasant ass with the ring fetish she'd had to deal with during their first meeting. She was convinced he'd been the one who had her excluded from the list of authorized guests, and tonight she was going to do a deep dive into his life and see if she couldn't dig up something to make him back off. While she was jacked-in, she also planned to delete her palm print from Astek's database.

Archer had been as unhappy about the requirement as she had been, and he'd made it clear to Tadeus that Astek had overstepped their authority. He had then gone on to remind the entire room that Astek had been offered the role of host as a courtesy, since it was their station, but if there were any more changes to security, the venue would be changed to the Interstellar Armed Forces temporary headquarters. She'd managed to resist the urge to clap when he was done laying down the law, but it hadn't been easy. She worked hard to ensure no one had access to her biometric data. No fingerprints, no retinal scans, not even DNA. She had spiders programmed to search for any trace of her personal information, and every time they found it, they sent her an alert so that she could nuke it from existence. It was the only way to stay ahead of the enemies she'd made.

When they were back on the *Santar*, she would explain it to Tyran. He'd sworn to protect her, then pushed her to do something that could allow her enemies to find her. It couldn't happen again. He had to start learning to respect her choices, even if he didn't understand them. She was trying to make this work, but he was making it harder than it had to be.

She set her food down on the table but didn't take a seat. It was a less than subtle message to their visitors, but they didn't take the hint. Instead, they were chatting away with Tyran and Braxon, though after a few minutes, Braxon returned to the table and sat down.

"What do they want?" she asked using her newly implanted throat mic.

"They want us to be their guests at a dinner tonight." Braxon replied.

She sat beside Braxon and started eating. "That'll be fun," she said in hushed tones before raising her voice to normal volume. "You should have something more to eat, we won't have long before we're due back for another round of talks."

Braxon nodded. "We still have matters to discuss, and time is passing. I'm sure our visitors will understand if we cut this short."

Tyr glanced over at them in surprise, then turned back to the two men and finished their conversation before accompanying them back to the door. Once they were alone again, Tyran filled another plate and rejoined them at the table. "Why did you encourage them to leave, Braxon? They had some interesting views on how things were proceeding."

"I'm sure they did, but they were also deliberately

intruding on what had been agreed would be our private time." Braxon turned to Phae. "How's your headache?"

"Bearable, but I'm going to need more of those pain-blockers before we start round two."

"I'm sorry, Phaedra. I forgot the toll this must be taking on you. You've been translating for us for hours." He reached for her hand. "Forgive me."

"I get it. This is what you came here for. I know how important this is to you, Tyr."

"For us," he corrected her. "But now I'm glad I chose to attend tonight's dinner alone. You will have more time to rest, and Braxon can stay to guard you."

"What?" both she and Braxon reacted at the same time.

"You're not going alone!" Braxon was out of his chair before he finished speaking, arms folded, wings outstretched, his golden skin suddenly gleaming.

"If you are with me, then who will watch over Phaedra? She's been attacked once, already."

"I can take care of myself," she retorted. "But I wouldn't have to if you hadn't agreed to go to this meeting alone." She hadn't been looking forward to it, but that didn't mean she wanted to be excluded, either. Not to mention the fact she had planned on talking to them about her hopes for River and her brethren tonight, and then explain about the palm prints. Tyran had already agreed to talk with her, but he'd gone and made other plans, anyway.

"I don't like it. Who will watch your back if I am not there?" Braxon said.

"I requested Colonel Archer be included. Neither of them seemed overly pleased by my suggestion, which makes me believe he is the perfect choice. Nothing will happen to me if he's present."

She couldn't disagree with Tyr's logic. Archer was a pain in the ass, but he was also honorable and deeply invested in brokering this alliance.

Braxon gave a grudging nod of agreement. "If you insist on doing this, then he's a good male to have at your side." He looked like he was about to say more, but he lapsed into silence instead.

"Is there a reason that you're excluding us?" she demanded. Braxon might not be willing to push for answers, but she wanted to know why Tyr was shutting them out.

"I wasn't excluding you. I was protecting you from that unpleasant male, Tadeus."

She took a slow breath before speaking again. "I know you meant well, but I've dealt with men like him my entire life. I can handle him, but only if you let me deal with him my way. Leaving me out of things will only make him think his little games are working."

"I do not like the way he speaks to you." Tyr's silver skin started to shimmer as he grew more agitated.

"Neither do I, but he won't stop unless I give him a reason."

"I'll give him a *fraxxing* reason," Braxon muttered.

It was the first time she'd heard either of them curse in any language but their own and it triggered a fit of giggles. She was still angry, but it was impossible to hold onto the feeling as the giggles turned into a bout of full-blown laughter. By the time she was done, she felt better.

"Did I say it wrong?" Braxon asked, and she lapsed into another round of giggles while trying to talk.

"No. You said it fine." She managed to get the words out eventually.

"Then why are you laughing?" Tyran looked so perplexed it almost set her off again.

"I'm not sure. Probably stress relief. It's been a weird week. I went to a wedding and wound up with two mates and a job I didn't apply for."

"Having regrets?" Braxon asked, his voice softer than she'd ever heard it.

She almost gave him a flippant answer, but something in his expression made her reconsider. Instead, she tried to be honest. "It's too early to for regrets. We're all still figuring this out, right?"

Her answer was met with silence. *Well, shit. Now I'm having regrets. I shouldn't have said that.*

The rest of the lunch break was a mix of awkward silences and brief conversations about what the morning had revealed, and what to expect next. Whatever progress they had made as a trio was gone, at least for the moment. It reminded her of another one of her mother's beloved expressions. "Beginnings are tricky things."

She could use some of her mom's wisdom right now. One of her strange truths that always came with a smile and scoop of ice cream. That couldn't happen though. Her mom had been gone for almost ten years, killed when a badly maintained bulkhead had given way. An entire sector of the station Phaedra grew up on had been exposed to the cold vacuum of space. There were no survivors, and no one left to give her advice. She was on her own.

——————

CHAPTER TEN

——————

FOR THE FIRST time in two days, Tyr was alone in his bedroom. He didn't like it. The space seemed too big and far too quiet. Without Phaedra's presence, everything went back to the way it was before, as if the last few days had never happened. His last contact with Neha wasn't helping with his mood, either. He'd hoped that putting distance between himself and his sister would force her to make her own choices. It wasn't working.

He sighed in frustration and got a lungful of Phaedra's scent. It was still everywhere, haunting him and arousing him every time her pheromones hit his senses. Leaving the ship would take care of that problem. It would also be a trial, because leaving Phaedra was not what he wanted to do. The idea of putting more distance between them didn't feel right, but he'd committed himself to this meeting and he intended to follow through. He had to, to prove that he was a being who could be trusted to keep his word.

At least she'd be safe here with Braxon. There wasn't

another male in the galaxy he would trust to safeguard Phaedra. She was too important to both of them, which was the other reason he'd chosen to go to tonight's dinner alone. Since she'd taken them as her lovers, they had always been together. It was time for them to spend some time with Phaedra alone. She needed to get to know them both as individuals, too.

Tyr had known Braxon most of his life. He knew his *anrik* faced constant judgment and jealousy from members of the court who deemed him unworthy of his position because of his parentage. Braxon needed Phaedra's acceptance, and to come to believe that she saw him as a worthy mate.

For him, it was different. What he wanted went against everything he'd been trained for. He didn't even know how to put it into words, yet, but he would have to at some point. Braxon wasn't the only one looking for acceptance.

He rolled his shoulders and flexed his wings, trying to rid himself of some of the tension that had built up over the course of the day. He briefly considered going to find Braxon and Phaedra to say goodbye, but it didn't feel right to intrude on their time together, not when he'd been the one to orchestrate it. Instead, he activated his throat mic and sent them both a brief message.

"On my way out. I'll see you both later. Have a good night."

"Watch your back, since I won't be there to watch it for you."

"Be careful," was all Phae said. Given how unhappy she was with him, it was more than he had expected. It wasn't until the day was done that he remembered his promise to speak with her tonight about bringing others to the colony. In the press of the day's events, he had forgotten. He'd apologized, but the damage had been done. He had always assumed that once they found their *mahaya*, everything would fall into place – but so far, it hadn't.

He was still musing over the many ways he'd messed up today when he reached the door that led to the station. It opened to reveal Colonel Archer and four IAF soldiers, all of them looking grim-faced and ready to go to war. "Good evening, Colonel. Do I want to know why you've double the size of our escort for tonight?"

"There's been another incident."

"Who and how?" Tyran fell in beside the colonel and they started walking, surrounded by their security detail.

"Dennis Davidson. He was the representative from Dazzle Enterprises."

"I remember him. He was interested in broadcasting rights and access to our entertainment programs, but he would not slow his speech enough for Phaedra to translate. It was difficult to understand him. What happened? Is he dead?"

"Corp-Sec received a distress call from Davidson's comm unit shortly after he left Astek headquarters. It was an automatic call initiated when his heart stopped beating."

"Cause?"

Archer's lips thinned for a moment before he answered. "All of this is unofficial for now. The investigation has barely started, but it appears that someone entered his quarters and reprogrammed his uh, well, his personal pleasure bot, would be the best way to describe it."

Tyr winced. That was no way for anyone to die.

"And it wasn't merely a malfunction? An electrical surge, perhaps?"

"It wasn't electrical." Archer's voice lowered to a pained murmur. "He bled to death from the violent removal of his genitals."

"*Qarf.*"

"Yeah," Archer muttered before continuing in his usual brisk tone. "Security is going to be increased everywhere. I've got two more soldiers on their way to the *Santar*. They'll brief Braxon and Kari, and then they'll be closing off that entire section of the docking ring. Oh, and ships will be patrolling the area around the *Santar*, just in case someone decides to get clever."

"I appreciate the efforts you and your people are making to keep us safe. When we came here, we didn't know what kind of reception we'd have, but a string of assassinations wasn't on the list."

Archer gave him an assessing look. "Your language skills have improved a great deal since the meeting today," he commented.

"Phaedra has been very helpful. As you may have noticed, she found a way to access our systems and is now quite fluent in our language. As she teaches the translation program, it teaches us."

Archer cracked a rare smile. "I noticed. She impressed a few people today."

"She is a most impressive female."

"She's also stubborn, defiant, and has more enemies than I do, which is saying quite a bit." He paused before asking, "I assume that once we join the others for dinner, your language skills will be less impressive than they are now?"

Tyr nodded. There was no point denying what they both already knew.

"I thought so. And after the games they played with the palm scanners, you don't trust them to be honest and straightforward with you."

"Would you?" Tyr asked.

"I've arrested far too many corporate representatives in the past few months to trust any of them any further than I could throw them."

"An interesting analogy, but I agree with it."

They walked on in silence for another minute before Tyr asked a question he doubted he was going to like the answer to. "These deaths and attacks, they're not going to stop, are they?"

Archer shook his head and sighed. "I don't think so, no. Whoever it is, and whatever message they're trying to send, I think they're just getting started."

Tyran held the same opinion, but unlike the man next to him, he didn't have to worry about protecting an entire station. The only one he needed to keep safe was Phaedra.

Braxon saw the two IAF officers off the *Santar* and then looked over at Phaedra. "This station is getting more dangerous by the day. First the ship exploding on its way here, then the attack on you, and now this."

"The ship exploding wasn't the first corporate death."

"Explain."

"While you and Tyr were busy prepping him for tonight's meeting, I started looking into that jerk, Tadeus. Turns out, he's new to his position. Only got promoted a week before you arrived. Care to hazard a guess as to what caused the vacancy?"

"Someone died."

"Aaron Snow was the victim of what Corp-Sec thought was a mugging gone wrong. His body was found in one of the roughest sectors, stripped of everything of value. Comm-unit, scrip, jewelry, even his clothes. The scene was made to look as if he was pushed and struck his head. With what's been going on, they're taking another look at the evidence."

"And how do you know any of this?"

"Like I said, I was doing some digging."

"Into the Corp-Sec database?"

She gave him a mischievous smile. "You say that like it's a bad thing. Now we know that at least one other corporate type has been killed lately. Information is key to everything. Eventually, we'll have enough to know what's going on."

"What's going on is that someone tried to kill you. Do you think it's a good idea for you to be involved?"

She lifted one shoulder and flicked her fingers in a dismissive gesture. "I'm already involved. They can only kill me once."

He grabbed her and spun her into his arms, hauling her up hard against him. "They are not going to kill you, *mahaya*. Not while I live."

She had to tip her head far back to meet his gaze. "I

don't want anyone to die trying to protect me. Not you, not Tyr. Not anyone. My life isn't worth more than yours."

"It is to me."

"It shouldn't be. I'm a cyber-jockey with a long list of enemies and a spectacular record for making bad choices. Just because I smell like sex and candy to you doesn't mean I'm a good person."

"You don't smell like sex and candy to me. You smell like every dream I've ever had. Every hope, every secret wish. You're the missing piece of my life, Phae, and I'm not letting anything happen to you." The words were out of his mouth before he had a chance to think about what he was saying, and in the silence that followed his confession, he started wishing a rogue comet would smash into the ship and save him from what he expected was coming. Laughter. Dismissal. Rejection.

Instead, she threw her arms around his neck and laughed. "I don't know if it's a translator thing, or the effects of the *sharhal*, or what, but that is the sexiest, most romantic thing anyone has ever said to me."

"It was the truth." Too dazed to say anything else, he leaned down to kiss her.

"I know. That's what made it so sexy." She whispered the words against his lips, igniting a fire so fierce it made the mating fever feel like a cool breeze in comparison.

He leaned down further, cupping her ass in his hands and lifting her without breaking their kiss. She moaned and twined herself around him, her shorter legs wrapped around his hips, pressing herself against his cock with an eager wiggle.

"Bed?" she asked as he started walking.

"Something better." He set off for the main lounge as an idea took shape in his mind.

"Better than bed? Are we going to take a bath together?"

"Tempting, but not now. Maybe later."

He sent a series of instructions to the ship, and by the time the lounge door opened, everything was ready. The lights were off, allowing the stars outside to appear that much brighter. The windows were in privacy mode, ensuring no one could see inside, and the various furniture had been reconfigured by the ship's servo-droids into a single sleeping platform in the center of the room. *Perfect*.

"Your furniture is huddling together in fear. Should I be worried?"

"I had the ship rearrange things in here."

"So, no sentient chairs. I'm not sure if I'm relieved or disappointed. Wait, how the *fraxx* did the ship move the furniture?"

"The droids moved the furniture." He lifted her higher and nuzzled her neck. "Is this really what you want to talk about right now?"

Her laughter flowed over him like a ray of warm sunlight. "No, it's not."

"Me either." He raised his head and looked into her eyes. "Do you trust me?"

"I wouldn't be here if I didn't."

It wasn't the perfect answer, but he'd take it. "Then I want to try something. If you want me to stop at any time, you just tell me."

Her green eyes narrowed, but she nodded. "This doesn't sound as sexy as I was hoping for."

"Oh, I think it will be." He set her down and started stripping her out of her clothes. She'd changed into a less formal outfit, but she'd chosen another Vardarian style-garment. He liked seeing her dressed this way, an exotic blend of the familiar and the new.

They left a trail of clothing from the door to the middle of the room. Once he had her naked he sat on the edge of the makeshift bed and drew her down so that she was straddling his thighs. "As much as I wish Tyr hadn't been foolish and gone without us, I'm pleased to finally have you to myself, *mahaya*."

She flushed with pleasure. "Same here. It's been so hectic we really haven't had time to be on our own. And I know some of that's my fault. If I hadn't been keeping so much distance between us..."

"This didn't go the way any of us thought it would." He speared his fingers into her curls and tugged her head back and to the side, baring her throat. He brushed his lips over her soft skin, pausing when he reached the spot where her neck and shoulder met. "Someday, when you are ready, I will bite you right here and claim you forever."

"How exactly does that all work?" Her question ended with a soft gasp as he ran the tips of his fangs over the spot.

"Your pheromones triggered the *sharhal*," he explained, continuing to taste and tease her with his mouth. His hands cupped her breasts, his thumbs stroking the hard nubs of her nipples as he spoke.

"I know that, but the biting thing. How will I scar if I have medi-bots?"

"Since the moment we caught your scent, we've been

changing. Part of that change is the constant desire we feel for you, but that's not all of it." He raised his head and curled back his upper lip to show his fangs. "When we claim you, we'll inject a small amount of an enzyme into the bite. It will cause you an intense rush of pleasure and ensure that there is a binding mark."

"What enzyme?" her voice soft and husky with desire.

"The one that started being produced the second we caught your scent." He ran his tongue along her collarbone, savoring the sweet taste of her skin.

"So, when you two bit each other, was there this enzyme present then, too?"

"No. For us, the scarring was caused by an ointment applied after the ritual was complete. We are *anrik*, but not mates." There were those at court who whispered that he and Tyr were more than *anrik*, that there was more than a simple blood bond between them. If there was, then neither he nor Tyr had ever acknowledged it.

"But some males are *mahaya*? Mated to each other as well as to a female?"

"Male mates are *mahoyen*. And yes, sometimes all three members of a trio are bound to each other. Sometimes they were born with those desires. Other times the desire comes only after we —I mean they— find their final mate and the *sharhal* takes hold. That kind of triple bond is rare, but intensely powerful."

"I think I've got it, now." She placed a hand on his bare chest and let it drift slowly downward. "Thank you for explaining."

"If you keep touching me like that, we're going to be done with explanations for awhile," he warned her.

"I think we've already agreed there's been enough

talking for now."

He kissed her hard as a jolt of raw lust tore through him. She moaned and opened her mouth to his, kissing him back with an urgency that matched his own. Tongues tangled, hands stroked, every breath shared, and every sound captured by the other's mouth. He released her breast to stroke lower, until his hand brushed over the trim set of curls that covered her pussy. His fingers slid between her slick folds, seeking her clit. Vardarian females were built slightly different, and he'd quickly learned that human biology was smaller, but far more sensitive.

She ground herself against his hand and groaned into his mouth as he found what he sought. He lightly pinched the delicate nub of nerves, then rolled it between his fingers. Soon she was trembling, her kisses wild and her breath coming in short gasps as he pushed her toward orgasm. He wanted her relaxed and pliant for the next part of his plan.

He worked a finger into her tight passage, then a second, using his thumb to continue working her clit as he fucked her with his fingers. She broke their kiss to utter a low, needy noise that made his cock twitch. As her orgasm struck she threw back her head and cried out, her inner walls pulsing around his fingers. With her head back, her throat was exposed, and his gaze fell on the spot where he had sworn to mark her one day. His fangs dropped, and lust fogged his thinking. It was an act of pure willpower not to bow his head and bite her right then and there. He hissed in frustration. He needed to know she would be with them forever.

She raised her head and lifted her hands to his

cheeks, cradling his face. "Thank you for letting it be my choice."

"I'm trying, *mahaya*."

"Then I think you should be rewarded." She raised herself higher and reached between them, wrapping her fingers around his cock. Within seconds their bodies were in position, and he gripped her hips as she slowly lowered herself onto his aching dick.

Instead of taking control, he stole a brief kiss and lay back. When she followed him down, he wrapped his arms around her and whispered in her ear. "This is the part where you trust me."

He used his link to instruct the ship to slowly reduce the gravity in the lounge to zero and waited for her to notice the change. Once he pushed down with his feet and set them adrift, it didn't take long at all.

"Braxon!" Phae froze as she felt the familiar stomach drop that always accompanied weightlessness.

"I've got you," he murmured, squeezing her a little tighter.

"That won't help either of us if the gravity comes back on." She wriggled, but all she managed to do was to send them into a slow spin.

"If that happens, we'll land on the furniture. He extended his wings, stabilizing their spin. "Well, I'll land on the furniture. You'll land on me. You're safe, my *jeza*. I promise."

She grunted. "It was still a dirty trick." She managed to glance down and noticed that they were only a foot or two in the air. If she sat up, her feet would almost touch the furniture. That made her feel a little better.

"I would never let anything happen to you." He rocked his hips, thrusting into her gently and reminding her what they had been doing only seconds before.

She made herself unwind one arm from around his neck and reached behind him to stroke the upper edge of one of his wings. "I've never seen them stretched out like this. Could you really carry me and take me flying?"

"Whenever you're ready to try it."

She stroked his wing again and he shuddered beneath her, his cock thickening in response to her touch. She squeezed her inner muscles, and he groaned her name. Feeling empowered, she gave his wing one last caress before easing herself out of his arms and slowly sitting up. The shift in positions pushed him deeper inside her. "So, how's this going to work?"

"No idea. I've never done this before." He grinned up at her. "We'll have to figure it out together."

"Rule number one, don't let go." She gave an experimental rock of her hips and once again he used his wings to compensate, keeping them more or less stationary.

"If I let go, we'll move apart. That is the last thing I want right now. I like you right where you are." His hands were already on her hips, but he increased his grip enough she felt even more secure. "Better?"

"Yep." She took hold of his wrists and started to move, slowly at first, but as pleasure replaced her worries and fears, she started rocking faster. They had to work together, her pushing up, him bringing her back down. She stopped staring down and looked out at the field of stars, and it was almost as if they were drifting among them. It was beautiful. As was the man stretched out beneath her. His skin glowed in the starlight, and he was staring up at her with fire in his pale green eyes.

He twitched his wings and they drifted higher, but she was beyond caring about heights or fears for the moment. All she wanted was him. His cock filled her with each thrust, the thick length hitting every sensitive spot she had. She curled her legs beneath him, adding more leverage and letting her take even more control.

"Yes, my beautiful little *jeza*. Just like that." He groaned and arched beneath her, increasing the tempo of their lovemaking until both of them were panting and flushed.

He shifted his hips, changing the angle between them so that his cock brushed against her clit as she rode him. It only took a few strokes to send her spinning into an orgasm so intense it took her breath away. Adrift in a haze of pleasure, she simply clung to him as he continued to fuck her until he came, too.

Afterward, she reached for his shoulders and drew herself close again. He cradled her in his arms, brushing kisses onto her hair and forehead as they drifted together. It was the most peaceful, intimate experience of her life and she never wanted it to end. At this moment, everything was perfect, but once reality intruded again...

"What is it?" Braxon asked, stroking her back gently. "You tensed up."

"I was wishing that we could stay like this."

"We can't, but we can do it again any time you wish."

"But will we? Right now, we're busy with the negotiations. Soon, we'll be busy organizing the new colony. Tyr isn't even here right now, and when he is, he rarely listens to me. How are we going to find time for quiet moments like this?"

Braxon sighed. "We'll find a way."

"But he doesn't always listen to you, either." She hesitated a heartbeat before asking, "It's rare for you to stand up to him, isn't it?"

"He's next in line for the throne of the empire. I might be his *anrik*, but back home, especially at court, I was never his equal. Not in public, anyway."

"You're not at court anymore," she reminded him.

He withdrew from her body and drew her upward so that they were eye to eye. "What are you saying?"

"To be honest, I'm not sure what I'm trying to say. I just know that he treats us both like we're not as important as he is. Like we're somehow less. I feel like he only listens to us when he wants to. Hell, he was supposed to talk to me tonight about my hopes for the colony, but he forgot his promise and went off to meet with Tadeus instead."

"You *are* important to him. He listens to you more than he listens to anyone else in the cosmos."

"If that's true, then he needs to listen more. To me, and to you. I'm used being the one making the decisions. I can't just hand over control of my life to someone else. That's not who I am. And if I'm being honest, I don't think that's who you are, either. If this colony happens, it's a fresh start for all of us. Some things need to change."

He was quiet for a moment. "This is about what happened today. The palm prints." It wasn't a question.

"That's a big part of it, yeah. I've explained this before. I've spent my life uncovering other people's secrets and making sure the galaxy knew what they were doing. I've made enemies. A lot of them. The only way I stay ahead of them is by making sure that none of them know where I am. I don't do scans, or voice prints, or let anyone have access to my DNA. I've already initiated a program that should track down and delete my biometric data from Astek's database, but it's Tyr's fault they had it at all."

"He didn't know."

"And he didn't ask, either."

"When he gets back, we'll talk to him. Explain." He kissed her gently and a moment later they were drifting downward.

"No more floating?" she asked. She'd stopped being afraid and actually enjoyed herself enough she hoped they could do it again.

He cracked a small, rueful smile. "Our moment is over, for now. If we're going to make Tyran listen, it would help if I knew everything you want to tell him."

That sounded like a good idea, but part of her was still sorry when the gravity returned to normal. They nestled together on the makeshift bed, and she waited for the feeling of heaviness to fade before she started talking. "Can I ask you some questions about the colony?"

"Anything you wish to know."

"When it's all set up, will it only be trios that live there, or do some of your people stay as couples?"

"Trios are the norm for my homeworld, but not everywhere in the empire lives, or loves, that way. Trios have been a tradition on Vardaria for centuries, and I doubt it will ever change. Why? Do you think that will be a problem during negotiations?"

"I doubt it. There will be some who will be judgemental, but they care about money and power. Offer them enough, they'll be fine. I was wondering because there's another group looking for a home, but I don't know how they'd feel about trios. They're…different."

"Tyr mentioned you had friends who might want to join us."

"Tyr assumed I was talking about friends he'd already met. It's more complicated than he knows."

He snuggled her close. "I'm here, *jeza*. Tell me, and together we can speak with Tyr."

She told Braxon all of it. About River, the cyborgs still in cryo-sleep, and what she'd seen while she was at Reamus station. When she was done, Braxon was quiet for so long she thought he was going tell her to forget it, that she was asking too much.

Finally, he nodded. "What kind of a fresh start would it be if we didn't include everyone who needed it? We'll find a way to include the cyborgs."

"Thank you!" She hugged him, feeling like she had finally made progress. "Tomorrow, I'll introduce you and Tyr to River. She feels like everyone has forgotten about her, and her group. This will make her so happy."

"First, we have to talk to Tyran. This isn't part of his plan."

"I know. That's what's worries me."

Braxon winked at her. "We'll find a way to convince him. That's our job."

She let herself relax again, but in her heart, she still harbored doubts. It felt as if Tyran only listened to her when they were in agreement. What if he didn't want the cyborgs as part of the colony? Would he refuse her? Ignore her? If he did, could she forgive him? She wasn't sure she could.

CHAPTER ELEVEN

Tyran paced the length of the meeting room, trying to relieve some of his agitation. After the meetings were done today, he intended to contact the cyborg siblings that owned the Nova Club and ask if he could use their training area. He needed an outlet for his energy, and not even sex with Phaedra was enough to take the edge off anymore. It wasn't just the *sharhal* bothering him. His frustration had several causes.

The meeting the night before had been a waste of his time. Tadeus and Raymond had talked a great deal, but they had offered nothing tangible. It was clear they were testing to see if he could be convinced to make side deals not part of the negotiations, and they weren't subtle about it. Not even Archer's presence had deterred them, and by the time the dinner was over he wished he'd declined the invitation and stayed on the *Santar*.

When he had finally gotten back, Braxon and Phaedra were waiting for him. Once he learned about River and the other cyborgs, the ones no one wanted, he had even more regrets. The two of them had made plans without him and approached him as a united front. It was good to see them working together, but it made him feel as if he was on the outside of what was supposed to be an equal relationship. Still, their plan was solid, and for once, someone else had done the work for him. All he had to do was agree. It was exactly what he wanted; the three of them sharing the work, but he didn't like being excluded.

Neha had been in contact again, too. He had spent too much of his precious time standing and listening to his sister, waiting for her to figure out the answers on her own, so he could return to Braxon and Phaedra.

The only good thing he had accomplished was to talk Colonel Archer into inviting River to the next round of negotiations. She'd be arriving at the *Santar* soon, and they'd have time for introductions and a brief planning session before heading to Astek headquarters. It would be rushed, but at least she would have a seat at the table.

Phaedra arrived, and his mood lightened the moment she smiled in greeting. She was dressed in the fashion of his people again, this time in a deep green top trimmed in black. She'd braided her hair back today, showing off the long lines of her neck. "That color suits you."

"I thought today I'd try to wear something other than black. This is one of the colors of the Imperial family, right?"

"It is. You honor me by wearing it."

"I thought today might be a good time to remind everyone whose side I'm on." Her expression was as fierce as any warrior headed into battle as she crossed the room and stood on her toes to kiss him.

"You're expecting more trouble?"

"You're going to learn, my *mahoyen*, that when I'm involved, there's almost always trouble."

It was the first time she had called him her mate. A surge of happiness and hope replaced his frustration, and he laughed as he kissed her. "You are worth any amount of trouble."

For a moment, he forgot about the multitude of challenges and pressures they were facing. She was what mattered most, and he was determined to prove it to her. She was pressed against him, her hands on his bare chest. That simple touch made him wish they had time to strip down and make love again. He nipped at her lower lip, and when she opened her mouth he slipped his tongue inside.

"Our guest will be here any moment. Is this how you wish to greet her?" Braxon's amused query made them both groan in frustration.

"She's already uneasy about meeting the two of you, so, probably not a good idea." Phae removed her hands and gave him a lopsided smile. "We'll revisit this conversation later."

"Yes, we will." Tyran released her, then helped to straighten her clothes before rearranging his own. "Why is she uneasy about us? You didn't mention this before."

"I told you, she's wary of everyone. After what she's survived, that's not a surprise. I just forgot to mention that the first time she saw you two, you were trying to knock each other senseless during that little sparring demonstration at the Nova Club."

"Then she also saw me save your life."

"No, she missed that bit. Once the violence started,

she couldn't watch. She doesn't talk about it much, but while she was on Reamus station I think she had to watch her friends fight each other, and they didn't stop at first blood."

Even after hearing Phaedra's stories and seeing vids and images of what she'd seen, it was hard to believe such cruelty existed. It was harder still to understand why no one wanted to help them. After all they'd been through, they deserved to find peace.

"What can we do to put her at ease?" Braxon asked.

"Be yourselves. She's a cyborg, so she can read body language incredibly well. Mostly, she'll need time. She's barely warmed up to me and I've known her for weeks."

"We don't have weeks," he reminded her.

"No, but considering that if these talks go well, you'll have helped her find a home for herself and the others, I think you might have an advantage." She placed a hand on both his and Braxon's chests. "Thank you again for agreeing to this. This is important to me."

The moment was interrupted by the chime of Phaedra's comm device. She pulled it out and read the incoming message with a smile. "She's on her way and requests that I meet her since the guards are giving her grumpy looks."

"We'll meet her together," he and Braxon spoke in near perfect unison.

"When you're both in sync, that's a sure sign I shouldn't bother arguing, isn't it?"

"Yes, it is." He held out his hand to her. "Let's go meet River."

"WHEN PHAEDRA SAID you wanted to invite the survivors from Reamus station to join your colony, I didn't believe her at first. This is an incredible offer. Thank you." River said in Galactic Standard. She hadn't said more than hello until they had returned to the ship, but the moment the doors closed, she seemed to relax a little. No doubt because the guards were no longer watching her with suspicion.

"You're welcome," Tyran said, while both Braxon and Phaedra nodded in agreement.

She glanced at Phaedra, her dark eyes still shadowed with worry. "And we'll be free, right?"

"Everyone will be equal citizens on whatever planet we manage to talk that bunch of corporate blowhards into giving us. There's still a lot we'll need to figure out, but we can work on that after the colony is a sure thing," Phaedra assured her.

Phae was almost bouncing with excitement as she spoke to River. She was so happy she glowed as she gestured and described some of the ideas she'd already talked over with himself and Braxon. Seeing her like this made him even more determined to make the colony work. Not just for his people, but for River's.

"And I'm really invited to the negotiations?" River asked.

"I spoke to Colonel Archer myself and confirmed everything. You will be our guest, but you will also be the official representative for your people."

River's expression softened. "Thank you so much."

"Don't thank us, yet." Phaedra warned her. "A few hours from now you're going to be wondering what you agreed to and how soon it will end. You have no idea how much these corporate types can *talk*."

Phaedra continued to update River on what had happened so far, and what their plans were. Tyran glanced over at Braxon, who was looking at their mate with adoration and pride. He knew exactly how the other male felt.

"Our ancestors chose well for us," he said, pitching his voice low to avoid interrupting Phaedra.

"They did, my friend. And to think, when I first saw her, I wondered how one so tiny could possibly be our mate."

Tyr stifled a chuckle. "And now?"

"Now I cannot imagine our life with any other female."

The two crossed arms and grinned at each other. "Neither can I."

THE SECOND DAY of negotiations started out much pleasanter than the previous morning. No one challenged her right to be there. The officious man from yesterday was nowhere to be seen, and there was no sign of the palm scanner. No one questioned River's presence, either. It gave her hope.

While she was getting settled a familiar voice came from behind her. "Can I get you anything to drink, Phae? They've got real orange juice! I've never even tried it before. It's delicious."

"Echo?" She turned around to see one of the cyborgs from the Nova Club standing behind her. She was dressed in a black vest and pants, and her shirt had old-fashioned buttons with sleeves long enough to cover the barcode on her wrist, and she had a white towel of some kind draped over one arm. "What the *veth* are you doing here, and why are you dressed like a penguin?"

The tall, statuesque blonde gestured around her. "I work here sometimes. As for the uniform, it came with the job."

"I thought you worked at the Nova?"

"I do. This is just a part-time thing when they need extra staff. Mostly for events like these. I spent every bit of scrip I had to get here to see Dr. Jefferies and get her to undo the fertility blocker. As you've probably noticed, this isn't a cheap place to live. I have a few side jobs to help refill my wallet."

Echo's gaze drifted to River, and her eyes widened in surprise. "You got her a seat at the table?"

"We did."

"Great. Though I confess I'm amazed you got her out of her room." One of the corporate reps waved at her, and Echo sighed. "And now I'm back on the clock. I'll bring you that orange juice in a minute."

True to her word, Echo reappeared a few minutes later and delivered a glass of juice to everyone, starting with Phaedra. There was no time to enjoy the exotic treat, though. She barely had time to take a sip before Archer brought the meeting to order. He started by updating everyone on the investigation into Dennis Davidson's murder, and then added that Corp-Sec was now looking into several other recent deaths that could be related.

The second he stopped speaking, the room erupted into a cacophony of voices. Accusations flew, angry words were exchanged, and several attendees started looking around them like frightened animals seeking escape. Concerned about River, she looked over to find the cyborg female staring blankly forward, her hands curled into fists on the table in front of her.

There was no way to be heard over the chaos, so instead of trying to speak to River, she sent a subvocal message to Tyran, who was sitting next to the cyborg. *"Check on River, please."*

"Of course." Tyr turned to River and after a few seconds she turned and offered Phaedra a weak smile accompanied by a tiny nod.

"Enough!' Archer's booming voice filled the room, finally restoring a semblance of order.

"Why weren't we informed before now? What else are you hiding?" Raymond Gunns, the representative from Torex, blustered.

Archer rose from his chair. "No one is hiding anything. In case you've forgotten, Corp-Sec is, as the name suggests, a corporate entity, not a military one. As they become aware of the facts, that information is being conveyed to your superiors as well as the IAF. I can tell you that if these other deaths are linked to current events, Nova Force will be called in to take over the investigation."

There were grumblings all over the room at that bit of news, though it shouldn't have come as a surprise. The rumors about Nova Force permanently stationing one of their teams to the Drift had been circulating since Erik's team had arrived.

"You people are taking over," Tadeus muttered. Unfortunately for him, there was a lull in the conversation right at that moment, and his comment was heard by everyone around him, including the colonel.

"We're taking over because *you* people can't stop breaking Galactic Law. The list of crimes being committed by the corporations keeps getting longer." Archer glanced at River. "Which brings me to my next point. The Vardarian delegation has added a new member. River will be representing the cyborgs recently recovered from Reamus Station. I'm sure you're all aware of the pertinent details of that mission."

"I thought all the cyborgs you recovered were placed in cryo-sleep because they're too dangerous to be around normal people? Why is she here? Are we safe?" The Bellex rep, Nadira Finn, was looking at River like she was going to leap across the table and tear her to shreds.

River answered, her voice flat and emotionless at first, but as she spoke, her feelings bled through. "I'm here because my people need a home. We didn't ask to be created. We didn't want to be tortured or experimented on. And now, you people, the ones who created us, the ones who used us to fight your wars won't even help us find a place to live in peace." She turned to Braxon and Tyran. "You wouldn't help us, but the Vardarians will. They've offered us a place in their colony. As equals."

"As friends," Tyran added.

Phae's heart swelled at the way he supported her friend. This was a man she could fall in love with.

Everyone started talking at once again, but this time Archer let them continue until the room fell into silence again. "So, are we done with the outbursts and drama now? Excellent, then let's begin where we left off yesterday. After all, the sooner these negotiations are finished, the sooner you can go back to your nice, safe offices on your fortified space stations."

She hated to admit it, but Archer was starting to grow on her. The man was almost as good at snark as she was.

THREE HOURS LATER, the pain-blocker started to wear off and her headache returned. Apparently, it had brought reinforcements, too, because in a matter of minutes it went from being mildly annoying to cripplingly painful. She'd been busy translating all morning. The more progress they made, the more complex the negotiations got. She had to make sure Braxon and Tyr understood every nuance before they agreed to anything.

She caught Echo's attention and pointed to her empty juice glass. Maybe a bit of sugar and a cold drink would help her stave off the worst of it until they broke for lunch. The cyborg brought over a fresh glass and set a couple of small biscuits down beside it.

All she could do was nod in thanks as she translated yet another bit of contractual wording for her lovers. She paused to take sips of the juice whenever she could, but it didn't really help.

She was reaching for her glass again when she suddenly felt like the room had tipped to the left. She grabbed the table, knocking the glass over as she struggled to stay upright. Her head felt heavy, and big black spots started dancing in front of her eyes. The spots multiplied until they blotted out everything, and then she was falling into nothingness.

TRY SAW Phaedra's glass spill and turned just as she started to crumple. He twisted in his chair and caught her before her head could strike the table. "Phaedra!" She was as pale as a corpse and just as still, and for one terrible, agonizing moment he thought she might be dead. He cradled her in his lap as Braxon rushed over and put a hand on the side of her neck, seeking a pulse.

"She's alive. What happened?"

It was hard to hear his *anrik* in the suddenly noisy room. There were sounds of panic all around them, but all his focus was on Phaedra. What happened to her?

"Med-techs are on their way. They'll be here in less than two minutes." Archer's deep voice cut through the noise.

"I want her back on the *Santar*." He didn't trust anyone else to take care of Phae.

"Too far away. And we don't know what's wrong with her. Let the humans examine her first." Braxon still had his fingers on her throat, no doubt to reassure himself that her heart still beat.

"Cyborg!" a female voice shrieked in fear. "That one. It gave her the juice and then the human woman collapsed. What did it give her?"

Tadeus' voice joined the female's. "Someone arrest her! She poisoned the Vardarian's translator."

"I did not!" Echo retorted.

River dropped from her chair to the floor, getting on her knees and lowering her head almost to the ground with her shaking hands palm down on the floor. It was an instinctive response, one that made it clear how badly she'd been treated.

"If we have to move quickly, I'll take River, you carry Phae." Braxon conveyed through their subvocal comms.

"S'okay. I'm good." Phae's answer was so weak it came through as a subvocalization. Her eyes were still closed, but there was more animation in her expression now.

"Thank the ancestors. Lie still, *mahaya*, medical help is on the way."

Braxon smiled down at River. "Phae's awake. It will be alright."

The cyborg raised her head a little and opened her eyes. "Are you sure about that?"

Tyr understood her concern, but he trusted Archer wouldn't let anything happen to River or Echo. He was about to tell her so when Phaedra's eyes fluttered opened and she uttered a low groan of pain.

"Headache." She managed to say the word aloud.

"You fainted because of a headache? The translation program?" He asked.

She started to nod, groaned again, and spoke. "Yeah. Bad one. Why the yelling?"

"Because they thought you were poisoned. Fear is making everyone foolish." Braxon stroked her cheek before straightening up and addressing the room. "No one has been poisoned. Our *mahaya* fainted from the strain of interfacing with our translation program. Echo did nothing but provide her friend with a drink."

"But, the juice..."

"Is not the cause." Braxon reiterated.

"You tell them, babe," Phaedra muttered.

"Babe?" Braxon gave her a look of horror. "I'm no child."

"It's a term of affection. I'll explain, later."

"No term of affection for me?" Now that he was aware of the cause of her pain, Tyr made sure to speak in her language. There would be no more translation work until they found a way to do it safely.

"Yours is a work in progress." She gave him a weak smile and then closed her eyes again.

"And yours is now officially Trouble, Kari." Archer commented, and for a second the older man's expression softened into one of affection as he looked down at Phaedra. "Take good care of her," he said and then he was gone, taking an anxious-looking Echo with him.

"Where's River?" Phaedra asked.

"I'm here," the cyborg answered in a guarded whisper.

Phae's eyes opened again and she looked around in confusion. "Where?"

"Under the table, out of sight."

"Which is probably the best place for you right now. Archer has taken Echo out of the room and away from these fools. You stay with us and we'll keep you safe," Braxon said.

The room quieted, and Tyr realized that while he'd been focusing on Phaedra, Corp-Sec officers had arrived and were escorting the other attendees from the room.

As the noise diminished, Phaedra's color started to return, but when she tried to sit up he tightened his grip, keeping her still. "Lie still, *jeza*. No moving until your medics say so."

"Are you bossing me again?"

"Yes."

She sighed. "I'll let it go, but only this one time."

He held her until the medics arrived, and even then he was loathe to let go of her until they insisted. They had her sit up as they scanned her and asked her questions. By then the room was empty and she answered their questions as candidly as she could. The medi-bots were already healing her. Once she stopped taxing herself, the nanotech was able to work fast enough to get ahead of the problem, and an injection of pain-blockers had her looking almost herself again in no time.

"Can I get back to work now?" she asked once they were convinced she was healthy.

"No." He, Braxon, and the med-tech all said at once.

"You need to rest, ma'am. At least for today. You know better than I do what's causing these headaches, but if you don't let your body heal, then it's going to happen again."

"I need to be here," she argued.

"We want you here, but not if it's going to risk your health. We're taking you back to the ship." Tyran helped her get to her feet, then bent and scooped her into his arms before she could take a single step.

"I can walk."

Braxon growled in frustration. "You could, but you're not going to. Resting starts now."

"Now you're both bossing me around?"

"Yes." They both answered together.

River uttered a faint laugh. "It's like they share a brain, at least where you're concerned. They're right, Phae. If your, uh, *enhancements* can't keep up with the strain, you need to take a break. What if you do permanent damage to yourself?"

"I won't. I just overdid it this morning."

"Which is why you won't be translating at all this afternoon," Tyr said.

Her green eyes turned stormy. "Who is going to translate for you if I'm not there?"

He lifted her higher into his arms and started for the door. "We'll manage. Anything we don't understand we'll bring to you to review tonight. Nothing is going to be signed today. In fact, given how uneasy everyone seems to be, I doubt we'll make much progress at all."

"I hate this. I feel completely useless."

"You're not," he told her. Tyran wanted to tell her that she was the most important thing in the world to him, to them, and they'd rather risk blowing a hundred negotiations than to let anything happen to her. Tonight, the three of them would find a way to either fix the issues with the translation program interface or make do without it.

CHAPTER TWELVE

TRUE TO HIS WORD, Tyran had carried her back to the *Santar* without ever letting her feet touch the ground. Thankfully, Archer had instructed their security detail to order a transport to take them most of the way, so the number of beings who saw her carried like a heroine from some over-the-top romance vid was less than it might have been if they'd walked the whole way.

Back at the ship, River had made herself scarce, leaving her alone with her two stubborn lovers. They'd gone to the med-bay first, running another set of scans to confirm there was nothing the med-techs had missed. She'd tried to argue, but there was no deterring them. As annoyed as she was with their attitudes, it was hard to protest when every demand they made was because they cared about her.

Once the scans confirmed that she was fine, Braxon picked her up and carried her to Tyran's quarters. They stripped her, kissed her, and then tucked her into bed.

"If you need anything, call us," Braxon repeated for

what had to be the fifth time. He was standing beside Tyran, the two of them so close they were almost touching.

She gave an airy wave of her hand. "I'll be fine. I'm going to take a page out of Tyr's playbook and make the droids fetch me stuff all afternoon while I lounge around and eat chocolate. That's what royalty does, right?"

Tyr turned a shimmering silver and flashed her a dangerous smile that showed his fangs. "You will pay for that remark, *mahaya*. But not until you are recovered."

"I'm recovered now. Blow off the meeting and I'll prove it to you." She patted the bed beside her.

"As appealing as that offer is, you haven't rested yet. If we join you in that bed, you won't get any rest for hours," Tyr pointed out, though the sheen of his skin told her he was tempted to give in.

Not that she wanted them to stay. She had plans for the rest of her day, and they didn't involve staying in bed. She needed to figure out what was wrong with the translation interface and fix it. Even more pressing, she had to jack-in and start looking into some of the other corporation reps. Some of them had shown a new and alarming level of fear of the two cyborgs present today. How could any of them think that Echo would poison her? Even if they weren't friends, the killings so far had all been carefully handled. No suspects. No evidence left behind, and all of them had been made to look like accidents. It didn't make sense to blame Echo.

She made herself stay in bed for ten long minutes after they said goodbye. She even shut her eyes, so if they asked, she could honestly tell them she'd rested. When she felt like enough time had passed, she hopped out of bed again and tossed on her favorite pair of pants and a comfy, too-big shirt. Vardarian clothes were pretty, but they allowed for a lot of drafts and bare skin sticking to the backs of chairs. For what she was about to do, comfort was key.

Her next stop was the med-bay. She needed to take another look at the scans and try to figure out why the interface was triggering her headaches. She had expected them to get better, not worse. If she and the ship's AI couldn't figure it out, she'd ask Alyson once she was back from their honeymoon on Vega-Axion station.

"Ship, call up my medical scans and display alongside the data from the translation program interface." She asked in Vardarian as she entered the med-bay. She'd spent enough time speaking the language that she didn't need the translator for basic communications.

"Access denied." The computer replied in Galactic Standard.

"What do you mean, access denied? By who?"

"That question has triggered a recorded message. Do you wish for me to play it?"

She gritted her teeth. "Yes. I do."

A projection shimmered into existence a few feet ahead of her. Tyr and Braxon's faces were clearly visible, as were the smug smiles on their too handsome for their own good faces. "If you are seeing this message, then you're not in bed, resting like you are supposed to be," Tyr said.

"To help remind you of what you are supposed to be doing, we have instructed the ship's AI to restrict your access to the translation program and your medical data for the rest of the day. Go back to bed, Phae. We'll see you soon." Braxon finished with a wave, and the projection vanished.

"Well, *fraxx*. Those two weren't supposed to get wise to my bad habits that fast." She sighed and briefly contemplated trying to hack in and override the computer, but it would likely take hours. That was time she could spend doing something else, like trying to find out why the Bellex rep, Nadira Finn, was so terrified of cyborgs. They were a shipbuilding company, and as far as she knew they hadn't even taken part in the Resource Wars. They made their money selling ships and tech to all sides, then waiting to see who was still standing when it was all over.

She left the med-bay and went back to the Tyr's quarters. She still thought of them as his, but as she looked around and saw her brush on the dresser, and her clothes hanging in his closet, she had to admit that it wasn't just his space. It was theirs. Bonded or not, their lives were blending into something new.

"Hey, ship, any other restrictions on my activities?"

"Negative. Is there something you wish to do?"

"Yeah, eat. Send a droid over with a couple of peanut and banana sandwiches, a glass of milk, oh, and a chocolate sundae. Two cherries, lots of fudge sauce."

"Affirmative. Your meal is being prepared."

One of the first things she'd done after moving onboard was to provide the ship with food dispenser programs with all her favorite things. While it wasn't able to replicate everything, there was enough selection to keep her happy, and when she had the time she kept adding more information and providing samples for the system to scan so it could improve. There were definitely some perks to all this new technology.

While she waited for her lunch to arrive, she dropped into one of the chairs by the windows and activated her computer. She'd claimed the sitting area as her make-shift office, and everything she needed to jack-in was laid out and ready for her.

She picked up the data jack and felt the same thrill she had the first time she'd jacked in - a mix of anticipation and adrenaline. Cyberspace was the one place she wasn't afraid to fly. It was a world without rules, one where even the laws of physics could be broken. It would take her a few hours at least, but by the time Braxon and Tyr returned, she was determined to have at least some idea why the Bellex rep was convinced the cyborgs were dangerous.

"I TOLD you she wasn't going to stay in bed." Braxon muttered as he spotted Phaedra reclined in a chair near the viewing area. She was still linked to cyberspace, and judging by the stale remnants of her meal, she'd been in there for hours.

"She is the most stubborn female I've ever met. Even my sister doesn't compare," Tyr replied, looking down at their mate with a mixture of frustration and affection.

"The day those two meet for the first time, we should probably ensure neither of them is armed."

"I'm not sure they should ever meet in person. My sister may try to blame her for my decision to leave. She's never experienced the *sharhal*. She won't understand that this wasn't Phaedra's doing, it was the will of our ancestors."

"But we have to go back. The diaspora. The plan…"

"Once we have the planet and permission to colonize, I will contact my sister and tell her everything. As scouts, we already had the authority to negotiate. As a member of the royal family, I have the right to approve such ventures. By the time Neha knows what we're doing here, it will be too late for her to do anything but agree. If she doesn't, then I will still declare a diaspora, and any trade agreements we've made will belong exclusively to our new colony."

Braxon hadn't realized just how carefully Tyran had planned this. Not until now. "That's brilliant. Neha will never forgive you, though."

"I think she will, in time. This is for the good of the Empire."

Braxon laughed. "And it just so happens to be very good for us, too."

"A happy accident." Tyr smiled. It was an expression he wore more often these days. "I will miss my mother, though. And Shen."

"I doubt you'll miss your mother or your father's *anrik* for long. Do you really think she'll stay on Vardaria and miss the chance to meet our mate? And when there are grandchildren to spoil, I imagine we'll see her often."

"True." Tyran's answering laughter was enough to rouse Phaedra from her fugue.

"Hey, you two are back early." She indulged in a bone-cracking stretch before unplugging herself.

"We're back exactly when we said we'd be. You must

have lost track of time." He frowned. "Did you get any rest at all?"

"A little." She got to her feet and stretched again. "How did this afternoon go?"

"Slowly. We spent most of it discussing the addition of River and the other survivors to the colony. Some of the corporations are very eager to see the problem resolved. Others are not pleased by the idea at all. I don't understand it. Even if they fear them, surely settling them on a planet where they'll spend the rest of their lives as peaceful colonists is of benefit to everyone?" Tyr said.

"I was wondering the same thing." She tapped the data-port on her neck. "So, I did some digging."

"And what did you find, my stubborn little *jeza*?" Braxon asked.

"Not much, yet. I managed to get into a few accounts. Mostly the mid-level reps. I didn't find anything useful in their backgrounds. What I have noticed is that some of the upper management types have some serious security protecting their data. Like, military level encryptions and coding that I've never even seen before."

"What if you're caught?" Tyr demanded, a concern that Braxon shared.

"I won't be. I was careful. Even if the hacks I did today are detected, they'll never trace it back to me."

Braxon sighed and reached for her, pleased when she came into his arms without argument. "Is all this truly necessary?"

"Something's going on. Nadira Finn is terrified of cyborgs, but there's no reason she should be. As far as I can tell, she's never even been in the same room with one before today. She's a minor executive for a company that didn't even take part in the Resource Wars. When I tried to take a closer look at her, I hit a wall. The same weird code and high security as with some of the others. It doesn't make sense. She's a nobody."

"You're putting yourself at risk again," he pointed out.

"Maybe. But if I don't, who will? They were ready to believe that Echo tried to poison me today with no evidence at all. If that fear is allowed to spread, soon my friends will lose everything they've worked for. I want to know why someone's trying to make that happen."

He didn't like it, but he understood her desire to protect her friends. Tyran didn't look pleased either, but he gave a resigned nod.

"Be careful. Every day seems to bring more complications and dangers."

"I'm always careful," she said airily. Then she looked from him to Tyr and spoke again, this time in a more serious tone. "I promise I'll take every precaution. I didn't mean to be glib. I just... I'm not used to having someone worry about me the way you two do. I like it, but it's going to take a little getting used to."

Tyr leaned in close and whispered just loud enough for Braxon to hear, "We will always worry about you, *mahaya*. You are the most precious thing in the galaxy to us."

TYRAN DIDN'T HAVE much of an appetite for their evening meal. He had too much on his mind to eat. Though Phaedra was much better now, he couldn't forget how pale and fragile she had looked as he held her unconscious body that afternoon. They spoke her language to keep her from accessing the translation program.

"I've been thinking about the problem with the translator program, and I have an idea," she announced near the end of dinner.

"I'm sure you have several. After all, you had all afternoon to think about it while you were blocked from accessing the med-bay files," Braxon said.

"And don't think I've forgotten about that, either. You could have just told me to stay in bed and rest."

"We did. Repeatedly," Tyr pointed out as he pushed his almost untouched meal aside.

"And we knew you wouldn't, because that's not who you are," Braxon finished.

"How's your headache? Do you need more pain-blocker before we start looking into this idea of yours?"

"I'm fine." She paused. "Actually, I'm really fine. No pain at all."

"Then let's go to the medical bay and figure out what's wrong."

"Great. Once we know it's working right, we can figure out how to connect you and Braxon, too. It shouldn't be hard, but if I'm right, we might have to make some changes, first."

"What kind of changes?" Braxon asked.

"I'll explain once we're in the medical bay. I need to look at my scans to confirm something, first."

They left the remains of their meals for the servo-droids to clean up and proceeded to the medical area. It occurred to Braxon that they'd spent more time in this room in the last six or seven days than they had in all the rest of the time they'd been on this mission. When they got approval for the colony, they'd have to be sure the list of colonists included a fair number of medically-trained beings for both species.

Phae went straight to the center console and placed her hand, the one with the data port, on the surface. After a moment she grunted in frustration and looked back at them. "One of you will need to tell the ship I'm allowed to access my records now. I'm still locked out."

Tyr chuckled. "One moment."

"And that's something else I want to talk about. When do I get to interface with the ship, too?" She arched a bright pink eyebrow at them both.

"Being linked to a single program is causing you crippling headaches. Do you really want to see what would happen if you were linked to the entire ship?"

She pursed her lips. "You have a point."

Several projections appeared in the air at the center of the room. "These are all the scans we took since I started getting the headaches. See anything?" she asked, waving to the images.

Braxon looked again, trying to see whatever it was she was talking about. They'd gone over these scans several times and seen nothing that would explain the headaches. After a minute or two, he shook his head in frustration. "What are we supposed to be seeing?"

"That's just it. There's nothing there, and I think I've figured out why. We've never taken a scan when the headaches first start."

"No," Tyran objected right away.

"You want to trigger an event here and scan it?" Braxon didn't like the idea any more than Tyr did.

"How else are we going to figure out what the

problem is? It shouldn't take more than a few minutes. It usually takes an hour or so for the pain to get bad. I'll be okay."

"No more than three minutes. I don't care if we have the data by then or not," Tyr finally said.

"But if we…"

Tyr cut her off. "Three minutes. You might be willing to risk more, but I'm not."

"And neither am I." Braxon pointed to one of the beds. "And you're going to do exactly what we say, agreed?"

"Agreed."

"And you'll tell us the second you feel any pain or discomfort?" Tyr asked.

Her shoulders tensed, her expression went blank, and she didn't answer right away. *Stubborn female.*

"This isn't going to happen until you agree to our terms," Tyr informed her.

Braxon tried a slightly different approach. "If it were Tyr or I having this issue, you'd want to know if we were hurting, wouldn't you?"

Her body language softened. "I would."

He managed to keep from smiling at her admission, but it wasn't easy. "We care about you, too."

"Okay." She raised her hands with her smallest fingers outstretched in an odd gesture. "I pinkie swear that I'll tell you if I get so much as a tingle."

He and Tyr looked at her hand, then at each other. "We're not familiar with this ritual."

"I'd be surprised if you were. Join your pinkie fingers with mine, yeah, like that." She curled her fingers around theirs. "If I feel any discomfort, I'll tell you right away."

"Witnessed," Tyr acknowledged, and a second later she was untangling herself and bounced over to the bed.

Braxon manned the scanner while Tyr took hold of their mate's hand. At Braxon's signal, Tyr began to speak to Phaedra in Vardarian. He was quoting a classic love poem and having her translate the complex phrases into her own language and repeating them out loud.

After only a few lines, the real-time scans showed a subtle change, but not where he expected it.

"Stop," he said without looking up. Within a few seconds, the scan returned to normal.

"Again." This time the change showed up even faster, and he knew exactly what the problem was. "That's enough."

Phaedra hadn't told them her theory before the test because she wanted their interpretation to be unbiased. Now, he wanted to hear it. "Before I tell you what I saw, what was your theory?"

"Feedback between my existing implants and the only new piece of tech I've added in the last six months." She sat up "Am I right?"

With a flick of his fingers, Braxon sent the images from the screen to be projected so they could all see them. "You were right. Somehow, the receiver is interfering with the translation program and it's affecting your neural pathways in the area around it."

"So, we take it out. Problem solved," she said.

"If we do that, you won't have any way to communicate with us if we're apart."

"Sure we will. You've both been given comm devices. And we're not apart that often. Not with security so tight."

"I'd rather you stop using the translator," Tyr said.

Her eyes narrowed and the set of her jaw shifted. "And I'd rather not be useless."

This again. It bothered Braxon that she still felt that she had to prove herself. Why couldn't she understand that she was part of them, now? "How many times will we have to say it before you believe us? You're not useless. Your contribution isn't being measured in terms of what you do, or how well you perform."

"You're not our liaison, Phaedra. You're our *mahaya*," Tyr said.

"Why can't I be both?"

Braxon got to his feet, seething with frustration. She was pushing them away again, and he didn't know how to stop it. All his life he'd struggled to be accepted by those around him.

"Braxon?" she called his name as he headed for the door.

He ignored her and lengthened his stride. He needed to be alone.

"Braxon!" this time her voice cracked. "Where are you going?"

"I need to get off this ship for a while."

"Take two of the guards with you."

"I will."

Tyr would already know where he was going. There were only two things that helped his *anrik* think. The first was flying, but so far, they hadn't found anywhere suitable to do more than a quick stretch of their wings. The other activity was to lose himself in the rituals of combat. Braxon was on his way to the Nova Club's training area to spar.

CHAPTER THIRTEEN

TYR COULD ALMOST SEE the walls around Phaedra's heart start to crumble as she watched Braxon walk away. She looked vulnerable and sad. As much as it hurt him to see her unhappy, it gave him hope, too. Her feelings for them were growing stronger... just as his were for her.

"He's coming back, right?"

He moved in closer and wrapped his arm around her shoulders. "He'll be back. It's always been like this. When he gets angry, he needs to be alone. Usually he goes flying. Since he can't do that, he'll do the next best thing to blow off steam."

She gave him a wild-eyed look. "Another female?"

"What? No! There are no other females for us. Not now, not ever. How could you even think we'd do that to you?"

"Because it's happened before," she confessed, her voice softer now.

"It will never happen again. Not with us. We waited a

lifetime to find you, and now we'll never desire anyone else."

"You say that with such confidence. I'm not so sure."

"You aren't Vardarian. If you like, I can show you the proof of it later. Studies have been done." He chuckled. "You are not the first female of a different species to be concerned."

"I'd like that. So, if he can't fly and isn't uh... seeking company elsewhere, where is he?"

"He'll be on his way to the Nova Club. The owners invited us to use their training area anytime we liked."

"Okay. Not thrilled about that option either. What is it with you males and the need to beat on each other?"

"It helps clear the mind and vent strong emotions."

"I didn't mean to piss him off – I mean, make him angry with me."

"He's not angry with anyone. He is caught up in feelings from his past. Tangled."

"Frustrated?" Phaedra closed her hands into fists and shook them. "Like you can't figure out all the things you're feeling?"

"Yes. Frustrated. Braxon has spent his life being judged by his parentage instead of his actions. Even as my *anrik*, he faced rejection and derision."

"But why is he angry now? No one here is rejecting him."

"No?" He gave her a long look.

"I'm not. I mean, that wasn't about him. It's about me. I need..." she trailed off, her hands fluttering in front of her like a pair of bewildered birds.

He caught her hands in his, stilling them. "You've

been alone too long, little warrior. You've forgotten what it's like to be connected to someone else."

"Maybe. Should I apologize? I can do it right now."

He shook his head. "Give him some time."

"Do you really want me to remove the receiver? I will, but if I do, you have to promise that you'll stay close to us."

She thought about it, then sighed and shook her head. "If it's that important to the two of you, then leave it."

"Your safety is what's important."

"Then leave it in for now. When Alyson gets back, I'm going to talk to her about having the three of us fitted with the same kind of devices the cyborgs use. I'm pretty sure Zale can build them for us."

"I'd like that. If we're sure it's safe for all of us." He touched the spot where her receiver sat behind her ear. "We were careless when we implanted this without testing what it might do. I won't take that kind of chance again."

"When you put it like that, I'm more inclined to agree with you. I'm not good with demands, remember?"

He chuckled and scooped her into his arms. "I'm learning more about you all the time."

"Where are we going?"

"You are supposed to be resting. Since you didn't do that today, I'm going to make sure you do so tonight."

"If you take me to bed, I don't see how I'm going to get any rest." She didn't sound at all concerned at the idea.

"Which is why we're not going to bed. I'm taking you to the most relaxing place on this ship."

She sighed happily. "The bath? I had planned on using that today, but the day got away from me."

"Well, you're not getting away from me. Yes, we're going to the bath. The water is already running."

"I really, really need to get myself wired to this ship," she muttered as he carried her back down the hall to their quarters.

"Take out the receiver and we'll discuss it."

"This would be so much easier if you would just say yes and stop arguing with me."

"Funny, I was thinking the same thing." It was the first time he'd been alone with her for more than a few moments since they had first met, and he intended to make the most of it. Even tonight had been full of talk of the corporations and potential deals, not to mention the constant shadow of danger that hung over them all.

"You're thinking too hard," she said, gently stroking a finger between his brows to smooth out the furrowed skin. "I'm not the only one who needs to rest. In fact, I don't think I've seen you really relax since we met. Don't you ever want to just stop and let someone else take over? Braxon's more than capable, but you never let him take the lead."

"Braxon's a fine leader, and so are you." She had no idea how much he wanted to step aside sometimes, but he didn't know how. Not, yet. His sister might have been the heir, but he always had duties of his own. Their father's accidental death had put Neha on the throne before she was ready, and she'd leaned heavily on Tyran, relying on his guidance and their mother's wisdom. The problem was, she hadn't *stopped* relying on them. This entire plan, the scouting mission, the dream of a colony of their own, it was all so that he could finally step away from his sister's shadow and claim a life of his own.

He thought that leaving court would be enough for him to start finding a new way to do things. It hadn't. Braxon still defaulted to him. The beings from this part of the galaxy assumed he was the one in command because of his title. The only one who didn't expect him to be in charge was Phaedra, and he kept trying to tell her what to do, anyway. He really needed to stop doing that, but the habits of a lifetime were harder to break than he'd expected. The only change he'd managed to make was finding the strength to defy his sister, or at least, ignore her.

The order to return home had come yesterday. He hadn't responded yet. Hadn't told Braxon or Phaedra, either. He'd have to tell them soon, and then he hoped the three of them could decide on a plan, together. But before that happened, the three of them needed to be in the same room and thinking clearly. Maybe tomorrow morning.

"If we're such fine leaders, why are you still calling the shots?" she asked as they entered his quarters.

He set her back on her feet and cupped her face in his hands. "Because I don't know how to step back, and Braxon has never been in a position where he could lead. Not until we came out here."

A spark of annoyance flared in her green eyes. "I have to say, I'm not a fan of your homeworld or the way they do things there. When we create this colony of ours, a lot of things are going to have to change."

"Yes, they will." This was why the ancestors had chosen this pink-haired female from another world to be their *mahaya*. Not only did she understand their dreams, she had the strength of will to make it happen. Buoyed up by hope, happiness, and something far stronger than either, he leaned down, intending to kiss her when a phrase he had never uttered before fell from his lips. "I love you."

Her brows raised in surprise. "You're not supposed to say that, yet. It's too soon."

"Not for me, it isn't."

She reached for him, her fingers clasping the back of his neck and pulling him down closer. "If there's anyone in the galaxy I think I'd ever fall in love with, it's you and Braxon. I'm just not there yet."

Disappointment pricked his heart like a thousand tiny needles, but he also remembered what the cyborg males had told him about human courtship. He needed to be patient. She'd said it herself. She wasn't in love with them, *yet*. He dipped his head and sealed her mouth with his. He needed her. Not just her body, but her fire. She was the brightest star in his universe, a blaze of light and glory that would guide him through the rest of his days.

PHAEDRA'S HEART was doing backflips and her head was spinning as Tyr kissed her. His mouth was as hot as freshly welded steel as he claimed her, his fingers tangling in her hair to draw her head back as he took the kiss deeper. A low, primal growl rumbled up from the depths of his chest, the vibration traveling from his body to hers. She stood on her toes and leaned into him until they were fused together from thigh to chest.

Pheromones flooded the air between them, and the fires of the mating fever ignited like an open flame reacting to rocket fuel. Heat and need consumed her, along with emotions she wasn't ready to acknowledge. He started easing her out of her clothes, uttering a low groan as his hands slid over her hips, pushing her loose-fitting pants down with ease. She started undressing him, too, her need for him at war with the pleasure she took in exploring his hard body. She heard the now familiar sound of his wings unfurling and reached around to stroke the sensitive skin normally hidden beneath.

"You have no idea how good that feels."

"I think I do. Sometimes when you or Braxon touches me, I can't breathe it feels so right."

He stepped out of his pants and gathered her back into his arms for one last kiss. "That's exactly how it feels."

They didn't let go of each other as they made their way back to the luxurious bathing room, both of them already lost in a fog of desire and need. Warm mist shrouded her body as they moved toward the tub. The air was scented, and it took her a moment to recognize it. "Vanilla?"

"I did some reading. This scent is one your species finds relaxing."

She was touched that he had even thought about it. It was one of his many surprising traits. He was arrogant and driven, but he could also be sweet and attentive. "It's also one of my favorites. My mom wasn't really the domestic type, but every once in a while, for birthdays or if I'd had a really bad day, she'd bake cookies for me. Vanilla always reminds me of her."

"You miss her. I miss my father, too." He stepped into the tub first, then lifted her beside him. The water was the perfect temperature, and there were bubbling currents flowing around her legs and feet.

"I do. I think we'll always miss the ones we've lost."

He moved behind her, sweeping back her hair to brush a gentle kiss to her bare shoulder before sinking down into the water with a sigh. "When I fly, sometimes I can hear his voice in the wind. It's been too long since I've flown."

She joined Tyran in the water, submerging herself and then pushing back so that she was curled into his side. One of his wings curled around her back, and his arm encircled her waist as he leaned down to kiss the tip of her nose.

She turned and captured his mouth with hers and he hauled her into his arms.

"No more talking," he muttered between kisses that grew more demanding with each second that passed.

There was so much raw need in his tone that she shivered in delightful anticipation of what was to come.

Instead of letting her settle across his lap so that she was facing him, he turned her so that her back was to his chest. He buried his face in the crook of her neck and reached around to cup her breasts. "Need you."

"You have me," she whispered back.

"Not yet. Not until we're bonded." He let his fangs touch her neck, exerting just enough pressure to dent her skin without breaking it.

"Soon."

"Don't make us wait too long, little warrior. We're not as strong as you think. Not when it comes to you."

His skin brightened to a gleaming silver and his fingers closed on her nipples, tugging and pinching them with just enough force to add a bit of pain to her pleasure. His cock jutted up between them, and each time she wriggled, it pulsed and thickened.

His touch was turning her brain to molten slag. She couldn't think anymore. Didn't want to. The subtle, spicy musk of his scent blended with the vanilla. Every breath she took pushed it deep into her lungs, marking her. Making her ache with needs and wants.

"You smell good," she murmured.

"As do you. Like the most amazing meal in the world. A feast of all my favorite things. From the first time I caught your scent, I knew you were mine."

"That's because you're used to getting your way, your Highness."

He nipped her throat as he stroked his way down her body, until he reached the apex of her thighs. "I am. Now, open for me."

She parted her legs wider and laughed, lying back so that her head was on his shoulder.

"I never thought I'd be with a pushy male. Why am I here with you again?"

"Because we're destined for each other." He stroked his fingers through her curls, teasing her for a moment before pushing deeper into her folds. "I never imagined my mate would have so much fire and strength."

"Or pink hair."

He flicked a finger over her clit. "Or such soft skin. Like sun-ripened fruit. So sweet." He started a coordinated assault on her senses, his fingers working her clit and nipples in synch as he kissed and nibbled up and down the column of her throat. He played her like a maestro might work his favorite instrument, sensations building and building until she was vibrating with need and poised on the brink of orgasm. Instead of giving her release, he slowed his touch, softening each caress until she was acutely aware of every contact. The water swirled around them, adding another level of sensuality to the moment.

She made a soft mewl of protest and wriggled against his hand. "More."

He gave in to her so fast she nearly came on the spot. His cock twitched between them as he started to fuck her with his fingers, stroking over her clit with every thrust. "Tell me what you want me to do to you."

She caught the urgent need in his voice, the sex-roughened edge to his words, and started to understand what he craved.

"Make me come, Tyr. Let me ride your fingers. Two of them, no, Three. I want you to do it hard and fast, and don't stop until I scream your name."

He continued to fuck her with one hand while he reached down with the other, moving her legs so that they were positioned outside of his. Then he stretched his legs wider, taking her legs with him. She was totally exposed now, his fingers moving with breathtaking speed and skill as he pleasured her exactly how she'd told him to. Her hips bucked against his hand, the water sloshing up the sides of the tub. The jets below them suddenly grew much more powerful, one of them sending a turbulent wash of water hard against her clit.

"Cheater!" She managed to utter the single word as

her world shattered and she went spinning into an orgasm that seemed to go on forever.

"You said hard, fast, and not to stop. I didn't cheat, I obeyed."

She was still dazed and trembling as he withdrew his hand and the jets died back down to a relaxing burble. He had obeyed. Quickly and eagerly. She filed that information away for further thought.

He only gave her a few moments to regain her senses before he shifted again, closing his legs and gently turning her around so she was facing him again. Her legs straddled his hips as he rotated his body in the tub so that he could brace his feet against the far wall.

"Ready for me?" he asked.

"Always." She set her hands on his powerful shoulders and moved in to kiss him. As their mouths met, he drew her down onto the thick head of his cock, filling her with exquisite slowness until there was no room between them. He rocked his hips in a slow rolling motion that fanned the embers of her passion back into an inferno in seconds.

Skin to skin, they moved together as Tyr's cock stroked her g-spot again and again. She gasped and tightened around him, milking his cock with every thrust.

"Slowly, *mahaya*. I want this to last. This is our first time alone together, and I never want to forget what it's like to have you in my arms like this."

"You won't forget. Any time the memory starts to fade, we can recreate this moment."

His blue eyes gleamed with an inner fire. "Any time? Does this mean you've finally accepted that we're going to be together for the rest of our lives?"

"It means I'm starting to believe it."

Despite what he'd said only seconds before, Tyr's thrusts grew faster as he stared into her eyes, his hands gripping her hips hard enough she would bruise if she didn't have medi-bots. She didn't care. All she wanted was more. More of his words, his touch, his cock...his love.

"Yes!" she moaned as their bodies came together at the perfect angle, sending a jolt of pleasure coursing through her.

He captured her mouth with his and their kisses fell into the same mad pace as their bodies, tongues dancing in time to each penetration, breath blended, pleasure shared. His thrusts became uneven, the rhythm unraveled, then turned into a passionate claiming that pushed them both to the edge of their control. She tumbled over the brink first, but Tyran was right behind her, snapping his hips up in one last powerful thrust as he came.

They flew together, clinging to each other as they rode out the last moments of ecstasy together.

"If flying feels anything at all like that, then maybe we can try it someday," she murmured as she finally lifted her head to look at him again.

He wrapped his arms around her and snuggled her against his big body. "Nothing feels as good as what we just did, but flying comes a close second."

"Maybe one day."

"We have time. To find a thermal air current, we'd have to be on a planet. I don't see that happening yet."

"Not yet, but it will happen."

"When you say it like that, it's easier to believe it will happen. But then we go back to those meetings, and I start to wonder if that's how we'll spend the rest of our lives – talking."

She sighed and nodded in agreement. "I know the feeling. So many words, and most of them are being used to obscure what they're really after. This would be so much simpler if I knew their end game." A thought started to gel in the back of her mind. That information had to be somewhere in cyberspace. Probably buried in encrypted messages and cyphered memos, but there was no reason she couldn't take a look around and see what she could piece together.

"I know that look, my little warrior. You're thinking of going into that cyberspace place of yours again."

"I might be able to find out what their real goals are. It could speed this whole stupid process up."

"And you might get caught. You are a member of the imperial house of Varosa now. What you do reflects not only on yourself, but on Braxon, myself, and the empire."

"Are you telling me you want me to stop—" The entire ship shook like it had been struck by a giant hammer, sending her and Tyr tumbling into the bathwater.

She came up for air, spluttering and stunned. The bathing room was full of strobing lights and screaming alarms, and somewhere in the distance she heard a sound that set her teeth on edge - the strident scream of twisting metal.

The computer started speaking in Vardarian. "Warning. Warning. Explosion proximity alert."

"Damage report!" Tyr snapped as he stood, spread his wings and leaped from the tub. She was only a few seconds behind him, but by the time she was standing on the tile he had a towel ready for her and wrapped her in it as the computer spewed a report so full of technical information she couldn't keep up.

"We need to go. Now." He didn't bother toweling off himself, he just headed for the bedroom with her following right behind.

"Go where? What the *fraxx* happened? Where's Braxon?"

"*Tyran? Phae? Are you alright?*" Braxon's transmission came in at full volume, making both she and Tyr wince.

"*No need to yell. We're fine. The* Santar *has some hull damage. We need to leave until repairs are complete. You?*" Tyr replied.

"*Unhurt. The shock wave rocked the area, but no damage. At least, I assume that's what hit us.*"

"*The ship keeps screaming about an explosion proximity alert, so I'd say you're right.*" She said, relief that Braxon was alright hitting her like a second shock wave.

"*Since I can't come back to the ship, meet you here? It's probably the safest place to wait for information.*" Braxon suggested.

"*We'll be there as soon as we're dressed.*" Tyr replied.

"*Dressed?*"

"*We were in the tub. It was supposed to help me relax. It didn't,*" she said.

"*I don't think there's a relaxed being on this entire station right now. I'll see you both soon.*" Braxon said and the link went silent.

Tyr went to the closet and grabbed clothes for both of them. She put them on as fast as she could, only registering that he'd chosen a Vardarian outfit for her as she drew the green and silver top over her head. It reminded her of what they'd been discussing before the explosion. *"You are a member of the imperial house of Varosa now."*

When things settled down again, she'd need to think about that. After they'd gotten off the ship and found out what in starsfury had happened.

The computer continued to give updates as she pocketed her comm device, which was buzzing and chirping with incoming messages. She'd check in once they were clear of the ship.

She snagged her favorite pair of boots off the floor and caught up with Tyr at the door. "How bad is it?"

He grasped her hand. "The ship will be fine. The shockwave hit our underside and caused some minor damage."

"Is that what I heard? The hull buckling?"

"I don't think so. I think that was the station. The *Santar's* hull is cracked, not buckled."

Wonderful. "I'm really starting to miss the slow, quiet days when all I had to worry about was staying ahead of my enemies and figuring out where my next meal was coming from. Those were simpler times."

"You are a strange female," he muttered as the door opened and they stepped onto the station.

CHAPTER FOURTEEN

PHAEDRA STARED at the bottom of her mug of cocoa and wondered if she should order another one. Her medibots kept her from feeling fatigue, but they couldn't stop the chill that sank into her bones as night slowly changed into what passed for morning out in the darkness of space. Usually the station was quiet at this hour, but not now. Everyone was awake and sharing what little information they had about the explosion that destroyed the Bellex corporation's cruiser, the *Blitzer*. The ship's crew were killed, along with Bellex rep Nadira Finn, and her guest, Tadeus Grasi of Astek. It had also turned the docking arm around the ship into a mess of twisted metal, venting part of it to space.

The club's kitchen staff were busy making meals for the rest of the employees, as well as the cyborgs and fighters that called the club home. Kit, and his security team were patrolling, looking for anything or anyone out of place. The doors were locked and guarded, and only a handful of beings, most of them wearing IAF or Corp-Sec uniforms, had been allowed inside. Despite the fact that there were no strangers in the club, Kit had assigned Owen Connors to watch over her. He was at the next table, chatting with Royan Watson. Well, Owen was chatting. Royan was flirting again.

At the moment, Braxon and Tyr were in one of the back rooms of the club in a meeting to discuss the future of the trade talks. Archer wasn't there, but one of his aides was, along with some low-level employees from various corporations and governments. The meeting rooms were small, and while no one asked her to go, she had chosen to make room for someone else. She couldn't translate for them at the moment, and as much as she wanted to know what was going on, she believed they'd tell her everything once they were together again.

So, here she was, mulling over the day's events and trying to make sense of it all. Why blow up Nadira's ship? Was this all the work of one group, or several taking advantage of the chaos to even old scores? She was itching to get back to cyberspace and look for answers, but her gear was still on the *Santar*. For now, all she could do was think.

"You look like you're trying to find the answers to the galaxy's problems at the bottom of that mug. I've stared into enough glasses to know the only things you'll find down there are regret and a need for a hangover cure." A familiar woman's voice drawled.

"I've never gotten a hangover from a mug of cocoa before." She set down the glass and smiled at Phylomenia Harrington, captain of the *Beacon*.

"Cocoa? Girl, after the day you've had you need something stronger than that." The tall, muscular woman sat down and set a heavy glass of something reddish-brown and bubbling on the table between them.

She eyed the contents warily. "I thought your poison of choice was Torskian ale. What in the name of glory is *that*?"

"This? This is my nerve tonic. I only break it out for special occasions, like when some idiot sets off a bomb and ruins my beauty sleep." Phyl tapped the glass. "Want some? Even with those medi-bots, I promise you'll feel it."

"I'm good. I need a clear head."

Phyl snorted and ran a hand through her close-cropped black and gray hair. "For what? You planning on solving this whole *fraxxing* mess by yourself? I'm pretty sure Scott thinks this is his mess to fix. He always did have a bad habit of taking on too much."

"Wait, Scott? As in Colonel bossy-brass Archer?" Phae leaned in and fixed the former smuggler with the best glare she could muster. "How are you on a first name basis with him of all people?"

"When you've been around as long as I have, you'll discover the galaxy is smaller than you think it is. I've known Scott since he was a hot-shot flyboy who thought he was the best pilot to ever sit in a cockpit."

"I thought that was your title?" Phae asked with a grin.

"It is. Who do you think I beat to get it?" Phyl took a drink, then glanced around to make sure they were alone. Since Phae had claimed one of the booths near the windows there wasn't anyone else around. Apparently, everyone else wasn't keen to be that close to open space after what had happened to the *Blitzer*. The explosion had damaged parts of the station and a number of ships that had been in range of the shockwave. Everyone was feeling vulnerable right now.

Phyl lowered her voice. "I only got back a few hours ago. Zura brought me up to speed, but she didn't mention anything that explains why you're here alone, in the wee hours of the morning looking like someone banned you from cyberspace for a year. So, what's up?"

"It's a long list."

"Do I look like I have somewhere else to be right now?" Phyl pushed the glass of 'nerve tonic' across the table. "Drink that, then tell me what's going on inside that highly enhanced head of yours."

"I don't—"

"You do. Don't argue with me, girl. I've been getting my own way longer than you've been breathing."

Phaedra took the mug and lifted it to her lips. She was expecting a hit of powerful liquor, but instead she got a mouthful of something fizzy, sweet, and tasting slightly of...*cherries*? She took a deeper drink, then another.

"Good, isn't it?" Phyl asked with a smile that softened her normally hawkish features.

"What is it and what am I supposed to feel if it isn't alcoholic?" she asked.

"Cherry cola, or as near as I can manage to replicate. The kick comes from the sugar, and the caffeine. There's enough in there to make a Jeskyran's thorns quiver. When I was a kid, I loved the stuff, but every corporation that made it got wiped out in the Resource Wars."

"If you're willing to share, I'd like the recipe before I go."

Phyl cocked her head. "Where you going? I thought you were sticking around here for a bit longer."

"Zura didn't tell you about Braxon and Tyran?"

"The new aliens? She said you were hand-picked to be their liaison and you've been helping them negotiate trade deals in exchange for a colony."

"She left out the good part. They're also my mates. Pheromones and some other chemical mojo is involved, but yeah. Mates."

Phyl whistled. "Mates, huh? Mojo or not, they better be treating you right."

"They're trying. I'm trying. It's all...trying."

"But you think you'll be leaving when they do? Back to their homeworld?"

"Or to start working on the new colony. That is, if we can ever get the corporations to agree to give up one of their precious planets. They are literally killing each other for the chance to get access to Vardarian tech, but not one of them is willing to part with the real estate." She gestured out the window to a docking spar that had been filled with ships only a few hours ago. "Now, I'm not sure we'll ever get a deal. They're running scared." And as they fled, they were taking her hopes for a future for River and the others with them.

Phyl's fingers started tapping on the tabletop, and then she chuckled. "You need a planet? As it happens, I might know someone who can help. Hang on a second, I need to check something. She dug into a pocket of her battered and worn jacket and pulled out a comm-device that looked like it had been made when Earth still had a breathable atmosphere.

"Does that still work?"

Phyl snorted. "Better than yours, I bet. You should know better than to judge something by its appearance. Old cover, shiny new insides. The circles I run in, it's best not to flaunt things if you don't want 'em stolen."

"I suspect we've run in some of the same circles." While Phaedra wasn't a full out criminal, she never claimed to be a meek, law-abiding citizen of the galaxy, either. She knew smugglers, hackers, pirates, pharma dealers and thieves. Some of them she considered friends, of a sort, anyway. She'd heard about Phyl long before the two ever met. The older woman was something of a legend. She had been running contraband for decades without getting caught, and then she'd simply given it all up one day and started working for Zura... another reformed smuggler.

"I suspect we have." Phyl had her eyes on the screen when a server wandered past, but Phaedra caught his attention and requested two fresh mugs of the cherry cola.

He wrinkled his nose before agreeing to bring it out. "That stuff will rot your insides."

"It was that, or Torskian ale," she shot back.

"In that case, two carbonated, caffeinated sugar bombs, coming up."

Phyl glanced up at her. "They've been telling me that stuff will kill me since I was six. I'm still here. And now I've had Zale's little booster shot, I plan on being here for a whole lot longer." She set down the comm-device and tapped it. "I think I have a planet for you."

"What? Where? How?" Questions tumbled out of Phaedra's mouth in a tangle.

"I have connections, girl. Lots of them. Now, does this

colony of yours need anything special, or will any goldilocks type planet do?"

"Nothing special. Breathable atmosphere, close to standard gravity, no existing colonies or intelligent native life forms. The usual stuff." She couldn't believe they were having this conversation.

She hummed thoughtfully. "There's a colony of sorts there, but I'll get to that in a second. This place isn't even close to civilized space. No trade routes, no IAF around to protect you if things go sideways."

"Coordinates?"

Phyl held up her comm device so the screen was pointed at Phaedra. A star map appeared, showing locations of the Drift and a system she'd never heard of. It would take weeks to get there even with FTL drive engines...and if she was reading this right, it was in the general direction of the Vardarian empire. She was starting to believe that Braxon and Tyran's ancestors really did know what they were doing.

"Who does it belong to?" she asked.

"Torex claimed the system, but the colony there has met every qualification. Torex is fighting their claim, though, greedy bastards that they are."

Phaedra leaned in. "I sense there's a story behind that statement. Tell me everything."

CHAPTER FIFTEEN

The station had switched to daytime mode by the time it was safe for them to return to their ship. The promenade had been full of beings, and they'd parted like a living sea as the three of them and their heavily-armed escort of IAF soldiers made the walk back to the docking ring. For Braxon, it felt a lot like being back at court, where even a simple walk turned into a procession. Then again, there were a few differences. For one he'd never carried a female into court.

Phaedra had given in to exhaustion by the time they found her. Cynder had convinced her to rest on the couch in the cyborg female's office. She had barely stirred when he tried to wake her, so he had picked her up and carried her instead. Apart from an incoherent murmur and a contented sigh as she snuggled into his chest, she hadn't moved again for the entire walk. It wasn't surprising. She'd put constant pressure on herself the last few days. Between that, the pain from her implant malfunctioning, and the nightmares that woke her at least once a night, she needed to sleep.

They had put her to bed with care, smoothing out the wild mane of her hair and easing her out of her clothes so she would sleep in comfort. There was something deeply satisfying about tending to her like that. They worked together in silence, their hands occasionally brushing against each other as they soothed and settled their mate.

They should have left Phaedra to sleep and started to discuss the myriad of challenges facing them. The future of any negotiations now that the corporation reps were leaving in fear, the growing threat to Phaedra, and whatever it was that Tyr was trying to keep secret. After spending most of his life as the prince's *anrik*, he knew when Tyran was hiding something. It was likely something to do with his sister. Neha had many gifts, but patience was not one of them.

Instead of talking, they'd stripped and joined Phaedra in the bed, snuggling her between them. She had sighed in contentment and reached for them both. That small, unconscious response filled his heart with emotions too powerful for him to deny. He didn't simply need this female because she was his mate. He loved her.

The words settled into his soul, and as he drifted off to sleep, there was a smile on his face.

THE REALITY they woke to didn't offer many reasons to keep smiling. He and Tyr slipped out of bed without waking Phaedra. Sleep would speed her healing, and there was no reason for her to be up yet. There would be no meetings today.

The corporate reps had fled like frightened *kerr*, leaving only a handful of underlings behind. Most of the government officials were still on the station, no doubt hopeful that with the corporations out of the picture, they could negotiate a better deal for the worlds they represented. All meetings were canceled for the moment, and the remaining reps were under guard while Archer's IAF and Corp-Sec did all they could to find the suspect and end the killings.

Braxon showered, changed, and then joined Tyran in the galley to eat and talk about the updates and news that had been waiting on their comm devices.

"We might be light-years from home, but some things are still universal. It would seem bureaucrats are spineless cowards no matter what their species," Tyr said by way of a greeting.

"Bureaucrats and money men are only interested in risking other people's lives, not their own," Braxon agreed before making his meal selection. Phaedra had introduced them to a number of new dishes and beverages since she'd come onboard. He wasn't impressed by coffee, but there was another one he'd found much to his liking - Earl Grey tea.

"Should we order something for Phaedra, too? I can't imagine she's going to sleep much longer," Tyr asked.

"Good idea. Our *mahaya* claims she cannot think until she's had her coffee. Not that there's much to think about today." He added the coffee to his list of requests and then placed it on hold until the ship's AI detected Phaedra had woken up.

Tyr grimaced. "There's more than you know."

"Neha?" he asked as he sat down across from Tyr. The ship's passengers normally ate in the more elaborate dining hall, but since it was only the two of them, they had taken to eating in the galley, instead. It was utilitarian but comfortable, with several long tables and bench-style seating that lined three of the walls. The fourth wall was full of food replicators, along with a chilled compartment for storing fresh fruits, vegetables, other perishables.

"My sister's patience has reached its end," Tyr confirmed.

"Then it's time to tell her what we're doing here."

Tyr scoffed, his expression one of frustration and doubt. "And what exactly is that? Negotiations are stalled. No one seems to be willing to offer us the one thing we came here to find, and our mate has not yet fully bonded with us."

"I choose to trust our ancestors. We found this place, and these people, against odds I couldn't begin to calculate. When we first got here, I had my doubts. About the plan and then about Phaedra. How could she be our mate when she was so different, so tiny."

"Our roles have reversed, my friend. Now I'm the one with concerns, and you're the one telling me to trust our ancestors."

"Not only our ancestors. Phaedra. Our *mahaya* is amazing, and she'll find a way to make this work."

"How come you never say such nice things when you know I'm in the room?" Phaedra was standing in the door dressed in one of her too-big shirts and nothing else. Her bare feet made almost no sound as she jogged over to him and threw herself into his arms. "Say it again."

He wrapped her in his arms and lifted her into his lap as he pushed the table back with one foot to make room for her. "You are amazing, and I trust you."

Her eyes filled with joy and she leaned in to kiss him, her hand coming to rest over his heart. "I think you're both pretty amazing, too. I'm sorry I made you doubt that. I didn't mean to. It's just that I'm not used to belonging anywhere. I've had to prove my worth every day since I left home. This is..." she trailed off and smiled at them both. "This is new, but I like it. And I like both of you, a great deal."

Tyr rose to fetch her coffee. "We thought you'd need this once you were awake."

She reached for the mug the moment she realized what it was. "Sweet words and you made me coffee. That's almost enough for me to forgive you two for leaving me to sleep the day away. In fact, I don't remember getting back to the ship, either. Did I sleep through that, too?"

"You were so deeply asleep that you didn't wake when I carried you all the way here with an escort of eight guards. You needed to rest," Braxon said.

"Eight? How could Archer afford to send eight soldiers with us and still protect the rest of the station?"

Tyr joined the conversation. "He told us last night that he has commandeered every ship in the area. He said it was as close as he could come to enacting martial law. I'm not sure what that means, but it sounded serious."

Phae groaned. "It is serious. Martial law would put the entire Drift under the direct control of the IAF. The corporations are already unhappy about the military presence here, but they can't push back too hard because they brought it on themselves. But if Archer took direct control of the Drift...that would be tantamount to declaring war on the corporations."

"He's too wise a man to do that. He knows this is all balanced on the edge of a cliff. One errant gust of wind and everything could fall apart."

She took a piece of fruit from Tyr's plate and nibbled at it, looking oddly pleased considering the dour news they were discussing. "Do either of you happen to know which corporate reps are still on the station?"

"Why? Negotiations are on hold for now."

She shrugged. "*Official* negotiations are on hold. That doesn't mean we can't keep talking to the ones that are left."

"True enough." Tyr checked his comm device, scrolling through various updates until he found what he was looking for. He read off the list of names and who they represented. It wasn't a long list.

"Gunns, the guy from Torex is still here? Good." She said, looking pleased.

"Do you want us to meet with him for some reason?" Braxon asked.

"I've got an idea. Maybe a way for us to salvage some of this mess. I need to talk to some of the reps still here." She grimaced. "Then, I need to ask Archer for a favor."

"What are you planning?" Tyr asked.

"It's not even a plan yet. It's just an idea. I was talking to a friend last night, Phylomenia Harrington. She was at the Nova while you were in meetings. I don't think you've met her, she's one of Zura's pilots and was on a cargo run until last night."

"I do not see how a cargo pilot would be much help to us or our situation." Tyr wasn't ready to believe again, but Braxon was. He believed in Phaedra.

"It's all a matter of connections. I swear Phyl has more connections and friends than there are stars in the galaxy. She suggested something that got me thinking, that's all."

"I have faith in you, Phae," Braxon murmured.

"I hope it's justified. I want to make this dream happen. The colony. The fresh start. All of it." She smiled at them both. "Our dream."

Tyr blinked, then got to his feet and came around the table to slide in beside them, grinning from ear to ear. He hugged them both, then kissed Phaedra tenderly. "Our dream, yes. A new home for all of us."

Without thinking, Braxon leaned in and kissed Tyran's cheek. "It's going to happen. Believe it."

Tyr froze and Phae made a soft sound of delight. Without a word, she pulled back so she wasn't between the two of them, but was still holding onto them both.

Tyr locked gazes with him, then he wrapped his hand in Braxon's unbound hair and kissed him with a bruising passion. Years of denial fell away in those seconds, and Braxon lifted his hand to stroke his *anrik's* face as he kissed him back. It was unlike any other kiss he'd ever experienced. Fiercer. Harder. Tyr's grip on his hair was hard enough to sting, but it didn't distract from the pleasure of their kiss. Instead, it added to it.

"I was wondering when you two were going to figure it out," Phae whispered, her voice thick with laughter and joy.

Tyr jerked away as she spoke, his breath ragged. "You are not angry?"

"Why would I be angry? It's not like you stopped loving me the moment you kissed him."

"You told her you love her?" Braxon asked, surprised and somehow stung that he hadn't been part of that moment.

"I did."

"And do you love him?" He asked Phaedra.

"Yesterday, I wasn't ready to say so." She kissed first Tyr, then him. "Then last night, there was a moment when I thought I might have lost you. The fight. The explosion. It made me realize that as scared as I am of loving you, I'm even more terrified of losing you. So, I'm ready to say it now. I love you both."

Her words wrapped around his heart, and for the first time in his life, it felt like everything had fallen into place. This was where he was supposed to be, and these were the beings he was destined to spend his life with. He knew it.

"I love you, too, my *jeza*."

TYRAN'S HEART was slamming against his ribs so hard it surprised him that he could hear Phaedra's declaration. He'd kissed Braxon. More than that, Braxon had kissed him, and instead of being angry or jealous, their *mahaya* was pleased. His thoughts were whizzing around his head like a swarm of meteors and the *sharhal* was burning like liquid fire in his veins. He needed to regain control. This wasn't the moment to explore this new facet of their relationship. He had to tell Phaedra that Neha had demanded their return. He sank a fang into his lip, using the pain to help him focus.

"Don't." Phaedra stroked his mouth with her soft fingers. "I don't like seeing either of you in pain. I think we've all had enough of that in the last while, don't you?"

"I fear there's more to come. My sister contacted me yesterday. She is demanding that Braxon and I return home."

"Why would she do that when we've not finished negotiations?" Phae asked, confused.

"Because she doesn't know about them, or you." Braxon's answer was blunter than Tyran's carefully planned response, but at this point Tyr didn't think it mattered much. He was certain she would be hurt and unhappy that they had kept her a secret from his family.

"Why wouldn't she know what you're doing?" She asked, then answered her own question. "Because she's part of the court you're trying to escape from. You can't let her know until the deal is done."

"You're not angry?" Tyr asked.

She winked at him. "You keep asking me that. Trust me, highness, when I'm mad at you, you'll know it. I'm not angry about you and Braxon finally figuring out you're more than friends. I wasn't sure, but I had a hunch. I just don't understand why you didn't act on it before now."

"Because it took being affected by the *sharhal* for it to manifest," Braxon told her. "That happens sometimes with our species. The bond is not complete until we find our *mahaya*, the one who binds us all together."

"So, you didn't feel this way about each other before?"

She quirked a pink brow at them both. "Are you sure about that?"

Neither of them spoke for a long time.

"And that's my answer. You sensed something but decided to ignore it, didn't you?" She huffed. "Males. It doesn't matter what species you are, you're all stubborn when it comes to your feelings."

"We're stubborn about our feelings? Are you sure the ground beneath your feet is firm enough to be hurling such accusations, little warrior?" Tyr asked.

"Probably not," she conceded, then changed the subject. "What are we going to do about your sister and her command to come home?"

"I think it's time we used a phrase you taught us," Tyr glanced at Braxon who nodded.

"Which one?" she asked.

"The one that states sometimes it is better to ask for forgiveness instead of permission."

"Oh! I like that one," she was beaming now, a warrior's grin that should terrify any sane male. But he wasn't sane. He was in love.

"I thought you would approve. Once we've eaten and bathed, we'll help you get started with this idea of yours."

Phaedra's smile broadened. "Good, because I think it's going to take all three of us to convince everyone to come back for one more meeting."

"We'll find a way." Braxon leaned in to gently kiss her cheek, then turned and brushed a whisper of a kiss on Tyr's lips as he moved away. He still wasn't sure how it was all going to come together. They didn't even know what Phae was planning, but in his heart, he knew it was going to work out. Their ancestors hadn't brought them all this way to fail.

THEY HAD BARELY STARTED on their day when the high priority message had arrived.

"What do you mean, she's demanding to see us now?" Phae had been enjoying a blissfully hot bath when Tyran had arrived with the news. The only thing she'd accomplished so far today was to eat and convince her mates to remove the subvocal communicator tech so that she could access the translation program without discomfort.

She climbed out of the tub and started toweling herself off, but Tyr took the towel from her and started doing it for her. A second later Braxon left the bath too, and soon she was being petted and stroked by soft fabrics and strong hands as they both took over. "How long have we got?"

"Long enough to dress and see to one other small detail. Then we'll speak to my sister."

"What other detail?" she asked.

Braxon kissed the curve of her shoulder. "We'd be honored if you would agree to wear your mating band to this meeting."

The idea made her stupidly happy. "You want her to know you're mated to me?"

"Yes." They both answered at once.

"I'd be happy to make that clear to anyone who might be watching. What about the two of you? Will you be wearing yours?"

"We will," Tyr confirmed.

"But I don't have scars, yet. Won't she notice that?"

Braxon unpinned her hair, letting it fall around her shoulders. "Wear your beautiful hair down and no one will be able to see if you bear our marks or not."

"Good idea." That would work for now, but she was ready to take that step. Soon, they'd bond and she'd have their claiming marks as well as the armband to mark her as their *mahaya*. She suspected that she wouldn't be the only one getting new scars, either. Her lovers were more than *anrik* now, or they would be, very soon.

Braxon left them to get dressed. That was another thing that would change. They were together now, in every sense of the word. It made no sense for Braxon's things to be in another room. She said as much as she donned the most ornate of her Vardarian outfits, the one with gems embedded in the collar.

"We'll help him move his things in here later today," Tyr agreed.

He was wearing the same green and black outfit he'd worn the first time she'd seen him, and she realized the two of them matched. It made sense, they were both wearing the traditional colors of his family line.

Braxon reappeared as she was putting on her shoes. He was also dressed in green and black, and his collar was inlaid with what looked like black diamonds.

Tyr looked up and nodded. "So, this is what it takes for you to actually dress the part of a courtier?"

"I'm doing this for Phaedra, not your sister."

She looked at her men and sighed happily. "You both look amazing. I have to say that I'm all for Vardarian fashion. Especially on the two of you."

Tyr retrieved an ornately etched metal box from his

things and set it down on the bed. "Our bands," he explained as he opened the box.

Inside were three gold and silver armbands, one significantly smaller than the others. All three were made up of two flat hammered-metal strands that formed an interlocking pattern that reminded her of the figure-8 style symbol for eternity. "They're beautiful."

Tyr lifted the smaller band from the box, revealing there was a gap between the two ends, so it could be fitted properly. "Hold out your left arm."

She did, and the two males carefully placed it on her upper arm, using the strength of their hands to close the gap enough that it stayed in place.

Tyr offered his arm to her, and she copied what he'd done, setting the band in place and allowing Braxon to press it closed. Then it was Braxon's turn, and she swore he stopped breathing until the band was in place.

"You're ours now, *mahaya*, and everyone who sees that band will know it." Tyr was so smug it was almost radiating off him in waves.

She looked down at the elegant bands of precious metal and smiled. "Or they'll think I'm seriously spoiled by the two of you. Which is also true."

She touched their new bands. "And you both belong to me." She paused a second before adding "And to each other."

"We do," Braxon agreed. He leaned in to kiss her but was interrupted by a warbling alarm that made both he and Tyr sigh.

"What the *fraxx* is that?"

"My sister is awaiting us in the audience room. She's made the connection early."

"I haven't even met her yet, and I'm already starting to dislike her."

Both males looked at each other. "I told you it would be this way," Tyr muttered.

They made their way to a room near the front of the ship. It wasn't large, but what it lacked in size, it made up for in opulence. It was a bit like a movie theatre designed for the richest beings in the galaxy. Every surface was polished, and there were thick falls of what looked like dark green velvet on the walls. Pictures of regal looking Vardarians, all with silver skin and solemn expressions, were carefully placed between the velvet hangings.

There were a number of silver chairs with black cushions set out in rows, all of them facing a much larger chair set on a dais at the front of the room. On the throne sat a silver-skinned Vardarian woman with gems woven into her dark hair. The image was so perfect it was hard to believe that it was only a projection.

Tyran stepped toward the throne and bowed slightly. "Empress Neha, it is good to see you."

Neha sniffed. "I doubt you truly feel that way, given that you haven't responded to my messages in days."

Tyran stiffened. "It was one day, and the delay could not be helped."

"I look forward to hearing about your reasons, along with confirmation that you are on your way home." Neha glanced over at Braxon, and her eyes widened when she realized there was another being standing just behind him.

"You found another species?" She asked. "Why wasn't I told of this? Introduce the female and tell me what you've found."

Braxon sketched a quick bow and brought Phaedra forward so she was standing between her mates. "Your Imperial Highness, this is Phaedra Kari, a female of the species known as humans. She is also—"

"She is strangely colored." Neha interjected.

"I could say the same thing about you, Your Highness," Phaedra shot back in Vardarian.

Neha's brows shot up on surprise. "Who are you to speak to me that way, human? And how is it you know our language?"

Phaedra turned to show Neha the band on her arm. "I am your brother's *mahaya*. Which makes us family. I assumed that since you felt it acceptable to interrupt Braxon a moment ago, that things were more informal among family members. Was I wrong?"

Neha's eyes narrowed. "What is this female talking about? You're a member of the Imperial family, Tyran. Your mate has to be Vardarian."

"It would seem the ancestors disagree with your assessment. Phaedra is our *mahaya*."

Neha's expression tightened into a mask of fear and spite. "Show me her scars, then, brother. I know you would never allow your mate to go with her scars hidden. If the *sharhal* has possessed you, then surely you've claimed her already?"

All three of them stood in silence.

"As I suspected. If you haven't claimed her, then she's not your mate," Neha sounded triumphant.

"We were waiting until Phaedra was—"

"She is not your mate. You will not claim the female. I forbid it," Neha snapped. "Send me your coordinates and I will send a negotiating team to continue what you've started. Say goodbye to your little pink pet and come home, now. Your empress has need of you."

The hologram vanished and the three of them were left alone in the room.

"Your sister is..." Phaedra didn't know a strong enough word in Vardarian to describe her.

"*Vipa*. The word you're looking for is *vipa*."

"If that's your version of bitch, then yeah, that's the word." She looked at the two of them. "Now what do we do?"

Tyr reached out a hand to both of them. "I believe I'm about to commit treason. Care to join me?"

CHAPTER SIXTEEN

PHAEDRA TOOK Tyr's hand and hung on tight. She wasn't letting go of either of them. Not now. Not ever. "I've been accused of a lot of things in my life, but until now, I haven't been able to claim treason. I'm game."

"And that attitude is one of the many reasons I love you." Braxon scooped her into his arms without any warning and started carrying her back toward their quarters.

"Where are we going?"

"To commit treason." Braxon told her.

"Naked," Tyr added.

"But with the armbands. I don't want to take mine off yet."

Both men rumbled in approval.

"That's not all I want." She paused before putting her deepest desire into words. "I want to be bound to you both. Not even the empress can deny a bonded mating, right?"

Braxon came skidded to a halt. "Say that again."

"He meant *please* say that again," Tyr said.

"I know it'll piss off your sister and probably land us in more trouble than we're already in, but I want to be bound to you both. Forever. I want the scars that go with my mating band." Zale had confirmed that there was no risk to her if they bound her and shared their nanotech. Either the Vardarian tech would replace the medi-bots, or the two would work in tandem. It was time to find out.

"So do I," Tyr said.

She looked over at him, then at Braxon. "I can't give you those scars, but I know a way around that little problem."

"How?" Braxon asked.

"You could bond with each other, as well as with me. Give yourselves the marks that I can't give you. Make it so we can never be parted."

Braxon's green eyes were as bright as lasers as he looked at Tyr. "Mine?"

Tyran didn't hesitate. "Yes."

"Then let's make this happen. I think we've all waited long enough." Braxon was already moving before she got all the words out, but it didn't matter. They were all thinking the same thing.

Tyr couldn't think straight at the moment, and for once, he didn't care. There was no one around to judge him, no one to prove himself to. It was just him and the two beings that had become the center of his universe. He was so distracted by what had just happened he failed to notice that Braxon had stopped until it was too late and he ran into him. Their bodies slammed together, and instead of stepping back, he wrapped an arm around Braxon's waist and buried his face in the crook of his neck.

"In a hurry, highness?" Braxon asked.

Reluctantly, he lifted his head. "You stopped before we got to our room. I ran into you."

"We're not going to your quarters. We're going to mine."

"Why?"

"Because I said so." It was the first time in their lives Braxon had ever taken charge. Did he know how much Tyr wanted that? No, he couldn't. No one suspected that his greatest desire was to let go and let someone else take command. His cock hardened instantly, and he had to step back before he gave away the secret he'd lived with for so many years.

They entered Braxon's quarters, and Tyran looked around him in surprise. He'd forgotten just how different their quarters were. The furniture was similar, but there were none of the luxurious touches he had in his quarters. It was barely half the size of his, too.

"You're moving in with us. Today," Phaedra announced.

"Agreed, but not now. Right now, we need to be in here."

"How come?" she asked before Tyr could.

"You'll see." Braxon set Phaedra down and then turned to Tyr. "Phae, will you help Tyr out of his clothes while I check on something?"

She bounced on her toes with barely repressed eagerness. "I can do that."

Braxon moved out of his line of sight as Phaedra moved in. She slid her hands up his bare stomach, moving slowly upward until she reached the clasp of his shirt. She undid it and pushed the fabric off his shoulders, and he let it fall to the ground. Instead of removing his pants, she walked around behind him, running her fingers over his furled wings. He opened them, exposing the sensitive skin of his back to her touch. She placed one hand between his wings and reached around with her free hand to cup his cock.

He uttered an explosive groan and rocked his hips, grinding himself against her fingers. "Don't stop."

"I've no intentions of stopping," she promised as she undid his pants and slipped a hand inside to grip his hard length.

Braxon walked back into view. He was already naked, his cock as hard as Tyr's. He was holding something behind his back. "Give me your hands."

Tyr's brain started to melt around the edges as he offered Braxon his hands while Phaedra continued her sweet torments. He'd been so certain Braxon didn't know his darkest secret, but now he wasn't sure anymore.

Braxon's hands closed on Tyr's forearms, and something heavy and cold clicked into place, encircling his wrists. "Phae, finish stripping our mate, now."

"What's this?" Tyr asked. There were two identical metal bands around his wrists. There were no markings on them, and they looked more like shackles than anything else.

"Get on the bed and you'll find out."

There was no hiding the affect Braxon's behavior was having on him. Not when Phaedra pushed his pants down over his hips, leaving him naked and exposed in a way he'd never allowed himself to be before.

Braxon reached up to stroke his cheek. "Trust me," He whispered, then gave him a hard but brief kiss before stepping back and pushing him toward the bed. "Go."

He could hardly breathe as he managed to nod, then made his way to the bed with Phaedra at his side.

"Lie down. Arms at your sides. Eyes closed." There it was again, that no-nonsense tone that made his breath catch in his throat.

He did as instructed, his heart beating like a hammer against his ribs as he settled onto the bed. A few seconds later, two pairs of hands took hold of his arms and lifted them over his head. There was a sharp click, and when he tugged at his hands, they didn't budge.

"Magnetic cuffs. You'll get your hands back when we decide, not you." Braxon's voice was coming to his left, which meant Phaedra was on his right.

"No peeking," Phae said. "And if it gets too much, all you have to do is say stop."

He nodded. "How long have you known?"

The bed sagged to his left, and then Braxon was whispering in his ear, his lips brushing over his skin with every word. "We've been friends for most of our lives. Did you think I didn't know?"

"I thought I'd done a better job of hiding it," Tyr confessed.

Phaedra joined them, her whispered words caressing his cheek. "There are no secrets between the three of us. Not anymore."

Braxon's large hand stroked down his stomach, not stopping until his fingers brushed over Tyr's aching cock. He arched his hips, craving more of Braxon's touch, and Braxon obliged him by fisting his dick in one hand.

"You're not in control, right now, remember? Lie back and enjoy." Braxon pumped his hand several times in a row, but this time, Tyr didn't move.

"That's better. As a reward, would you like to taste Phaedra? Make her come with your mouth?"

"Yes."

He caught the scent of her pheromones a split second before she kissed him, and he groaned into her mouth. When she raised her head again, she helped him into a better position, while Braxon continued stroking his cock and balls. It was hard to focus on either one of them. Especially when Phaedra moved above him and then straddled his face, lowering herself until her pussy was over his mouth.

He devoured her, licking and sucking her tender flesh until she was quivering. Just as he had her at the brink of an orgasm, Braxon's tongue swiped over the tip of his cock and Tyr released her clit to groan aloud.

He fought the restraints for a moment, wanting to be free, but Phaedra placed her hands on his arms. "If you want it to stop, all you have to do is say the word."

He didn't want to stop, though. Not really. Once he realized that, Tyr let everything go but the pleasure they were giving each other.

Time stretched out into one seamless flow of sensations. He was drunk with pleasure, the *sharhal* setting fire to his blood. Every sense was overloaded. The scent of pheromones and sex, the taste of Phaedra's flesh, the heat of Braxon's mouth and hands. He could hear the three of them breathing hard, gasping and moaning as they moved together.

He wanted to hear Phaedra's cries of pleasure as she came, and he used all his skill to make it happen. This time, Braxon slowed his sensual assault on Tyr as Phaedra started to moan and grind herself across Tyr's mouth, allowing him to stay focused on giving their *mahaya* what she needed to bring her to orgasm.

The moment she cried out, Braxon sucked the entire length of Tyr's cock into his mouth, and Tyr saw stars. He was on the verge of exploding when everything stopped. Braxon withdrew, and Phaedra moved away, though he could still feel the bed dip near his head, indicating she hadn't moved far.

He opened his eyes to find her staring down at him, her face flushed and green eyes gleaming with desire. "No peeking," she scolded him.

"If he can't keep his eyes closed, we'll have to do it for him," Braxon said. Something sailed through the air to land beside his head and before Tyr could turn to see what it was, Phae placed a hand over his eyes. A second later a swatch of soft fabric touched his face and Phaedra removed her hand. He still couldn't see. Without thinking he tried to remove it, but his hands were still cuffed over his head.

"Lie still, lover. I promise you'll enjoy this next part." Phae stroked his chest and then moved over him, straddling his hips so that his cock was pressed along the seam of her pussy.

He groaned and fought the urge to thrust his hips upward.

"Do you want to fuck our mate, Tyran? She looks so

beautiful right now, perched on top of you, waiting to take your cock."

Braxon's crude words almost broke him, and his dick twitched and swelled so much Phaedra had to know how close he was to the edge. She leaned forward, her breasts caressing his chest as she nibbled on his lower lip before whispering. "Say yes, Tyr. Tell me you want me, and I'm all yours."

"Yes!"

She lifted herself over him, and someone's hand reached between them to position his cock at her opening. It was Braxon's, he was sure of it, and that awareness broke what was left of his control. He thrust into Phaedra's welcoming heat, and she tore the blindfold away as he claimed her body.

PHAEDRA HAD NEVER FELT SO powerful as she did at this moment. Tyr's submission had been intoxicating to watch, and so had the moment that Braxon had joined in their play. She knew exactly what Tyr was experiencing, the push and pull of being pleasured while giving pleasure to someone else. Now, though, it was her turn to be the focus of her lovers' attention. They'd told her what they wanted already, preparing her mind and her body every day since they'd first taken her to their bed. She was ready.

She leaned forward to kiss Tyr as he thrust into her, hard the first time, then slowly and gently as he got himself under control again. Braxon moved in behind her and she caught the familiar orange-and-spice scent of *uli* oil. He drizzled some of it into the small of her back, massaging it into her skin in slow, tingling circles as he worked his way lower until his fingers were stroking over the puckered rosette of her ass.

Her legs were trembling by the time he started to work a finger inside her, keeping her well lubricated with the pleasure-enhancing oil as he prepared her for his cock. He added a second finger, and she tensed for a moment as her enjoyment morphed into something closer to pain, but then Tyr kissed her hard, and she let herself relax again. He fucked her mouth with the same slow rhythm as his cock, and she got so lost in the pleasure of it all that when Braxon added a third finger, all she felt was a tingling burn that rode the edge between pleasure and pain without ever crossing the line.

She moaned, her inner walls flexing around Tyr's cock as a flood of cream flowed from her pussy, soaking them both.

"Are you ready?" Braxon asked.

She lifted her head to look over her shoulder at him. "I am."

He withdrew his fingers and then something thicker was pressed against her back opening.

"Look at me, *mahcya*. All you have to do is look at me and breathe. You know we'd never hurt you." There was a low clicking noise, and then Tyr's hands were cradling her face and he was looking up at her with adoration. "I love you."

"I love you both," she replied, then exhaled slowly as Braxon pushed inside her. She felt impossibly full, but gradually the feeling faded, and she started to relax.

"I can feel you both," Braxon said, his voice raw with need. "This is…"

"I know," Tyr reached around her to grip Braxon's hand as they started to move in unison.

"Oh hell, that's incredible," she gasped as they found their rhythm. It was a slow, sensual dance that carried all three of them to the heights of ecstasy and then higher still. They weren't just making love to her, they were connected to each other through her, and it made everything even more intense. When she thought it couldn't get any better, they proved her wrong.

In one fluid motion, they rolled to one side, keeping her between them. Then, Tyr ended their kiss and moved his mouth to one side of her throat while Braxon gathered her hair in his hand and pressed his mouth to her neck.

She braced for the pain of their bites, but instead of pain, she was rocked by a flood of pleasure so intense she screamed as their fangs sank into her neck. She was lost in a delirium of ecstasy, and by the time she came back to herself she was being rocked between them, wrapped in two pairs of strong arms.

"Ours now," Braxon murmured, sounding smug.

"Forever," Tyr agreed, smiling up at her.

"Now it's your turn," she informed them, squirming just enough to make them both groan. "I want you both to come inside me as you claim each other the way you just claimed me."

"For someone who doesn't take orders well, you certainly seem to be good at giving them," Braxon said.

"I'm learning from the two of you," she shot back.

They both chuckled, and then Tyr raised his arm. "Cuff needs to come off first."

Once he was freed from the cuffs, both males reached around her, offering their already scarred wrists to the other. Their cocks twitched and swelled inside her, and she was already riding the first waves of another orgasm as Tyr bit Braxon's wrist and they both lost control.

It was like being caught in a storm of pure passion, both of them crying out as their orgasms tore through them. They bucked and thrust into her, lost to everything but the bliss of the moment, and before they were done they catapulted her into yet another orgasm of her own.

When at last they could speak again, it was Tyr who broke their breathless silence. "I waited my whole life to find you, Phaedra. I had started to believe you didn't exist. You are our mate in all ways, and I will thank my ancestors every day of my life for guiding me to you. You've helped me find everything I dreamed of, and some things I didn't know I needed."

"It's the same for me, *mahaya*." Braxon said before kissing her cheek. "I love you."

Cradled between her mates, surrounded by their love and strength, Phaedra knew she'd be thanking their ancestors, and hers, for bringing them all together. The odds had been against them ever finding each other but somehow, they had anyway. The odds were still stacked against them, but as long as they had each other, they'd find a way.

CHAPTER SEVENTEEN

PHAEDRA WALKED into the meeting room with her head high. This was their last chance, and she was determined to make it work no matter what the risks. *Re'veth*, the risks. When they'd approached Archer, he'd rattled off the dangers of meeting again until he'd run out of breath. She had expected Braxon or Tyr to try and talk her out of it, but instead they'd stood their ground right beside her, even though they still didn't know what she had planned. Their faith in her was the best feeling in the galaxy.

It had taken hours and more fast-talking then she'd done in her life to get the agreement of the major corporations to meet again. Their reluctance was annoying, given that they were only going to be present as holograms. While the reps who had fled were in transit and couldn't make an appearance, replacements were going to sit in via the wonders of modern technology. The only beings that would actually be present were the four members of the Vardarian contingent; herself, Braxon, Tyr, and River, along with the handful of representatives still on the station. Getting them to agree to meet again had been another long process, but once they understood what they could gain from it, everyone agreed. They were going to pressure Torex Mining into giving up their claim to the planet Phyl had told her about.

She refused to tell Braxon or Tyr what she was planning until she was certain it would work. There was no point in building up their hopes only to dash them again if her plan fell apart. There was too much at stake. Now, they were here and everything was in place. It was time.

"Well?" Tyr asked. "Are you ready to tell us your plan? Why are we here?" He gestured around them. The only place that had the technology and the security to make it all work turned out to be at Astek's headquarters. Archer hadn't been happy with that, either. Until they got more information, he couldn't eliminate the possibility that it was Astek's rep who had been targeted. All they were certain of was that the blast had been caused by several micro-explosives detonating at the same time - somewhere near the stern of the ship, where the meeting rooms were located.

"We're here because Torex has the perfect planet for us, and we're going to make them hand it over."

"What?" Braxon asked.

"How?" Where?" Tyr added.

"Phyl and her connections. One of her friends is a scout for Torex. She had to make an emergency landing on a planet recently and discovered there was a cyborg living there. Turns out, he's been there long enough to be able to claim it as a colony. Torex is fighting it, but we're going to apply some leverage and make them give in."

"How?" Tyr asked again.

Braxon caught on right away. "The cyborgs. River and the other survivors. The colony founder is another cyborg. It's likely he'd be agreeable to having others of his kind join him."

"Exactly. This gives the IAF and the other corporations a reason to pressure Torex to agree, and none of them have to give up anything. And..." She beamed at them. "It's located in a system not far from the path you took to get here."

For a moment, Tyr looked like he'd been hit with a stun ray. His mouth was open, his eyes wide, but he neither spoke nor blinked.

"Tyr? What's wrong?" Phae asked, trying not to laugh.

Braxon didn't bother hiding his amusement. "He's lost his ability to speak. I didn't know that was possible."

"Well he better get it back, soon. We're all going to have to do a lot of talking if we're going to make this work."

"The others are in agreement?" Tyr finally asked.

She nodded. "They are. Even the IAF. That's the favor I asked Archer for."

"You are amazing. I wished you'd told us sooner, though. I thought we'd lost our chance. I thought..." Tyr pulled her into his arms for a hug and a toe-curling kiss that told her more clearly than words how he felt.

Braxon threw his arms around them both and they had a brief moment of hopeful celebration. It was all they had time for.

"Does everyone know?" Braxon asked.

"Everyone but River and Raymond Gunns from Torex." She hoped to be able to tell River before the meeting, but she hadn't wanted to give her false hope. As for Gunns, the first he'd hear of the offer would be at the meeting where he would face the combined pressure of his fellow corporations, the galactic governments, and the IAF.

River arrived just after they finished hugging and kissing. She looked uneasily around the room as they all got seated and Phaedra gave her a quick update on the reason they were all here.

River was thrilled, but even Phaedra's good news wasn't enough to ease all of her concerns. "You're sure this is safe?" River asked, her voice tinged with doubt.

Phae knew River wasn't asking about the safety of the group. She was concerned that there'd be a repeat of yesterday and the others present would turn on the only cyborg present. "The fool who caused the panic yesterday is dead. Most of the others present are holograms. No one here can hurt you."

"No, but they can destroy any chance we have of finding a home for the others. I promised them I'd find a place for us." River's voice cracked.

"I'll keep you safe, River. You have my word, you'll be able to keep your promise," Zale's words were a muted rumble as he joined them at the table.

"Thanks for coming, Zale." Phae smiled at the big half Torski. She had a theory that one of the issues the corporations were having was their fear that the medi-bot technology would spread into the general population. Zura's pregnancy was one of their nightmare scenarios. Zale, Archer, and the others had all agreed. It was time that the truth came out. There were beings of almost every race already carrying nanotech, including the Vardarians. Today was the day the corporations would learn that their worst-case scenario had already happened.

A glass of orange juice was set down in front of her and she turned to find Echo standing there smiling. "You're looking better," the cyborg female said.

"Feeling better, too." She tapped her temple. "Minor malfunction between some of my newly installed hardware."

Echo snorted with laughter. "I keep forgetting you're more like us than them."

"And now I'm insulted. I'm nothing like them." She gestured to the still empty area on the far side of the table. They were in a different room today, though they shared a similar décor. The only real difference was that this table was larger, and there were no chairs at all on one side. Overhead was a bank of holographic projectors and audio equipment that would allow the various reps to be present without risking their precious skins.

Something dark and sad flashed in Echo's eyes, then was gone before Phaedra could decipher it. Regret for the inadvertent insult? An unexpected memory? "You okay?"

Echo nodded. "All good. I better get back to work, though. Can't have the other guests thinking I'm playing favorites."

Before she had time to take more than a few sips of her juice, the rest of the representatives still on the station arrived and took their places. Once they were settled, Archer moved to the head of the perfectly polished wooden table and waited for silence. His eyes were slightly bloodshot, skin sunken, his face unshaven for the first time she could recall. Only his uniform looked the same as always, perfectly fitted, every button polished until it gleamed.

He nodded to an Astek employee, who tapped on a datapad and then stepped back. The holographic projectors lit up, and soon the space on the far side of the table was filled with the rest of the attendees.

"Can everyone hear me?" the colonel asked.

The translucent images all nodded.

"Good. Then we'll begin. As you all know, last night an explosion destroyed the *Blitzer*, which was built and owned by Bellex shipyards. Six crewmembers were killed, along with corporation representatives Nadira Finn and Tadeus Grasi. All findings are still very preliminary, but I can tell you that there were multiple micro-explosives involved in the blast. The IAF and Corp-Sec are working together to determine how the explosives got onboard, and who put them there."

The Pheran representative sat straighter, his blue tufted ears twitching in agitation. "The Pheran government has a message for any corporation that wishes to continue doing business in our sector. These attacks between rival corporations must stop. We will protect our worlds and the beings who live on them by whatever means necessary, including ending trade agreements and banning corporations from doing business in our part of the galaxy."

Every corporate rep present started talking at once, drowning each other out with their denials and accusations. Archer didn't let it go on long before he slapped a hand down on the tabletop with enough force to make every glass on the table jump. "The purpose of this meeting is not to air grievances or cast blame. We're here to finalize the trade deal with the Vardarians, including providing them with a planet to colonize."

The Torex Mining rep chuckled softly. "Do you really think we're going to reach any conclusions by the end of the day?"

The new Astek rep looked over at him with smug satisfaction. "Actually, Raymond, we do."

"That's our hope, yes. But before we speak about that, there's something else you all need to be aware of. Something I believe will move things along." Archer raised a brow and looked at Zale, who nodded and got to his feet. "This is Astek's robotics expert, Zale Fel."

Holtzman, the new Astek rep, frowned. "I was not aware you were going to be part of today's meeting. Why wasn't I told?"

Zale shrugged his massive shoulders and stared down at the much smaller human. "Because what I am here to discuss was, until now, a secret only a few were aware of."

"You're keeping secrets from your own employer?"

"Damn right I was." Zale looked around the room. "I was one of the original creators of the medi-bots used by every surviving cyborg. When I left the program, I didn't destroy my research. I designed a variation of the nanotech. One that didn't require a genetic match in order to work."

Horrified gasps and outraged mutterings filled the room.

"I'm not done!" Zale raised his voice to the point the walls reverberated with the sound.

Silence fell, and Phaedra braced for what would happen when he told them the rest. They'd talked about this. All of them. About what it might mean, and what might be gained. For River and her brethren, it might help get them a new life. For Zura, it would make it more likely the corporations would leave her and her unborn twins alone. For the rest... it meant they were about to become even less popular with the corporations than then already were. They were all okay with that.

"That nanotech has been injected into a number of beings, myself included. You can't stop it from spreading, now. This technology could have been used to help billions of beings live better, healthier lives. Instead you used it to prolong the suffering and extend the life of your slaves, the cyborgs."

"You're fired," the new Astek rep snapped. "I'll have you up on charges. Theft of property. Corporate espionage!"

"No, you won't. Zale Fel is under IAF protection. Am I clear?" Archer looked like he was ready to start cracking skulls, and Phaedra wondered if this is what he'd been like back when he and Phyl had first met.

Then, all hell broke loose.

"Phae, run!" Echo's scream caught everyone off guard.

Braxon and Tyr grabbed her arms, pulling her up out of her seat.

"River!" She turned back for the cyborg, and saw Echo standing over River, who was staring into the barrel of a weapon Phae had never seen before. Echo's hands were shaking so hard the firearm kept jerking in her hands. Her knuckles were white, and her teeth had sunk so deep into her lip that blood was trickling down her chin.

A mobile mountain flew in front of her as Tyr hauled her out of the way. Zale hit Echo like a rogue comet, his massive body generating enough force to knock her off her feet.

They went down together, and as they hit the floor, Phae heard another sound. One that made her heart scream in denial. Blaster fire. Once. Twice. And a third time. Then, a split second of silence before everyone reacted at once. Security poured into the room, fighting to get past the panicky attendees using the same doors to escape the carnage.

Neither Echo nor Zale moved.

River flew out of her chair and dropped to her knees beside Zale's body. She pushed him off, revealing what Phae had feared most. Two bodies, both devastated by whatever weapon Echo had used. Bloodied and shattered, there was no way either of her friends could have survived.

She tore out of Tyr's grip and ran to join River, hot tears scalding her cheeks as she knelt beside her friends' bodies. She barely registered that her lovers followed her, standing guard over her and River as they mourned.

River closed Zale's eyes with a sob, and Phaedra gripped his lifeless hand. How had this happened? Why had Echo done this?

"No choice." Echo's words were barely more than an agonized gasp.

"Echo! Hang on. We'll get you help." Phaedra turned to call for a medic, but Echo grabbed her free wrist with desperate strength.

"No. Too late. For me." She went still for a second, then shifted her grip on Phaedra's arm so her hand covered Phaedra's data port. "Sorry. For...everything. Please. Save her."

"Save who? Why did you do this?"

"Gray men." A surge hit Phaedra's internal processors as Echo transferred a data packet to her through the port on her arm, and then her hand relaxed and fell to the floor. Phaedra grabbed it and hung on tight, her vision swimming with tears as she watched the last spark of life flicker and fade from Echo's eyes.

She was gone. Both of them were gone. Grief cracked her heart into pieces and it seemed like the world went dark. It took her a moment to realize that it *had* grown darker. Braxon and Tyr stood on either side of her, their wings outstretched to form a barrier between the four of them and the rest of the world.

She looked up at Tyr and managed a broken smile. "Thank you."

Tyr had one hand on Phaedra's shoulder and the other on the hilt of his blade. He'd almost taken Echo's life when she reached for his *mahaya*, but he'd stayed his hand at the last moment when he realized she was apologizing. He didn't understand why she'd done it, but he'd swear by his wings that she hadn't wanted to. Why else would she have warned Phaedra, or delayed pulling the trigger as she fought whatever compulsion drove her?

He and Braxon gave the two grieving females a few minutes with their friends, but soon they were surrounded by highly agitated and heavily armed Corp-Sec officers. "I'm sorry, Phae, but we have to go and let the investigators do their jobs."

"She was sorry. She didn't want to." Phae's voice quavered.

"I know. And we'll find the answers, but not here. Not now."

She looked up at him with haunted eyes. "Promise me you'll let me look for the answers my way. Royal family or not."

"Whatever you need to do, however you need to do it. I saw how she fought against herself. Something is..." He switched to his own language to convey his point. "Things are not how they appear to be. There is a mystery here."

For a moment, she brightened, and her next words were in his language. "Thank you for understanding, *mahoyen*."

"Always."

She let go of her friends' hands and got to her feet at the same time as River. Once they were on their feet, he and Braxon furled their wings and allowed the others to approach. He drew Phaedra into his arms, holding her as Archer approached them.

"I take it none of you are injured?" he asked.

Everyone shook their heads in the negative.

"That's something, at least." Archer glanced down at the two bodies, his jaw set and eyes hooded. "Zale and I were friends for a lot of years. I'm not going to stop until I know why he died and who ordered it. I'm tired of always being two steps behind whoever is orchestrating this *fraxxing* nightmare."

Phaedra looked up at the colonel. "Then let me help you find them. I know you have your own cyber-jockeys, but Erben's your best and he's not here. I am."

He stared down at Phae, then nodded. "Insane times call for insane measures. Fine, you're in. The room next door has been secured and investigators are waiting for you. Give your statements, and I'll have security teams standing by to escort you home afterward." He paused. "I expect you'll want to be there when I tell Denz about Zale?"

She uttered a soft sigh and nodded. "I want to be there. He's going to need all the support he can get. We all are."

"I'll see you at the Nova, then. Better clean up before you come."

She glanced down at her hands. They were covered in the blood of her friends. She started to tremble, and a moment later Tyr handed her a napkin so she could wipe some of it off her skin. He gave one to River, too. She started scrubbing at her hands so hard he worried she'd hurt herself. Apparently, so did Phaedra.

She reached out to touch River's hand. "It's okay, River. We'll go wash up together before we give our statements."

"Right. You do that. I'll have someone clear the room so you can both have a private moment." Archer called over one of the Corp-Sec officers and barked a few terse orders.

"Give him a minute to get it cleared. I don't want any more surprises today." Archer turned his attention to Tyr. "I'm sorry you didn't get to finalize the deal you wanted."

Tyr hadn't even thought about that. Not when there was so much death and grief to contend with. "We'll find a way to make it work. Just, not today. Today we have more important things to deal with."

"Mourning," Archer said in agreement.

"And revenge," Phae added.

"There will be a time and a place for both, my little warrior. For now, let's start with mourning." When his father died, he had been too busy supporting his sister and mother to grieve. He'd buried himself in work instead, denying and delaying his grief for too long. When it had finally hit him, it was a howling maelstrom of hurt that brought him to his knees and left him reeling. Only Braxon knew the price he'd paid for his denial. He wouldn't let Phaedra make the same mistake.

THEY LET River give her statement first, and once she was done she said a brief goodbye and left with her escort. No doubt she wanted to be alone for a while. According to Phaedra, River had been distant and struggled to trust anyone who wasn't a cyborg. Now, one of her own had tried to kill her, and Zale had given his life to protect her. It was a lot to deal with.

Then the Corp-Sec officer had tried to separate the three of them to give individual statements. They refused. After what had happened, none of them were interested in being out of each other's sight. It had taken a call to Colonel Archer to make the officer back down.

They gave their accounts, which were more or less identical, though each of them had noticed different details during events. They were asked to go over things several more times, but eventually they were escorted back to the *Santar*. None of them spoke, but Phaedra didn't let go of their hands until they were back onboard.

When it was only the three of them, she turned to Braxon, leaned into his chest and uttered a heartrending sob of pain and sorrow. She didn't let go of Tyr, though, and after a moment she pulled him in behind her. He knew what she needed. What all of them needed. He wrapped an arm around Braxon's shoulders and they both bowed their heads over Phaedra, holding her between them.

Braxon reached around to grip Tyr's hip, pulling him in even closer. The three fit together perfectly. He nuzzled Phaedra's hair, murmuring comforting words as Tyr did the same. He wasn't even aware that he'd started to stroke his thumb across the back of Tyr's neck at first. He was only trying comfort their mate, but as he stood there, wrapped up in them both, he realized he didn't have one mate any longer. He had two.

CHAPTER EIGHTEEN

IT WAS strange to see the Nova Club empty during the day. Phaedra couldn't recall it ever being so still and quiet. Usually there were at least a few diehard gamblers at the tables, music would pulse and pound the air, and staff would be on hand to make sure that everything ran smoothly. Today, there was no one to serve. The club was closed.

She opened the doors with her access code and then made her way in silence to the door that led to staff only areas. Zura had sent a message to her comm device letting her know they were waiting for her, but that they already knew that Zale and Echo were gone.

She knew which room they were in, but even if she hadn't, it would not have been hard to guess. It was the only open door, and the only source of sound in the entire place.

There was a moment, just before she crossed the threshold, that she thought about turning around and walking away. Maybe if she did that, she could pretend for a second that none of it was real.

"We're with you," Braxon's murmured words gave her the strength to take the next step.

Zura reached her first, throwing her arms around Phaedra in tearful silence. The others appeared. Her co-conspirators, her friends, all of them heartsick and stunned by the news of what had happened.

When the hugs and quiet words finally stopped, she looked around until she found Zale's cousin, Denz. He was sitting in the corner of the room, his massive frame looking small and somehow frail. She crossed the room and stood in front of him, but he didn't seem to see her. Finally, she set a hand on his shoulder and squeezed.

He looked up then, his black eyes full of pain. "You were there. Tell me they got it wrong. That he's going to walk through that door any minute."

"I wish I could. All I can tell you is that he died a hero. If he hadn't acted when he did, River would be dead, and I might be, too."

"Who did it?"

She knew she should wait for Archer to debrief them all, but Denz needed to know. She leaned down and whispered Echo's name in his ear in tones so soft that not even cyborg hearing would be able to detect it.

"Why would she do that?"

"I don't know yet, but I'm working on it. I'll let Archer explain the rest." She hugged Denz and stepped away to let him have a moment to absorb what she'd just told him. She didn't go far, though. If he had questions, she'd be close by to answer them. At least, the ones she could. Her hand absently brushed over the shoulder bag she carried. Her computer and other tools were inside. She wanted to get started working on the encrypted data Echo had given her as soon as possible, but she didn't want to be away from her friends. At least, the ones who were here. They'd have to tell Alyson, Lieksa and their husbands soon. Lieksa was going to be devastated. *Veth.* They were all devastated, and they didn't know the worst of it. Not yet.

She set the bag down in an out of the way corner and considered taking a seat but opted not to. She had too much emotional energy churning through her to stay still for long. Braxon and Tyr stood on each side of her, their arms overlapping across her shoulders.

Tyr had worried that she'd be jealous of their attraction to each other. She wasn't. It felt right. Like this was how the universe had always intended them to be.

The colonel arrived not long after, and it was obvious by his appearance that he hadn't taken even a second of time for himself since she had last seen him. If he didn't rest soon, the man was going to break. No one was that strong.

He wasn't three steps into the room before everyone went silent. They knew why he was here. He came to parade rest and scanned the room, giving Phaedra a brief nod as his gaze met hers. Then, he began to speak. He kept the news brief, minimizing the horror and chaos. He managed to find the words to make it clear that while Echo had been the one to pull the trigger, she seemed to be just as much a victim as Zale.

When he was done, Denz got to his feet. "Where is my cousin's body? I want to see him."

"I thought you would. There's an officer outside

waiting to escort you to the med-center. His body is there."

"I want to see Echo, too," Denz said.

"I'm not sure that's—" Archer started to speak, but Denz raised his voice and cut him off.

"I have to see her. I need to tell her she's forgiven."

There were soft sounds of grief and pain from all around the room, and then everyone moved at once, converging around Denz, hugging and holding onto him and each other. Even Archer was part of it, and Phaedra swore she saw him rub his eyes more than once as they leaned on each other.

Later, after Denz had left, Archer and Phyl found their way to where she was standing and talking with Cynder, Jaeger, and Toro. All of them were guilt-stricken and wondering how they had missed the truth about Echo.

"I don't think you missed anything," she told them.

"I agree," Archer said as he joined the conversation. "You weren't the only ones who employed her. She worked for Astek, too, and they vetted everyone in the room for the negotiations."

"And those corporate types are so high strung they'll reject anyone they even *think* might be dangerous. More delicate than a shipment of Tiskalian ice orchids, that bunch." Phyl chimed in.

"Then why?" Cynder asked.

Toro wrapped an arm around her waist and hugged her to him. "I think, maybe, Echo's like Vic and Ward. Only not exactly the same." The big cyborg shrugged awkwardly. "I'm probably wrong, though."

"I don't think you're wrong, T," Cyn murmured. "Stop doubting yourself."

It made sense. Vic and Ward had been freed with the rest of the cyborgs, but sometime later, they'd been captured and reprogrammed. For several years an unknown group had used them as assassins, and their handler had been a cold-hearted bitch who abused the brothers in every way imaginable.

"That thought has crossed my mind, too," Archer agreed.

"But how will we ever know?" Jaeger asked.

It was the pain in his voice that made her give up the secret she'd been hiding. She'd told Tyr and Braxon about the data transfer once they were back on the ship, but she hadn't planned on telling anyone else until she knew what Echo had given her. Normally she held onto information, but if she did that now, she'd be denying her friends what little hope they had. "I think Echo gave me the answers before she died. I won't know until I decrypt the data she transferred to me."

"When did this happen?" Archer demanded.

"It was just before she died, she used the data-port in my arm to transfer a large, encrypted file."

Braxon glowered, and she knew she was about to get another lecture about the risk she'd taken. "She could have killed you. Why did you trust her to touch you?"

"Because she was my friend. She told me to run, remember? Whatever happened, she did everything she could to stop herself and protect us. I trusted her because she was my friend. And if either of you had stopped her from grabbing my arm, we would never know the reason any of this happened."

"How long until you can decrypt it? Why didn't you say anything before?" Archer asked. He looked like he wanted to strangle her.

"I didn't say anything because I don't know what's on it. Echo entrusted this information to *me*, and I intend to live up to that trust."

"But the investigation..."

She cut Archer off. "The investigators can have any relevant information once I've figured out how to access it. I have no idea how long that will take."

"You'll need the key," Toro said.

"Yeah, I know. It's going to take me some time to work out what it is, though."

Cyn smiled a little. "Not a key. *The* key. Most cyborgs are given a standard set of encryption programs. Think of it as default programming. Echo wanted you to be able to read what she gave you, so I'm going to bet she used one of the defaults."

A spark of hope flared in her chest and she held her arm out to Cyn. "Give them to me. Please. Then maybe we can get some answers."

"We could all use some answers right now," Archer agreed. "Not that I am in any way sanctioning your decision to hide this from Corp-Sec and the IAF."

"I'm telling you now, aren't I?" she pointed out.

He closed his eyes, pinched the bridge of his nose, and sighed. "This is why I don't work with civilians." Then he walked away before she could respond.

"That man annoys me on so many levels," she muttered.

Phyl snorted with laughter. "He says the same thing about you. Can't imagine why."

IT TOOK a little time for her and Cynder to find the right decryption key to unlock the data. "I'm nearly there," she announced as she looked up and finally registered that one of her males was missing. "Where's Braxon?"

"He was talking with Archer last I saw him." Cyn looked around the room. "No idea where they got off to."

"I'll contact him," Tyr said.

Phaedra waited, her fingers itching to start delving into Echo's final message.

Tyr frowned, then pursed his lips. "He says he'll be back soon, but not to wait for him. He knows how important that information is."

"He's not here?" It bothered her that he'd left without saying anything. Where was he, and why had he gone?

"He must have gone with Archer," River said.

"Then, I guess we're ready to find out why Echo and Zale are gone. Should we tell everyone else?"

Jaeger shook his head. "Not until we know what's there."

Tyr, River, Cynder, and her two husbands gathered around, and Phaedra tapped her keyboard. Documents and file icons filled the screen. They had strange names and some of the icons were unfamiliar. "What the *fraxx* is that?" she asked, pointing to one of the icons.

"That's a memory transfer file. She's sent you her memories. Dozens of them." Cyn said.

Phaedra filtered the data, looking for some clue as to where to start. It didn't take very long to find it. There were three files that caught her eye. One was a document called "targets,", there was another marked "For

Magi." the other a memory simply named "For Phaedra."

She took a second to move the one for Magi to her internal drives without opening it. She'd send it to Eric later, along with a note telling him what had happened while he was gone. After that, she clicked on the memory and a vid started to play. An old-fashioned pad of paper appeared first, then a woman's hand, writing in simple block letters.

I can't tell you any of this. I want to, but the ones who programmed me made sure I could never speak to anyone about what I am, or the program, or the ones who run it. The only reason I can write this down is because I've been on my own long enough the conditioning is weakening. Not enough to defy my orders, but maybe it's enough to explain why.

The hand on the page stilled, the fingers gripping the pen tightly for a moment before it started to move again.

Even this is painful. I'll have to be quick.

The Reaper project wasn't unique. There are more of us. Other versions of the program. We don't know how many. They've gotten better at programming us. Not all of us have barcodes. Or handlers. We gather intelligence. Create chaos. Commit murder. All on their orders. The faceless ones. The Gray men. That's the only name we know for them.

A drop of blood fell to the page, staining the paper.

"I included a list of my targets. Some were mandatory hits, others were targets of opportunity. I was supposed to gather intel, but once a name was activated, I had no choice but to take their life, including yours, Phaedra. The Gray Men know you were the one who stole the proof of what they had done. They won't stop coming for you, or anyone else on that list. Protect yourselves.

The words got harder to read as Echo's hand started to shake and twitch. Another splatter of blood obliterated some of the words near the top of the page.

"I can give you one name. Nyx. She's my batch sister. She's stronger than I am. She's found a way to fight back against the programming and conditioning. They keep her to run tests on. She suffers more than any of us. Find her. Save her if you can. Please.

I have so many regrets. If you're seeing this, then I'm dead, which means I likely took another life, or tried to. I hope it wasn't a friend. I fear it will be because the names of friends are the only ones left on my list.

Don't mourn for me. They can't make me hurt anyone else, now. I'm finally free.

"*Re'veth*. There's more of them." Toro muttered.

"And they're coming after Phaedra." Tyr pointed to the list of targets. "Open it."

She knew every name on the list. River, Victor, Ward, Zale, Alyson and Lieksa, along with the names of the dead corporate executives. Echo had been sent to the Drift to spy on them and kill them if she could.

They looked at the other files. Echo had included documents, images, and even fragments of her memories. Voices. Locations. The faces of her victims. Anything she thought might help. There was a file marked "Finn." Phaedra opened it, then sat back in shock. It was a brief piece of footage from a security feed, clearly showing Nadira Finn submitting to a palm and retina scan before being allowed past a security post. To one side were stencilled letters that Phaedra recognized - "Reamus Research Station." With the file were several dates and times that appeared to show more visits to the station. No wonder

Nadira had been afraid of cyborgs. She'd seen what they were capable of becoming with the right programming and pressure. This conspiracy just kept getting deeper.

"There's a treasure trove of information in here. Archer needs to see this," she said.

"Everyone needs to see this." Cyn gestured around them. "We're at war with an enemy we didn't know existed."

She copied the data and attached it to an encrypted message for Corp-Sec, then sent it. Once it was gone, she pointed to the screen, then looked at Tyr. "This is why I can't stop doing what I do."

He nodded. "I know. I don't like, it, but I won't stop you."

Cyn scoffed. "Like you ever had a hope in hell of stopping her."

"I've figured that out. I may be a prince, but as my little warrior has pointed out to me more than once, I am not *her* prince."

"You're right. You're not my prince, you're my mate."

"Yes, I am, *mahaya*."

"Speaking of which, where is our other mate? He said he'd be back soon."

Cynder pointed across the room. He's coming this way, and judging by the smile on his face, I'd say he has good news. I sure the *fraxx* hope so, because we could use some."

BRAXON HAD INTENDED to stay and watch over Phaedra as she worked, but there was nothing to actually see and he quickly grew restless. He wanted to be doing something useful. She had lost friends. Tyr's dreams of a colony were unraveling. They'd been on the verge of having it all, and now nothing was certain anymore. Well, not nothing. He looked at his mates and smiled to himself. He was certain about one thing – the three of them were destined to spend the rest of their lives together. All his doubts about that were gone.

When Archer had come by and tapped him discretely on the shoulder, Braxon had followed him without a second thought.

"The Torex Mining rep just informed me that he's making ready to leave the station. He knows what we're going to ask for, and he's willing to talk, but it has to be now," Archer said.

"I'll get Tyran."

"Leave the prince here. The time for careful diplomacy has passed. If you want to get this done, it's going to have to be quick and dirty. I get the sense that's your strength, not his."

"It is."

He followed Archer out of the room, determined to make this happen.

The colonel hadn't been exaggerating. The meeting was quick and ugly. There were four of them present, himself—Archer, an older human female that turned out to be Phaedra's friend, Phylomenia, and Gunns. There were no pretty words or false promises. The three of them stated the facts about the existing colony, and the fact that the planetary governments, the military, and the other corporations were all in agreement that it was the ideal location for the Vardarian colony. Gunns hadn't put up much of a fight once he realized the odds were against him, especially not when Archer revealed what Torex would be granted if they agreed. They'd be allowed access to a new, unexplored area of the galaxy, with full claiming rights and no competition. After that, it had been relatively simple.

He returned to the Nova Club and found his way back to the room where he'd left Phae and Tyr. Everyone was still there, talking in quiet groups. It was how every species seemed to deal with tragedy. They came together and supported each other.

Phaedra hadn't moved while he'd been gone, but she did get to her feet as he made his way to her. "You look happy," Phae said by way of greeting

"You don't. Did something else happen while I was gone?" He had left believing that after the day they'd had, things couldn't get worse. Had Echo left them more bad news?

"I decrypted Echo's files."

He folded her into his arms. "What was on them?"

She started to explain, and he listened intently as she told him about the lists of targets, Echo's explanation, her apology, and her warning. Others gathered around as she spoke, and he realized that this was the first time many of them had heard the news. She had to go back to the beginning twice, but eventually the story was told.

"Now that I've caught you up, you can tell me where you've been and why you were smiling when you came back."

He'd let her go while she told everyone what she'd discovered, but now he pulled her in with one arm and grinned at Tyr. "I got us our planet. Torex agreed, and it's all arranged." Braxon turned to River. You'll be able to keep your promise. You and your people finally have a home."

The mood in the room lightened in seconds. Questions and congratulations came in from all sides, but the only ones that mattered came from his mates. Phaedra squealed with happiness and launched herself into his arms for a kiss, and when he raised his head again, Tyran was there, gripping his shoulder. For a moment they looked at each other, and then Tyr leaned in and whispered, "thank you, *mahoyen*," before sealing his mouth with a kiss.

Phaedra was laughing and smiling as she held them both. "I love you both so much. You've helped me find a new cause to fight for and given me the one thing I never thought I'd have again."

"What's that?" Tyr asked.

"A home. Wherever the two of you are, that will always be my home."

"Where are we going? The sun's not even up yet." Phaedra was still bleary-eyed despite the mug of coffee Braxon had handed her when they'd woken her up at some unholy hour of the morning and insisted she get dressed.

Now they were walking through the dew-soaked grass as the sky overhead slowly lightened. She was still adjusting to the idea of there being an actual sky above her, and grass under her bare feet. They'd only landed on the planet yesterday. She'd been on asteroids and moons before, but none of her experiences prepared her for the vastness and beauty of being on a full-sized planet, with atmosphere and gravity and life. *Veth*, there was so much life here. Every breath she took was scented with dirt and plants and living things. Instead of the background hum of machines there was the wind, and the bleating of the creatures their hosts called noats.

They'd stayed up much of the night talking with Raze and Sevda, the only two beings on the planet. Raze was a cyborg, but he wasn't like any other cyborg she'd ever met. He was rougher around the edges, with long hair and a gruff voice. He'd slowly warmed up over the course of the evening, but it was clear he wasn't used to company. Sevda was as different from her husband as night was to day. Where he was quiet, she was chatty and upbeat. By the time they'd all gone to bed, she, Braxon, and Tyr all agreed that Raze and Sevda would be valuable assets when it came time to welcome the rest of the colonists to their new home – the planet Liberty.

She took another few steps and then came to a halt. "I'm not taking another step until I know what we're doing out here. Even the chickens are still asleep, so why aren't we?"

Tyr looked down at her with amusement. "Because despite their wings, chickens can't fly. We can."

"Will you come fly with us?" Braxon asked, his wings unfurling as he spoke.

For a second all her old fears returned, but all she had to do to banish them was take hold of their hands. She trusted them with her life, her heart, and her future. "Show me our new home."

Raze's farm was on a plateau partway up the mountains that enclosed the lush, fertile valley below. They walked to the edge, and she gripped their hands tighter as she looked down the steep mountainside to the shadow-filled depths at the bottom.

"We've got you." Braxon said.

"You better," she muttered, but she didn't back away.

Tyran picked her up and cradled her next to his chest, and she threw her arms around his neck, gripping as tight as she could without choking him.

"Ready?"

She closed her eyes. "Yes."

He launched them into the air, and the next few seconds felt like they lasted forever as she waited for something to go wrong. She kept expecting to feel the familiar stomach lurch that came when the gravity was shut off, but instead, the wind rushed by her face, tangling her hair as they soared.

"You should open your eyes, mahaya. You're missing the view." Tyr's voice sounded inside her head.

Before leaving the station, Alyson had found a way to fit all three of them with a modified version of the internal communicators the cyborgs all used. She and Lieksa designed them together, using notes and sketches Denz had found among Zale's possessions.

She cracked open one eye, gasped, and turned to look out at the vista unfolding below them. *"This is paradise."*

"No, love. This is Liberty," Braxon said. She looked over and spotted him not far away. He and Tyr were both beaming with enjoyment. It had been a long time since either of them had been able to manage more than a brief moment in the air. Circling the loading bays of Astek station was as close as they'd been able to get.

They climbed higher, and with every flap of their wings more of the world was revealed. They left the shadow of the mountains behind and flew into the sun-drenched morning air. It was more open space than she had ever seen, and every meter of it was breathtakingly beautiful. It was green, and wild, and it belonged to them. All of it.

So much had happened in the last two months. When she tried to look back on it all, everything was a confusing muddle of happy memories and painful good-byes. Zale and Echo's funerals. Making contact with Raze and Sevda for the first time to start making plans for the colony. Saying goodbye to Alyson and the rest of her friends. One of her favorite moments was the day that Tyran's sister finally accepted the fact that her brother was never coming home. There were tears in Neha's eyes as she apologized for her behavior and promised to support the new colony in any way she could. Tyran's mother was at her daughter's side, and Phaedra had no doubt that the older woman had a lot to do with Neha's change of heart. At least Neha had embraced her destiny as leader of the empire and freed Tyran to find his own path. That path had led them here.

"Our home is beautiful," she sent the message to them both.

"Yes, it is." Braxon pointed to the point where the river left the valley. It passed through some low, rolling hills that eventually leveled out into a plain on either side of the river. *"That's the spot Raze was telling us about last night. We'll build there."*

"There's so much space," It was hard for her to absorb how much land they had to work with.

"One day, there will be a city here. If we're blessed, it will be the first of many. This continent is massive, and the one further north is even larger. There are resources there that will ensure we have all the ore and wealth we need to prosper." Tyr was almost gleeful as they looked over their new home.

They'd be leaving in a week or so, but they wouldn't be gone for long. Colonists were already signing up, ships were being prepared, and within a few months the empty land below them would become the first city on Liberty –

Zale's Landing. They'd decided on the name before they left the Drift, and their announcement had been met with approval from everyone.

Denz had already decided to join the new colony. He'd be accompanying River on the IAF ship full of cyborgs still in cryo-sleep. They'd arrive within days of the Vardarians, and while everyone hoped that the newly freed cyborgs would be able to adjust, those that needed more time to accept their freedom would be encouraged to colonize the other side of the river, where they'd have the support they needed and the solitude to heal.

"You're quiet. Do you want us to take you down?" Tyr asked, speaking normally.

"I'm fine." And she was. There was so much to see she'd forgotten to be worried.

"You sure?" He asked.

She switched to their internal channel so Braxon could hear her. *I was thinking about Zale, and Echo. They'll never get to see this place. And then I was thinking how amazing it will be when everyone arrives, the colonists and our friends. I can't wait to see Zura's twins running around in all this space.*

Braxon and Tyr had issued an invitation to all their friends to visit or stay on Liberty. The Gray Men were still out there, and the colony was a potential sanctuary for anyone who needed protection from them, or the corporations, or anyone else who threatened innocent lives. Sevda had made the suggestion that once the colony was set up and running, they could start inviting human females who wanted to escape the hive cities of Earth to come to Liberty as mates for the cyborgs and Vardarians. It would take time and more negotiations to make it happen, but they'd find a way, and they'd do it together. She wasn't alone in her battles anymore, and she never would be again. Her lonely time out in the shadowy fringes of the galaxy was over. From now on, her life would be full of sunshine, free air, and a love that knew no limits.

THE END

Want to read more stories with book boyfriends
that are out of this world?

**Check out Susan Hayes' other Science Fiction
Romance Titles**

<u>The Drift</u>
Double Down
All In
Wild Card
Three of a Kind
Full House
No Limit
Aces Over Queen

<u>Nova Force</u>
Operation Phoenix
Operation Cobalt

<u>Star-Crossed Alien Mail Order Brides</u>
Joran
Vader
Kash

<u>3013: The Series</u>
3013: RENEGADE
3013: STOWAWAY
3013: TARGETED
3013: FATED
3013: SCARRED

ABOUT THE AUTHOR

Susan lives out on the Canadian west coast surrounded by open water, dear family, and good friends. She's jumped out of perfectly good airplanes on purpose and accidentally swum with sharks on the Great Barrier Reef.

If the world ends, she plans to survive as the spunky, comedic sidekick to the heroes of the new world, because she's too damned short and out of shape to make it on her own for long.

You can find out more about Susan and her books here:
www.susanhayes.ca

www.ingramcontent.com/pod-product-compliance
Lightning Source LLC
Chambersburg PA
CBHW061612190726
48288CB00007B/2279